AGAINST THE RHYTHM

Jacob Grey

Contents

CHapTer 1

I can't count on my hands the number of times my best friend has asked me to look at her boobs. So it was no wonder my selective hearing wasn't paying attention.

"Can you tell I'm not wearing a bra?"

I flicked the pages of my new text book, not really reading anything, just scanning as my mind wandered to the scent of coffee and cologne.

"Elle?"

"Hmm? Looks great on you," I mumbled. He stood in line behind me at the campus café today. I hadn't been expecting it, not considering there was another week before classes started.

"Elle! A little attention please."

I looked up at my friend Sascha posing with one arm over her black hair, leg propped against the bathroom door. She pushed out her petite chest, looking down at the silky red camisole.

"Am I wearing a bra or not?"

I looked her over. Petite, gorgeous and a man-eater. There was no other way to describe her. And apparently nipples could be barred after all. "The stag is real," I said with a serious tone.

"Perfect!" She flicked her long hair over her shoulder and went back into the bathroom, leaving the door ajar so we could still hear each other.

I shook my head as my friend continued. "I've got small tits, right? Who's going to notice them if they don't put on a little show?" That was her well-rehearsed philosophy; make the most of your assets, even if they were itsy bitsy. Small boobs, no cleavage? Free the nipple. Little bum, long legs? Bare the booty. Simple.

"Hasn't your target audience seen that show already?" I questioned carefully. She hadn't told me in so many words, but if history was any indication, then her new crush had surely been an interactive member of the Sass Show.

Sascha tore the door open and fixed me with a blistering glare. "I'll have you know, Miss Prim and Proper, that Dale has been the perfect gentleman."

I raised a brow. "By his wish or your command?"

She pressed her lips together and thought about it. "A little of both, I think." She gently folded the silk and put it back in the shopping bag. "I don't know, Elle, I think it's different this time." Her voice was quiet, tone serious.

"How do you mean?" It was an unusual statement coming from Sascha.

She sighed. "He just... he treats me different. Better. Than previous guys, I mean." She fell onto the couch beside me. "I really like him, like really like him! In the I want to bare his children way."

I smiled. Her giddiness was infectious. I hadn't seen her like this since we were teenagers and she fell for her first boyfriend. He was older, rode a motorcycle and seemed a little dangerous. Worse, he hit on all her friends. He was a creep, and it took Sascha a while to figure that out. Since then, she'd dated a range of guys, each one different but each one entirely wrong for her.

"And that's why you have to come tonight. I need my best wing woman," she continued with pleading eyes and a puckered lip. "You promised."

In Sascha's quest to lock down her new man, she invited me to one of his shows. He was a musician and frequently performed at the bar on the edge of campus. I'd never set foot in the place, it just wasn't my scene, but she begged me to come along to one of his gigs. I usually rejected her invitation and used work or assignments as an excuse. That wasn't going to fly this time. The new semester didn't start for another week and Sascha worked at my family's hotel. She'd seen this month's roster and knew I was free.

"Pretty please?" She fluttered her eyelashes.

I sighed. "You know I don't like bars."

"That's a lie and you know it."

"Guys getting drunk and being jerks..." I continued with disdain.

"You'll be with me; I'll fend them off."

"Uni is a place to learn, not party."

Sascha scoffed. "Sure they are."

I frowned. Between work and classes, I barely had time to eat dinner with my dad, let alone waste time partying the nights away.

I crossed my arms and huffed. "Fine! I'll go, but only because I love you."

Sascha bounced on her cushion and clapped. "This will be great, you'll see. Maybe we'll even find you a musician of your own."

I groaned in annoyance. Typical. "What did we just talk about? You're fending off the vultures, remember, not encouraging them." I reached into her shopping bag and pulled out the red camisole. "Speaking of which, if you're only interested in Dale, as you so adamantly claim, I'd be wearing a strapless or pasties with this. You attract guys just walking into a room. In this, they'll be flocking towards you. If Dale likes you the way it seems he does, then there's no need to free the nipple. And making him jealous could seriously backfire."

Sascha rolled her eyes. "Pasties are so not sexy." She shrugged her shoulders after thinking about it for a moment. "You're probably right though. Okay fine, I'll saddle the girls if you come."

I glanced sideways at her. She knew I'd go regardless of the bra situation. She must be serious about this guy if she was taking advice from me.

"I'll need to go home after work to change, then I'll come pick you up." It would be easier if I drove. That way we'd both have a way to get home. Whether she'd be coming home with me or not would be a question for later tonight.

She gave me a coy smile. "Thank you."

"You're welcome. Come on, we're going to be late." My response was dripping with sarcasm. As if we'd be late. We were already here.

Sascha grabbed her belongings and put them in her locker. I did the same, gathering the textbooks I'd brought this morning, smiling at the memory of his reflection in the cake display window. I wondered what he was doing there a week early, and if he'd gone to buy his new course material before the rush next week, like I had.

"Get your head in the zone," she said, taking my empty keep cup and putting it in the staffroom sink. "The Boss Lady doesn't like it when we're late," she laughed before ducking back into the bathroom.

By Boss Lady she meant me. I wasn't manager on duty today, but my father owned the hotel Sascha and I worked at. By extension and my part-time managerial position, I was often referred to as the Boss Lady. It was ridiculous considering I worked the same shifts as everyone else on the front desk and only shouldered a few extra responsibilities by my father's request. He wanted me to learn on the job, hoping the experience would help me figure out if I wanted to stay in the family business. I wasn't a boss lady, not yet.

I walked down the hall and entered the foyer of Twenty-Nine on Queen. Sawyer greeted me with a warm smile.

"Did you have a good break?" he asked, moving in beside me at the desk where I quickly scanned today's arrivals. He leaned his elbows on the counter and his muscled arm brushed against mine, the rolled sleeve of his button down exposing the veins on his forearm. I couldn't help my wandering gaze.

I turned to face him, coming dangerously close, so close I could smell his sweet cologne. He was smirking, all gorgeous blue eyes and luscious lips. He knew what his proximity did to me.

"You know you shouldn't be doing this," I whispered, eyes darting around the foyer. There was no one here, but someone could walk through those doors any minute. Our heated moment was too unprofessional for my liking.

"You don't mind as much as you think you do," he leaned a little closer.

Sawyer McKinnon. Hot, sexy, tall and lean, and oh so frustrating. That slight Scottish accent inherited from his parents who migrated to Australia when he was young did wild things to my body. But he was also my father's prodigy and completely off limits. Not that it proved to be much of a barrier.

Sawyer reached his arm around me, placing a strong hand on my hip before giving a gentle squeeze. "Are you coming over tonight?" He asked in a deep voice close to my ear, his warm breath tickling my skin.

I grabbed his arm and glanced around. "Sawyer! Anyone could see." The last thing we needed was for another employee to spot us, or worse, for my father to walk in.

He let go and took a step back, chuckling at my discomfort.

"It's not funny," I stated bluntly, turning back to the computer screen. "If Dad finds out we've been... well, you know what, he'd murder you."

"Oh please, he loves me."

That he did. When my father hired Sawyer straight out of university, he'd admired his intellect and drive. I'd crushed on him when he first started working here. Now, the six-year age gap was least of our concerns. My father may treat Sawyer like the son he never had, but he certainly wouldn't appreciate him hooking up with his only daughter.

I rolled my eyes. "It doesn't matter how much he loves you; he would never appreciate..." I waved my hand between us. Sometimes I didn't know how to explain what Sawyer and I were doing. It was what some might call a 'friends with benefits' situation. We discussed it the first time, deciding it was better not to label it, whatever it was. Hanging out, hooking up. Having a good time.

Sawyer's glistening eyes swept my body and he leaned back, arms bulging as he pushed his weight against the counter. "Appreciate what? Me fu-"

"Ew! Do not finish that sentence!"

I jumped as Sascha appeared, interrupting Sawyer mid-sentence.

"As hot as I'm sure that would be, let's keep it in our pants at work please. Some of us are PG-13."

I blushed and Sawyer scoffed. "Sass, you're anything but PG."

Sascha knew about my little rendezvous with Sawyer. After the first time I went back to his place, I had to spill to someone.

Sawyer turned back to me as Sascha busied herself with the brochures on the counter. "So, tonight?"

"I can't tonight," I apologised.

Sascha turned around. "Yeah, she can't tonight. I'm kidnapping her. She's my wing woman."

Sawyer laughed. "Going hunting?" he queried with a smirk.

"More like going in for the kill," Sascha winked.

He pressed his lips together in an amused smile. "Good for you, Sass."

"Thanks babes."

Sawyer turned back to me. "Where are you headed?"

"Just to the Uni Bar. Sascha's been seeing a musician and his band is playing tonight."

Sawyer nodded. "Well, if your night ends early, give me a buzz."

I looked up at him hopefully. "Not interested in coming, are you?"

He pushed off the counter and let out a low whistle. "I think I'll leave the good old uni days in the past. You have a good night though. Make sure you eat, especially if you drink. You're a lightweight." His gaze turned from admiring to concerned.

Sensing my annoyance before it even materialised, Sascha reappeared. "Don't worry, big boy, I'll take care of her."

Just then the entrance doors opened, and an elder couple walked in.

I glanced back to Sawyer as Sascha greeted them. "Have fun," he said with sincerity. "And if you want to come by after, let me know." He winked as he took a step back toward the office door.

I blushed. Oh, how tempting he was.

"I can't believe you've been a student here for two years and have never been to the campus bar," Sascha laughed as we walked through the doors of Uni Bar. The popularity of this place amazed me. How could a name as bland as Uni Bar hold such a big attraction?

I looked around curiously. "Does it have a coffee machine?" I queried in a serious tone.

Sascha rounded on me with a raised brow. "Babe, take a look around. Does this look like a place they serve coffee?"

I scanned the room. Uni Bar looked more modern than I thought it would. In my mind, I'd always imagined a university watering hole to be made of nothing but wood, beer-soaked carpet, and faux leather booths. Clearly Eastern University kept up with trends. It had a modern industrial vibe with exposed brick, wooden floors, and metal stools.

The crowd was exactly as I imagined though. Students laughing and drinking, heads bobbing to the background music as they socialised. Some patrons looked a little old to be prowling a campus bar, but who was I to judge?

I called her bluff. "Actually, it does."

She crossed her arms over the red silk camisole she tried on earlier today. She'd paired it with some high-waisted, skin-tight black jeans. With her hair curled and tied into a stylish ponytail, and her natural makeup accentuating her beautiful features, she was Sass the Man-eater, but also not. There was something differ-ent about her tonight.

"Okay, they do have coffee," she admitted. "But you're not al-lowed to have any. It's strictly tequila or Jägerbombs for you, young lady."

"Do not bring Jägermeister anywhere near me!" My stomach turned at the unforgettable memory of a messy night. "Besides, I'm driving, remember."

Sascha groaned and rolled her eyes. "Right. Driving. You suck." She turned and glanced towards the stage, heels tapping on the wood as she bounced up and down.

I watched her carefully as she scanned the crowd looking for Dale. She was nervous. And she'd worn a bra. Sascha really was serious about this guy.

I reached over to hold her hand. "Where is this mystery man of yours? It's time for the Boyfriend Approval Panel to get to work."

She gave a little giggle. "Oh yeah, because you're so tough."

I faked offence. "Umm, I can be tough when I want to be, thank you very much."

"Mhmm," she laughed again. "Oh, look, there he is." Sascha pointed toward the stage where a few guys and a woman were setting up equipment. She took a step and then stopped, noticing how I still held her hand but was rooted to the spot.

My heart rate rose as I watched the movements of a guy on the stage. He was tall and had dark hair, and even though I couldn't see his eyes from here, I knew they were a piercing translucent blue.

Sascha followed my line of sight. "What's wrong?" When I didn't respond right away, she tried again. "Elle?"

"He... he's the guy," I stuttered.

"The guy? What guy?" Sascha seemed confused, glancing back at the stage. "Do you mean your guy? Hot Café Guy? Which one?" The worried tone in her voice brought me out of my daydreams. She was making connections in her mind that were nothing to worry about. Hot Café Guy was not Dale. I'd seen pictures of him, and she was the one who showed them to me.

"The guy at the back. Black hair, toned arms." The guy I'd been crushing on for the last two years. The guy I'd first seen at the campus café. The guy we'd dubbed the suitable nickname of Hot Café Guy because that was one of the only places I ever saw him.

"The guy of your wettest daydreams?" she finished for me with a smirk. I rolled my eyes at her, and she continued. "I can introduce you if you like."

I tore my eyes away from him to look at her. "You know him?"

"He's in the band with Dale. They're best mates."

"What's him name?" I asked. I'd been dying to know since the first time I saw him.

"Justin," she replied. "Justin Hart."

I froze.

Justin Hart.

He couldn't be. No way.

Sascha must have noticed the change in me. "Elle, what's the matter? Do you know him?"

I was shocked. Did I know him? Yes, I did. But how could I not recognise him? How much could a person change in twelve years? A whole lot, apparently. Surely I should have recognised something about him. Like the eyes! How did I not see it before?

"Who is he?" Sascha asked again.

I took a deep breath, a million thoughts running through my mind.

"Justin Hart is the son of the man who knocked up my mother."

CHAPTER 2

Okay, when I put it like that, it's no wonder Sascha's jaw hit the floor. It was true, Justin Hart's father did get my mother pregnant, but there was more to the story than that.

First, she wasn't really my mother. I knew that I was adopted from the moment I could comprehend the news. Knowing this seemed to make her leaving hurt more than knowing she wasn't my real mother. She had chosen me and then tossed me aside the moment a better offer came along. I considered her my mother, and when she finally gave birth to a daughter of her own, I felt like I'd been replaced. Which brings me to the next part of the story. Caroline lost the right to be called mother when she cheated on my dad with his oldest friend. The day she told us she was pregnant was the worst of my dad's life. He couldn't have children. It was the reason they chose to adopt in the first place.

I hadn't just lost my mother that day, my dad had lost his wife and best friend, too.

These memories flowed through my mind as I stood there watching Justin in all his tall, dark and handsome glory. He represented the fracture of my family. By no fault of his own, of course, but still. Caroline had left me and played mother to him.

I should hate him. I should turn around and walk out the door. And I shouldn't think twice about it. But watching him as he plugged in a microphone and set it on its stand, I couldn't. The way he ran his hand through his hair and nodded at someone as they walked by reminded me of other things.

Hot Café Guy.

A clicking sound in my ear made me jump. "Hello, Elle, you still with us?" I turned to Sascha who regarded me with concern. "Are you okay?"

I sighed. "Yeah, I'm fine. Just thinking."

"Do you want to leave?" She looked disappointed.

"No," I shook my head. "We're here for a good night, so let's have a good night."

She was sceptical. "Are you sure?" Sascha and I had been friends since kindergarten. She knew what happened with Caroline, among other things. We'd been there for each other almost our entire lives, which was why I couldn't let her down tonight.

I turned to her with a genuine smile. "Of course. The almighty Boyfriend Approval Panel is here and it's time to get to work."

Sascha laughed out loud. "Alright, come on then, but be nice." She took hold of my hand and pulled me through the assembling crowd. We bypassed the bar and walked up to the small stage where Dale smiled as soon as he noticed Sascha approaching.

He kissed her on the cheek in greeting and I witnessed something I hadn't seen in a long time. Sascha blushed. I squeezed the hand I still held in mine, showing her I was here for support. "Dale, this is my best friend, Elle. Elle, this is Dale."

Dale nodded a hello and smiled again. "How's it going?" He was cute. Only a few inches taller than Sascha, but she was wearing heels. Brown eyes. Short sandy hair styled to perfection. Stubble. Definitely cute.

I crossed my arms and made my scrutiny obvious as I looked him over, treating his greeting as an inquiry into his performance. The B.A.P. was serious business. "That depends on how well you do tonight," I replied with a smirk.

Sascha let out a nervous giggle and fixed me with a glare. "She's joking."

"Am I?" I continued, much to her horror.

Dale laughed. "I guess I've got someone else to impress tonight."

"I've heard all about you, Dale O'Donoghue. Hopefully you live up to the expectations."

"Okay! Wow!" Sascha interrupted, eyes wide. "We're going over there now." She took me by the shoulders and turned me around. To Dale she said, "I'll see you after?"

I tried looking back at Dale to say I'd definitely be seeing him after. Sascha wasn't having that and swiftly turned me away again, but not before I saw him press another sweet kiss to her now bright pink cheek. I felt a surge of joy spread through me. Maybe Sascha had found a good one after all.

She took hold of my hand again and pulled me away from the stage, and conveniently, towards the bar. "Oh my... I cannot believe you did that!" Her tone wasn't accusatory. I could hear the surprise she clearly still felt.

"Oh please, that was nothing compared to what you'd do to me," I laughed.

Sascha looked back at Dale with glistening eyes. "What do you think?"

We took a step closer to the bar as the line shortened. "I think he adores you," I admitted. I'd watched the way he looked her, and the way his lips lingered on her cheek as he kissed her. He was definitely smitten.

She smiled dreamily. "You think?"

"Yeah, I do. And I can see how much you like him." My words seemed to send her into her own world—a sappy, starry-eyed world—and so we waited in silence.

I took the chance to look around again. The crowd was steadily increasing, filling up the tables as people settled in before the gig. Dale's band had assembled at the edge of the stage and the overhead lights of the main area were dimmed. Justin was standing inside the ring of bright light on the stage, smiling and laughing along with his bandmates.

As if some embarrassing message from the universe was sent his way, he suddenly looked up, gorgeous blue eyes locking with mine from across the room. I felt my cheeks warm and my heart start racing again. I quickly looked away, mortified at being caught. After a few moments of trying to settle and mentally chastising myself for being a fool, I dared to look back.

Justin Hart was still staring at me, a smirk curving the corner of his lips.

Oh my... there it goes, pounding so quickly it might thump right out of my chest.

I turned away again, now completely ashamed at being caught staring twice in less than a minute. I tried focusing hard on the bartender, and while I was looking at him, I wasn't really seeing him. My mind was too busy thinking of all the times I'd come close to talking to Justin at the café. And those eyes. And that smirk. So cocky.

And then I thought about who he really was. My heart was still racing. Was it for the usual reasons when he was around, or was it because of something else now? Because I knew him?

Maybe I should have gone home.

Sascha nudged me out of my overthinking mind when it was our turn to step up to the bar. We ordered our drinks; a vodka cranberry for her and a sparkling water for me. Then we found a spare table near the front where Sascha could ogle her man candy for the next hour, and I could sit in mortification where Justin could see me front and centre.

This night was not turning out as I expected.

I was pleasantly surprised by their sound. Dream of Darcy that is. It was clear they were all about the lead singer. She was tall with long, sandy-coloured hair, and looked smoking hot in leather tights and red stilettos. I knew next to nothing about music but could tell she was the real deal. She was amazing. The others in the band were, of course, just as good. Dale played the keyboard, used his laptop for something, and at one point pulled out a tambourine. He did just about everything. Another guy played lead guitar and contributed some vocals. And Justin... Well, Justin was the drummer. He was good, as far as I could tell, and very much into what he was doing. He never missed a beat. Most of all, he really looked to be enjoying himself, grinning widely every so often as he kept time for the rest of the band. Altogether, they had this indie pop rock thing going on.

"They're good, aren't they?" Sascha yelled into my ear after a few songs. We were so close to the stage that invading personal space was the only way to communicate.

I nodded in way of agreement. Some people had even gotten up to dance on the tiny floor in front of the stage. As if she knew where my mind was at, Sascha grabbed hold of my hand and tried to pull me up.

I shook my head. "No way!"

"Come on!" she pleaded, a pout forming on her red lips. She didn't really give me an opportunity to object again and next thing I knew, I was standing right near the front of the stage. Sascha had no doubt chosen it to be in perfect view of Dale who winked at her when she blew him a kiss.

Rather than stand awkwardly in a sea of moving bodies I accepted my fate and joined in. I was no stranger to dance floors and it came just as naturally as anything else. I didn't even need alcohol to get moving, unlike one of the girls dancing near us. She probably shouldn't have worn heels like that if she'd planned on getting this wasted before 10 o'clock.

As we danced, I found myself glancing up at Justin again. He was lost in his own world. Looking a little closer, I noticed a slight sheen of sweat forming on what I could see of his chest under that black, V-neck shirt. And again, as if he could sense me staring, his eyes looked to the crowd and found mine. That same smirk from earlier formed as he watched me and continued drumming.

I was so entranced that I didn't notice a guy had swooped in behind me until Sascha pulled me to her. She kept her hands on my hips as she turned us around, placing herself between me and the potential vulture. She said something to him and he backed off. I mouthed a thank you and felt somewhat embarrassed as I looked back up at Justin, but he was no longer watching. He'd gone back to focusing on the music.

Disappointment flow through me, followed by a wave of confusion. There was no reason for me to think he'd still be looking at me. Nor should I want him to. He was Justin Hart after all.

How didn't I recognise him? I could have avoided this two-year obsession with Hot Café Guy if I'd known his true identity. Or if I'd just had the courage to talk to him, I would have known much sooner.

A thought occurred to me as the band wrapped things up and the lead singer thanked the crowd. Their set was over, and Sascha was going to introduce me. I'd already met Dale, but he said he would see her after, meaning after the gig. And with him he'd surely bring his band. And Justin, who was in the band.

"Why do you look so panicked?" Sascha asked as we sat back at our table.

"Panicked? I'm not panicked. I don't know what you're talking about."

She raised her eyebrows at my rambling.

"I need to pee," I announced, noticing the band step down from the stage.

"What?"

I took off for the bathroom before Sascha could protest further. What was wrong with me? I worked the front desk at a busy hotel. I was a people person. I introduced myself to strangers all the time. Why was this any different?

I knew why. Justin. He was no stranger.

I took the time to actually use the toilet. I might as well give some truth to my lame excuse for disappearing. While in the cubicle, I took a few deep breaths to calm myself. I could do this. I could speak to him. I mean, I'd been waiting for two years to talk to Hot Café Guy. That's a long time, and here was my opportunity. On the other hand, he wasn't just Hot Café Guy anymore, he was Justin Hart.

I'd met him before. Sure, it was twelve years ago and he looked like a different person now, but he was still Justin. Just Justin. That's how I had to look at him, like the ten-year-old I met at Caroline's wedding to his father.

Oh man.

I washed my hands in the cool water and looked into the mirror. Maybe primping alongside this terrible pep talk would give me some courage. I pushed my hands into my hair to neaten the natural honey-blonde strands of my long bob. I'd let it grow out a little recently and it now touched my shoulders when straightened. My natural makeup looked fine but did nothing to hide the terror in my brown eyes.

I took a few more deep breaths and straightened my navy smock dress. I looked perfectly presentable. With one more string of self-encouragement, I left the bathroom. As I opened the door, I almost ran directly into my best friend.

"Are you okay? What's wrong?" Sascha asked with a frown.

I shook my head. "I just had to use the ladies room."

She stared at me with a raised brow.

"I swear. I'm all good. Is Dale's gig finished? We shouldn't keep you away for too long or he'll start pining after you." I finished my rambling with a forced giggle. She knew something was up, but I wasn't letting her get a word in. "Let's go."

I walked beside Sascha as we approached our now packed table. The whole band was there, plus a few others. More importantly, Justin was there sipping a beer like he had no care in the world.

Sascha and Dale introduced me to everyone. I learned the beautiful lead singer's name was Darcy, namesake of the band, and that she and Dale were actually twins. As soon as he said it, it made sense. They looked eerily similar and their hair colour was exactly the same. I just didn't pay enough attention to notice earlier. The guitarist's name was Anthony and he gave me a wink as he looked me over, seemingly showing his approval. He was cute too, if not a little scruffy with his messy black hair curling around his ears. And Justin, well, he barely paid me any attention. In fact, besides a nod hello, he didn't look at me at all.

I felt my heart sink. It had been racing only moments ago, as the anticipation of our formal introduction rose. Now it was disheartened, and I felt embarrassed at my earlier freak out. He obviously didn't remember me, or if he did, then he had no significant feelings about this whole situation.

I was a fool.

To distract myself from these ridiculous thoughts, I let myself fall into easy conversation with the others. I played the best friend well and answered questions from Darcy with ease. She was clearly doing the same thing for her brother as I was doing for Sascha. Assessing the new girlfriend. I imagined a twin sister would have a lot of sway if she felt someone wasn't good enough for her brother.

After a short while, I excused myself to get a drink, offering to grab a round for the others. They all declined, having been to the bar while I was melting down in the bathroom. So I went up alone. It didn't stay that way for long.

As I leaned against the bar waiting for someone to notice me, I caught wind of the most intoxicating scent. I'd only experienced that sweet, woodsy aroma in one place before. The campus café as I stood in line behind Hot Café Guy. I was closer to him now than I'd ever been before.

My poor heart must have thought it was running a marathon tonight. It couldn't catch a break.

Sure enough, when I chanced a glance at the person next to me, Justin was standing there. He leaned an elbow against the bar and looked down at me. He was even taller now that I could see him up close. Those eyes were even bluer than I remembered. And was that a tattoo on his chest?

"Hey Ellie Bean," he said with that same smirk from earlier. My breath caught at the old nickname; one I hadn't heard in a very long time. "Can I buy you a drink?"

CHAPTER 3

Ellie Bean. The nickname that stuck when I couldn't say jelly-bean at three years old. Conveniently, it sounded like the beginning of my name, Elizabeth. From there came Ellie, and then as I got older, Elle. No one I knew called me Ellie Bean anymore, except Dad when he was feeling sentimental.

And now Justin.

Standing this close, I was finally able to take him in completely. As always, those eyes, which currently sparkled with a hint of arrogance, were gorgeous. His black hair, which was shorter on the sides and a little overgrown on top, shone with the remnants of sweat he earned throughout his time on stage. He was clean-shaven but looked a little scruffier than usual, also a result of the drumming, no doubt.

There was also a tattoo on his chest. I thought I saw a glimpse of it earlier, but now I could confirm that Justin definitely did have a tattoo. I could see the corner of it peeking out of his shirt. What it was exactly, I couldn't tell.

"So you do know who I am," I stated with a spark of confidence I didn't know I possessed.

He shrugged. "I wasn't sure at first but figured it out recently."

Recently? How recently? Ten minutes ago recently?

I took a chance, remembering the all-knowing smirks I'd received tonight. "And you never said hello?"

He licked his lips slowly as he thought about it. Oh, wow.

"You've always been a little standoffish," he admitted openly. "I wasn't sure how you'd feel about it."

Standoffish? "No, I'm not," I countered boldly.

The corner of Justin's lips curved up and he looked me over. "Are you sure? Your body language is telling me a different story, and you've always sort of been that way."

My body language? I took a moment to consider that. Crossed arms, a popped knee and a cold attitude. I quickly unfolded myself and tried to relax. That only made him laugh. "I'm not 8-years-old anymore," I reminded him, "and I'm sure I don't know what you mean."

He laughed again. It was nice, and I momentarily forgot that he was teasing me. "So, that drink?"

I shook my head politely. "I'm not drinking tonight."

"Alcohol's not a condition on the offer." When I didn't respond, he continued with an air of confidence. "How about a skinny macadamia latte?"

My heart picked up its uneven rhythm again. He knew my coffee order. "So you have noticed me." All those times in the campus café when I stole glances at him, watched him from afar, and daydreamed about things I shouldn't have be daydreaming about while trying to study, he noticed.

He spread his hands in a shrug. "It's a little hard to ignore the ogling eyes of a beautiful woman."

I had to look away to hide the beginnings of a smile that threatened to break through. So I was beautiful? The shock of that only lasted a few seconds as my eyes widened in realisation.

Ogling. He knew that I'd been watching him! Could this meeting be any more embarrassing?

Again, I didn't respond. I was coming up blank, not knowing what to say. Thankfully, he picked up the conversation. "So, that coffee?"

"Sure, thank you," I accepted, intentionally avoiding gaze. I seemed to lose my words when I looked at him.

Justin caught the attention of the bartender and ordered our drinks. While he was doing that, I glanced back at Sascha. She mouthed an 'are you okay?' from her position in Dale's arms. I smiled to let her know that I was. Somehow, despite the swirling storm of emotions and memories occurring inside me, I was okay.

With drinks in hand, Justin and I walked back to our group. It had grown again. He pulled another bar table over and then found me a stool to sit on. I took it gratefully and thanked him for the seat and the coffee. That was the only bout of grateful I could manage, though, because as soon as we sat down, Darcy pounced upon him with one of her friends.

It wasn't like I should be surprised, or have any feelings about it at all, but watching Darcy lean against him as they laughed at some inside joke, stirred something inside me. It was plain to see that they were friends. They were clearly close, and there was nothing sensual about their actions, but it still sent a wave of annoyance through me. Her friend, Emily, was far worse. She outright flirted with him, tossed those perfect brunette curls over her shoulder, pressed herself against his side, and touched him with a confidence he didn't knock back.

I had to look away, if only to hide my eye roll. I wasn't sure what I was feeling, or why I was feeling it. I'd always had minor bouts of jealousy when I saw Hot Café Guy flirting with girls at the café.

Surely that's what this was. Two years of obsession that needed to be thrown out.

Anthony, the guitarist, happened to be sitting next to me, so I decided starting a conversation with him would be a good distraction. It was, and I found myself falling easily into the group and tried to be confident.

Later in the night I caught Sascha's attention. She pulled herself away from Dale's embrace and came to stand beside me. She placed her drink—some blue concoction on ice—beside my now empty latte.

"What was the deal, again? Oh, right, no coffee!"

I held my hands up in mock surrender. "Hey, Justin offered. I could hardly refuse. That would be rude."

"Mhmm..." she mumbled with pursed lips. Then she lowered her voice. "Are you okay with all that? It looked a little awkward earlier."

"Yeah, I'm fine," I told her. I snuck a glance at him. Justin was now engrossed in a conversation with Emily but he looked a little stern. Sascha clearly wasn't convinced, so I distracted her. "You and Dale are cosy. How's that going?"

She brightened immediately. It was then that I could tell she was tipsy. The giddy smile and glassy eyes were a tip off. "I have no words," she admitted. "No, really, I'm speechless. I go completely blank." She placed her hands on my shoulders and looked me directly in the eye. "It's like nothing else matters." And then she giggled.

Definitely tipsy.

"Okay, I think I'm cutting you off now."

Sascha pouted. "Oh, come on, I need to drink for the both of us."

"Except you're more of a lightweight than I am," I chastised.

She folded her arms. "Yeah, okay Sawyer." Before I had time to respond to that little dig, Dale appeared. He placed a tall glass of water in front of her. "Now you guys are just ganging up on me." Sascha's hands went to her hips, but her attitude contradicted her eyes completely. They melted as she looked up at Dale.

He held her gaze and didn't back down.

"Fine," she moaned and reached for the glass.

I laughed and turned my attention to Dale. "I like you."

Sascha almost spat out the sip she'd taken.

"So you're impressed then?" he asked hopefully.

I held my pointer finger and thumb close together. "Just enough."

Sascha and Dale had been hanging off each other all night. I'd been mindful not to overcrowd her and gave her plenty of space to be with him. I was glad I did because it gave me a good view of them. Dale was very attentive. He was always touching her in one way or another: a hand on the small of her back; an embrace from behind; or a sweet kiss. And Sascha? Well, I'd never seen her so happy. She was no stranger to a good time, but the way she seemed tonight was on a new level.

My best friend was completely smitten.

When she'd finished her glass of water, Sascha spun and hugged me. I put my arms around her, a little stunned by her sudden burst of affection.

"We're getting ready to head off," Dale said as she turned to him. "You ladies are welcome to join us if you want."

"We have work in the morning," Sascha said reluctantly before I could respond. That was a surprise. She didn't normally mind working with a hangover. I would have to question her about this later. "Next time?" Her tone turned hopeful.

"Of course." Dale tried to hide the disappointment in his expression. "I'll walk you to your car." That was to both of us. What a gentleman. Yes, I definitely liked Dale. I'd only known him for a few hours but could tell he was a good guy. Sascha deserved a good guy.

We said our goodbyes to the group, and I made sure to pay Justin no particular attention. Then Dale walked us out. It was a chilly June night and I wrapped my arms around myself to keep warm. I'd parked in the lot around the corner. It was only a short walk, but the breeze wasn't very kind.

We'd barely taken a few steps when another body joined us. Justin.

Much like most of the night, he didn't say a word to me. I felt my frustration deepen. What could have been a nice stroll on a winter's night turned into one of awkward tension. To make it worse, I could hear Emily and co. giggling behind us. A brief glance back showed me that she, Darcy, and Ryan had joined our group. Their presence made me wonder. Was Emily his girlfriend or just a potential suitor?

I felt relief wash over me as we approached my white Audi. Safety and warmth at last.

I stood there awkwardly as Dale and Sascha kissed goodbye. It was probably a little too intimate for others to witness and I turned away to give them some privacy. Justin, apparently, was thinking along the same lines.

We had turned to each other, and he did nothing to hide his grin. I pressed my lips together trying to contain my own smile.

"Shame you're not coming with us," he said. "I'm going to be hearing about how perfect your friend is all night, now." I was both surprised and annoyed. If he wanted me there so badly than why had he ignored me? Why buy me a drink and then let other girls hang all over you?

I couldn't let him see my frustration, so I laughed. "Don't worry. I'll probably cop it as well. She's sleeping in my bed tonight."

His eyebrows rose and his lips parted in surprised. I had no doubts about what he was thinking. He pressed his lips together, deciding not to comment on the suggestive connection he'd just made in his mind. Smart boy.

Just then, Sascha and Dale resurfaced. Justin took that as his cue and gave me a nod. "I'll see you 'round, Ellie Bean." And then he turned and walked away.

That added even more confusion to this shamble of a night. He'd spent the better part of the last two hours ignoring me and then he calls me by my nickname as if we're old friends?

He was so frustrating!

Sascha seemed oblivious to my spiralling mood as we drove home. Possibly because she was lost in her own little world of romance, or because she was still drunk. Either way, she left me alone to my thoughts. I actively tried to push Justin Hart out of my mind by thinking of other things, like my new class schedule. It worked, sort of. I needed to figure out how I would fit shifts at the hotel into my timetable. I was going to be very busy this semester.

By the time we made it back to my place and I'd deposited Sascha in my room, she was almost asleep. She was going to have a thumping headache in the morning, but that should be all. On my way downstairs to grab her a glass of water and some aspirin for when she woke up, I poked my head into my father's room. He'd left the door slightly ajar, like he always did when I was out. He liked to hear when I got home, to know that I was okay. But tonight he'd fallen asleep, his light snores telling me he'd passed out a while ago.

Standing there watching him, I was reminded of who I'd been hanging out with tonight. What would Dad think if he knew I spent time with a Hart? He'd been so hurt by the actions of his ex-wife and best friend. Would he be upset if he found out I chose to spend time with Justin? Would he be disappointed in me? I quietly closed his door, deciding it was best he didn't know. Not if tonight was a once off. It was better not to upset him.

I fetched the water and painkillers for Sascha and then got ready for bed.

As I climbed under the warm covers with her, she spoke in a sleepy voice, very close to nodding off. "He couldn't keep his eyes off you, you know."

I turned to face her. She was curled up with the sheets pulled close to her chin. Her usually perfect hair was splayed across the pillow in an unruly fashion, but she still looked beautiful. "What are you talking about?"

"Your hot café guy," she went on. "He was checking you out all night. You didn't notice?"

Had he been? I'd made a pointed effort to avoid looking at Justin. Surely he was too busy flirting with his groupies to pay me any attention. Not that it mattered. He wasn't just Hot Café Guy anymore. He was Justin Hart. I didn't want him to give me any attention. That would be wrong, and it would stir up a lot of memories and pain. Not just for me, but for Dad if he ever found out.

"No," I whispered. "I didn't notice."

I received no response from Sascha. She was already asleep.

I tossed and turned most of the night, wondering about Justin and all the what ifs that came with him.

CHAPTER 4

"You should eat another slice," Sawyer said, holding the pizza box out to me.

We were cuddling on the couch in his small apartment watching a rerun of one of his favourite sitcoms. I wasn't really a fan of them, so I had no idea what was going on. It was something about a group of geeky friends and their wacky adventures. Not my cup of tea. I'd retrieved my date book from my bag twenty minutes ago and was more focused on figuring out when I could work between classes.

I shook my head without looking up from my schedule. "I'm all good. You probably shouldn't eat so late. It's terrible for your metabolism, and your sleep." The time was pushing on midnight.

He laughed. "I don't know, I'm pretty tuckered out," he replied with his husky, suggestive voice, the one he usually used in the bedroom.

I turned to him with a raised brow. We were sitting quite close, and his arm was already resting behind me on the pillow. My movement brought us closer together. "Oh yeah, why's that?" I asked, matching his tone.

Sawyer shrugged and scanned my body with hooded eyes. "Some chick wore me out." He always looked cute after sex, with his tousled blonde hair and sleepy blue eyes. And he wore nothing but his boxers, which was always a good sight. Sawyer worked out, and while he wasn't as well-defined as a Baywatch lifeguard, you could definitely see the slight curvatures on his abdomen. He also had bagpipes tattooed on his ribs, right below his peck. It was a small nod to his Scottish heritage, and it was kind of hot. "I'll sleep like a baby."

"Some chick? You're not helping your case." I leaned forward to put my date book on the coffee table, brushing my fingers over his thigh as I did. It brought us even closer.

His arm moved from the pillow behind me to rest on my lower back. "What case is that?"

"The one where you try to get me back into bed," I giggled softly.

He was only a breath away now. "There are other ways to do that."

"Oh, yeah?" I challenged, knowing exactly where this was going.

"Yeah." He pressed his lips to mine and I felt his familiar warmth spark the mutual lust between us. Kissing Sawyer always felt good. I found comfort in his arms and it didn't take long before he leaned me back against the couch and hovered above me. In the small space we had, he settled between my legs and turned up the heat.

Unlike Sawyer, I was fully clothed. He had a roommate that liked to come in and out at all times of the night. I had no interest in him accidentally walking in while I pranced around in my bra. While I was pretty sure he was snuggled up in bed right now, I wasn't going to risk it.

My clothes didn't hinder Sawyer. He confidently reached under my knit sweater to run his warm hands up my sides and under my bra. Then he moved to unbutton my jeans.

That's when I broke the kiss. Sawyer moaned and rested his head on my shoulder. He knew what was coming. It was almost a routine at this point. "It's late," I whispered. "I have to go."

He held himself above me, resting his elbows on either side of my head, and pouted. As if that would work. "Come on, old man," I teased, reaching between us to run by hand over his boxers. "I think it's too soon for round two anyway." It had only been half an hour since round one and he needed to recharge.

Sawyer's eyes widened in offense. "Ouch."

I rolled my eyes and smiled. "It's not personal, it's biology." I pushed myself up to give him a peck on the lips in the hopes it would reassure him. Science was science and his body needed to reproduce a few substances before we went again.

"I just need ten more minutes, fifteen max," he argued. When I remained silent, he groaned and sat up, pulling me with him. "Okay, fine."

As I straightened myself up, fixing my bra and the button on my jeans, I noticed the couple on the TV screen. They were in bed talking, clearly having just finished their intimate moment. Next thing, they were sidling back under the covers, less than a minute after round one. I giggled at that. How ironic.

Sawyer scoffed. "These shows are so unrealistic."

"Exactly. Unrealistic. So get over it." His pride was obviously suffering, but there was no point dwelling on something so minute.

I stood up and stretched a little, then started to collect my things.

"Did you figure out what you're going to do about work?" Sawyer asked as I put my date book in my bag.

"Yeah, it looks like it will have to be weekday mornings or weekends." My class schedule was spread over four days this semester and that meant less time at work. What it did mean was more time on campus, and potentially more time seeing Hot Café Guy. Normally this would excite me, but I'd tried really hard over the last week to push him out of my mind. So far, I was succeeding, but with classes starting in two days, it was becoming more difficult.

I took a deep breath. I couldn't think about any of that now. Not here.

Sawyer sighed. We wouldn't be seeing each other as frequently in the coming months, not at work anyway. "No office hook ups then?"

I had to laugh at that. "There are no office hook ups now."

"I know, and it's a damn shame." He was pouting again, making a show it. When he noticed that I was all packed up and ready to go, he asked, "do you want me to walk you out?"

"No, it's okay. It's cold outside." He was nearly naked. I leant down to give him a quick kiss goodbye and he tapped me on the butt as I turned around. "Goodnight."

"Night, lovely."

I made it home just before Dad went to bed. He was up late working on the books and was happy that I'd come to say goodnight. It also made things for me a little easier. If he thought I spent the night somewhere else without prewarning him, I would face a few awkward questions in the morning. He was never overbearing and was always respectful of my privacy—I was an adult after all—but he did like to know that I was safe. It was a father's prerogative.

I almost made it through the weekend without a single mention of Justin Hart, that was until the end of my shift crossed over with the beginning of Sascha's on Sunday.

"And where have you been this past week," she questioned as we went over the check-in list. She wore her Sass face, the one that told me she meant business. "It's like you dropped off the face of the Earth."

"I think you mean you haven't come back down to Earth in the past week," I laughed. Both were true, but it was probably best to focus on her so that we could avoid scrutinising me. I knew exactly where this conversation would go if I didn't keep the attention on her escapades with Dale, and I wasn't ready to talk about it. Whatever it was. "I've just been busy prepping for classes and working and stuff."

Sascha tapped her nails on the counter. "What prep? There's nothing to prep until classes start and you get your book list and assignment schedule."

I rolled my eyes at her, putting on an air of sarcasm. "We both know I've already looked up the course material."

"Nerd," she chuckled. There was not faulting that logic. Plus, I did look up the course materials for the semester. I knew what I needed to buy at the campus bookstore tomorrow.

I bent down to the key cabinet below the counter to slip the cards into their little envelopes for today's check-ins. "What have you and Dale been up to?" I played up a suggestive voice and wiggled my eyebrows at her. She was instantly distracted.

Sascha and Dale were official now. She was his girlfriend, and he was her boyfriend. I remembered what it felt like to get a new boyfriend. Granted, my last official relationship ended when I was seventeen and that was just puppy love. There was nothing spectacular about it now that I looked back. As a slightly more mature adult, and after witnessing the pain and let-downs Sascha experienced in previous years, it was plain to see that this was the real deal. Watching them last week at the Uni Bar showed me the intensity that could be experienced between two people, and not just of the animal instinct kind.

It was beautiful.

Sascha sighed dreamily and rested her elbows on the counter. "He took me to the beach the other day, it was so romantic."

"It's freezing." The beach seemed like an odd place to go in the middle of winter.

"We didn't go in the water," she laughed. "We just strolled along the sand and then sat on the rocks and talked for ages."

I smiled, standing back up now that I'd finished the room keys. Check-in started at two o'clock and everything was ready to go. "That's really nice. Have you guys, you know?" I wriggled my eyebrows again.

I was very invested in Sascha's relationship at the moment. It was like the Sascha buried deep inside her, the one who only came out with family, had surfaced. And for a guy. I'd never seen that happen before.

This new Sascha was intriguing.

"Not yet, and I'm kind of glad we haven't." Another surprise. My confused expression led her to elaborate. "You know how I've always jumped in too hard, too fast? Well, I don't want that with Dale. All those other guys only wanted my body or liked the idea of me hanging off their arms. But with Dale, I just want to make sure he really likes me before we get into that part of the relationship."

"Because you really like him?" I guessed.

Sascha's smile lit up her beautiful face. "Because I really, really like him," she admitted.

I reached for her and pulled her into a hug. "I'm so happy for you, Sass."

The phone rang then, and we let go. While Sascha spoke to the caller, I busied myself by making sure the counter was tidy. It really made things easier if everything was in order.

"Right," she began after hanging up, and I cringed at her tone. "Now that the plan to distract Sascha with her dreamy boyfriend has concluded, we can go back to you. What's going on?"

I should have known I couldn't fool her. "Nothing's going on specifically, I just have a lot happening right now."

She rose one eyebrow and stared me down. "There's a difference?"

I turned to her with hands on my hips, hoping some attitude would deter her. "Okay, you've got two minutes until my shift ends. What do you want to know?"

She rolled her eyes. I was being a little dramatic. "Classes start tomorrow. What are you going to do when your hot café guy shows up?"

What could I do? I spent the last week trying to ignore his existence, which proved to be a fruitless task. History told me I would see him this semester, just like I have every semester in the past. And it would likely be at the café.

I shrugged. "I don't know. I guess I would have to say hi now that we've met." And now that I knew I'd known him for over half my life. There was no ignoring that.

"That's it?"

"What am I supposed to do?"

"I don't know, I thought maybe you'd want to hang out a bit. He was checking you out, remember? Maybe we could double date." She looked hopeful.

There were so many things wrong with that. "He was kind of a dick last weekend. He knew exactly who I was and didn't care."

Sascha's enthusiasm dimmed. "Is that going to be a problem? What happened when you guys were kids?" Was she worried my hesitations about Justin would affect her life with Dale? "He's kind of been through a lot as well."

That he had. I'd been burned by Caroline's choices, and they'd had a profound impact on my life. But Justin? He experienced a world of pain before any of that. At seven-years-old, he lost his mother to breast cancer. I couldn't even imagine what that was like for a kid so young. And then two years later his dad married someone else. He suddenly had a stepmother and a little sister. It was an emotional rollercoaster I couldn't pretend to understand. Sure, I'd lost Caroline, but it wasn't the same. I could have seen her anytime I wanted.

I knew of Justin Hart, but I had no idea who he really was.

None of what happened in our mutual past was his fault, but that didn't mean seeing and interacting with him was easy. And then there was my dad to think about. I still hadn't told him about Justin, and I felt so guilty about that.

"Sass, I don't know what will happen when I see him," I admitted solemnly. "But the least I can do is not criminalise him for things he can't control."

This time, she was the one to pull me into a hug. I held on tight. "I'm proud of you. And I'm here, anytime you need me, okay? No more pushing me out and avoiding me."

Still in Sascha's arms, I nodded. I had been avoiding her because I knew she would make me confront things head on. But it also felt good knowing she was there, and that she noticed my struggles.

It was true, I didn't know how I would react when I saw Justin again, and of course I would see him again. What I did know was that I had a storm of emotions brewing inside me and I couldn't define a single one of them.

CHaPTer 5

On Monday morning, all my anxieties came barrelling in, breaking through the walls I'd spent a week building. I could feel tingles in my fingertips from the moment I woke up. Classes never made me nervous, so I knew, without doubt, what was causing this reaction.

The possibility of seeing Justin.

I'd well and truly accepted it was going to happen, but that didn't curve the paranoia pulsing through me as I stood in the line at the campus café. When I walked through the doors, I scanned the tables, keen to spot him if he was around. It would give me the advantage, or at least give me a few extra minutes to prepare. But he wasn't there.

I made it through my mid-morning coffee and croissant without seeing him. I had even chosen a spot in the corner where I could view the whole room and the two entrances. But no, he didn't show.

Then I walked to my first class and sat through an introduction lecture without event. It calmed me down somewhat, knowing he wouldn't be there. Justin was older than me and had started university a year earlier, so he was highly unlikely to be in any of my classes.

When I went to the campus bookstore, which was crowded with students eager to purchase their course materials, I was sure he'd pop up out of nowhere and surprise me like he had that time at the bar. But he didn't. In fact, I didn't see Justin at all on Monday.

Surprisingly, I felt disappointed, which was also frustrating. I shouldn't be disappointed, but I hyped myself up so much about what I would say to him that I couldn't help it. Now I was annoyed all the stress was for nothing.

On Tuesday, I felt a little better. Justin hadn't made an appearance and I almost forgot about him. I even managed to order coffee and lunch at the café and eat the whole sandwich without worrying he would walk through the door.

It was a nice day, so I chose to sit outside where the sun could provide a little extra warmth. I was flicking through one of my new textbooks when a familiar, intoxicating scent caught my attention. I sat upright as a shadow loomed over me. I knew exactly who it was without turning around.

Justin held a coffee out in front of me. "Hey, Ellie Bean. Can I join you?" Ellie Bean. I wasn't sure how I felt about him using my childhood nickname so often.

"S-sure," I stuttered, cringing at the fact I couldn't seem to function in front of him. At the bar, I was coming up blank and couldn't respond. Now I was tripping over my words, and we hadn't even started a real conversation yet. It was kind of pathetic.

I cleared my throat as he moved to the other side of the table, coming into full view. "Is that for me?" I questioned, trying to be confident and trying to ignore how good he looked up close. Sitting outside prevented me from keeping an eye on both entrances to the café. He obviously snuck in the other door without me noticing and ordered two coffees. One for him, and apparently one for me.

Justin's lips turned up in a smirk. "Skinny macadamia latte," he announced confidently as he sat down. I still couldn't believe he knew my favourite order. He really did pay attention to me all those times we stood in line together in awkward tension. At least, it was tense on my side. I had no idea what he was thinking or feeling.

I reached for it, and as my hand grazed his, I felt that all-consuming tingle return to my fingertips. My heart started racing and I did everything I could to remain neutral. It hadn't done that since last week. I couldn't let him see how his presence affected me.

Now it was Justin's turn to clear his throat. He placed both his hands around his coffee cup and shifted slightly. Did he feel the same thing? Unlikely. It was just me and my undefined emotions going haywire.

"Thank you for the coffee," I said awkwardly. "You didn't have to do that." It was the second time he'd bought me one, and the second time he caught me off guard.

"No worries," he replied. "I saw you sitting all alone out here and thought you might like a little company."

That was a daring assumption. "And what if I enjoy being alone?" I questioned boldly.

Justin shrugged, but gave me a smile. "Well then, maybe I don't like being alone."

I pursed my lips, finding it hard to tell if he was being sarcastic or not. I very rarely saw him on his own. He usually had a group of friends hanging around. If I saw him walking through campus, there was always at least one other person with him. It was one of the reasons I never approached him. That, and I was obviously a wimp.

I gave my own little shrug. "You are a people person." I also remembered what he was like at Uni Bar. However hard I tried to ignore him that night, it was impossible not to see someone so confident and outgoing. His presence was enough to draw anyone's eyes to him. I also remembered the girls giving him their undivided attention.

He took a sip of his coffee then, avoiding my eyes. "Not all people." What did that mean? Justin seemed to notice my questioning expression and changed the subject. "Is that the textbook for, what's it called?" he clicked his fingers, trying to remember the name of the class. "Something to do with business innovation and creativity?"

I nodded, wondering how he knew the class. "Have you taken it?"

"I have. It's a mandatory class in the hospitality management major."

Another surprise. We were doing the same business degree. Although, it did make sense considering his father's successful hotels. I was ashamed to admit that I'd given into temptation and googled his family business last week. The Harts now owned three major hotels. One in Sydney, another in Brisbane and a new one on the Gold Coast.

"I'm majoring in the same thing," I smiled. "Do you have a sub-major?" I was curious to know if he was only taking business classes or if he was branching out into something else, like me.

"Accounting. What about you?" he asked, now seemingly invested in our conversation.

I hesitated for a moment. Our fathers went to university together and went down the same path supporting each other before disaster struck. It made sense their children would follow in their footsteps. And I was, sort of. Would Justin find it odd that I was interested in other areas?

"Child and Community Studies," I admitted.

His eyebrows rose in surprise. "That's a little far out of the field. What made you choose that?"

"I don't know, I'm just interested in it, I guess." I was shrugging my shoulders a lot today.

He looked like he wanted to ask another question, but just then someone called out to him. Justin stood up to greet a guy in a heavy leather jacket and a manbun.

I took the chance to pack up my belongings. Justin briefly introduced us with no information other than our names and gave me a quizzical look as I lifted my bag over my shoulder.

He said goodbye to his mate, Jimbo. I had to assume it was a nickname for Jim, or James, or something of the like. When he turned back to me, he looked a little disappointed, or was it worried? "Heading off?"

I placed a palm on the textbook I held against my chest as I stood up. "My lecture starts soon."

"Ah." He still looked disappointed as he picked up his backpack and empty coffee cup. He threw it into the recycle bin close by. Somehow, during our short conversation, he managed to finish it. I'd only taken a few sips. "Is that class still in the north building? I'll walk with you."

Oh. How was I supposed to respond to that? I thought sitting together and discussing our majors was a huge deal. Now he wanted to walk me to class. Why? He probably just had a tutorial nearby. Instead of questioning him, I remembered what I said to Sascha yesterday. I would make an effort. "Okay."

We walked in silence until we were halfway. That was when he made me an offer. "You know, I ended up buying a book from the additional readings list for this class. It came in really handy for the group assignment. You can borrow it if you like?"

That brought me up short. Why would he offer to lend me something? We barely knew each other. The paste twelve years didn't count. "Yeah, maybe, thanks," I said, unsure if he really meant it. The book would come in handy, no doubt. I hated group assignments. There was always one slacker who barely contributed, and my perfectionism ensured I ended up doing the bulk of the work. Any help I could get would be a godsend.

When we reached a fork in the path, one way leading to the north building and the other to a smaller one full of tutor rooms, we said our goodbyes.

"Thanks again for the coffee, and for walking with me," I nod-ded, hoping I sounded polite and not uncomfortable. Even though I questioned his motives about walking me to class, I had to admit it was nice of him to buy me a coffee. His Hot Café Guy status was peaking now.

Justin smiled his gorgeous smile. "Anytime. Let me know if you want to borrow that book someday." Someday? Was that him saying he wanted to hang out again? No, that was probably just me overthinking it. "See you 'round, Ellie."

"Bye." I kept my eyes on him as he walked down the other path. He called me Ellie. Not Ellie Bean. Just Ellie.

Why did that disappoint me so much?

It felt nice to have dinner with my dad. Our schedules didn't always line up, what with him working so much and me working or in classes at odd hours. Today we managed to be home at the same time, so he made pasta and we sat down at the kitchen counter to eat together.

The counter was littered with my books and papers from class. I was writing due dates in my date book so I could keep on top of my workload while he cooked.

We spoke about his day and how he was considering a remodel of the penthouse suite at the hotel. It lead to a discussion about making sure finances were in the right place and how it would affect the off season. He brought up Sawyer's contributions at their meeting today and I felt a little guilty. I was lying to my father about seeing Sawyer. It made me wonder if he'd be more disappointed in me for seeing him or for getting involved with the Harts.

Dad mistook my worried expression. "How are your classes this semester? Did you take another social studies elective?"

I looked up at him, knowing I could be honest about this. That was something, at least. "I am. Only one this semester though, the rest are the mandatory classes."

He placed his utensils carefully on his plate and gave me his full attention. He was starting to look his age, with silver streaks running through the sides of his dark hair and crow's feet at the corner of his brown eyes. Mid-fifties still looked good on him. "Darling, I hope you know that I support you with this, with you exploring other interests."

I shifted uncomfortably. "I know, Dad." He had never forced me into a business degree and always made it known I could choose whichever path I wanted in life. I'd chosen my degree based on what would help me run his business one day. I was his only child. What would happen to all his hard work if I didn't eventually take over? Would all his success amount to nothing if I chose to do something else?

Dad placed his hand over mine. "No matter what, all of it's yours. You can be as involved as you want to be in the business, whatever you choose.. You will always own the controlling shares." He was overcompensating, reminding me of my inheritance. The disappointments I'd faced in life worried him and he didn't want to be another source of pain. He didn't want to force me into anything.

I took hold of his hand. "I know, Daddy. I'm still deciding what I want to do."

"Okay," he said eventually.

"Okay," I repeated, and then we continued eating the dinner he made for us.

When we were finished, we cleaned the dishes together. I was drying the plates when my phone rang loudly on the corner of the island bench.

I dried my hands and reached for it. Sascha. "Hey stranger," I answered.

"Girl, it's been two days," she said in mock annoyance. "I don't even know who you are anymore."

I chuckled. "Only you consider two days a lifetime," I reminded her. Typical Sascha being overly dramatic. I loved her for it. "What's up?"

"Well," she began, dragging out the word. That wasn't a good start. "How do you feel about going camping this weekend?"

"Camping?" I questioned in horror. My dad laughed, not needing to hear the other end of the conversation. She had to be joking.

Sascha launched into a spiel so I couldn't interrupt, knowing how I would protest. What a ridiculous thing to suggest. "So, Dale and his mates go on this annual camping trip in memory of his brother Daniel. Don't ask now, I'll tell you all about it later. It's a long story." I felt my stomach drop. In memory? I didn't know Dale had lost a brother. "Anyway, he invited me along this year and suggested to bring you as well, so that I had a close friend. There will be other girls there, of course, like Darcy, but it wouldn't be the same. I know classes just started, but that makes this time great because nothing is due yet, and we can find a temp to replace you at work on Saturday. And you know, I don't know what to say or do. I've never had a boyfriend who's lost someone so close to him before."

I shook my head. That was a lot to take in. "I wouldn't know either," I assured her.

"It would be really good if you came, to support me, supporting him, if that makes sense." It did, sort of.

"Sass, we don't camp. We don't even glamp." My dad laughed again and I threw the dish towel at him. It was true.

"I know," she whined. "But we won't have to get anything besides sleeping bags. Dale has a tent and an air mattress for us. Please? I'd really like to be there, but it will be a little weird without a friend. Plus you'll know Darcy and Justin as well, so it won't be just me to talk to."

She didn't need to beg, or to ask again. Of course I would go. "I guess we're going camping then," I said with as much enthusiasm as I could muster.

Camping. In a tent. Overnight. With Justin.

I now had a whole new set of worries.

CHaPTer 6

Our lack of survival skills was starting to show, and we hadn't even made it to the campsite yet. "What do you mean you don't know where the turn off is?" Sascha's panicked voice filled the car.

"I mean the internet dropped out a kilometre ago and the GPS on my phone is no longer tracking us." What else could it mean? I paid attention to the roads we passed since the connection cut out and was matching what I saw with the map that no longer functioned on my phone. I was quite certain our turn off was the next one on the right.

Sascha shook her head. "Maybe this was a bad idea. We are so not cut out for camping."

"We're going to be fine," I reassured her. "We have everything we need, I think, and once we're there, I'm sure Dale can help us with whatever we panic about next."

I looked into the backseat of Sascha's little Toyota. We went shopping on Thursday night to get sleeping bags and had come home with a few extra things. We now had an esky, which was currently filled with alcohol and snacks, as well as a camp light for inside the tent. Our pillows and overnight bags were there as well.

I'm pretty sure we overpacked, but we wanted to be prepared for anything. Besides, we would leave our second bags in the car and no one would be the wiser.

"Turn right up here," I instructed when I spotted the small gap in the tree line. We were driving through a dense area. Luckily, it was only midday, and we could see everything clearly. When Sascha made the turn, I started getting some seriously creepy Wolf Creek vibes.

The bush was incredibly dense and there were dilapidated wooden signs with the faded names of bushwalks and their distances. There was also an empty car parked to the side of the narrow dirt road.

As if she read my mind, Sascha asked, "Are you sure this is the right place?"

"Mhmm," I mumbled, not wanting to formally admit it in case I was wrong. "Just keep going. I think it's at the end of this road." I hoped it was at the end of this road.

Thankfully, it was. A group of cars was parked at the end, just outside an open gate. We drove through that gate, not sure what to do, and just to stay safe. We spotted Dale almost immediately and a wave a relief ran through me.

"You made it," he greeted proudly as we stepped out of the car. Sascha ran straight into his arms.

"Barely," I muttered.

"Let's grab your stuff and put it in the tent. Justin set it up for you earlier."

Of course he did. At the mention of Justin's name, I felt my usual heart phenomena start up, but I didn't pay as much attention to it now. After our little coffee date on Tuesday, or whatever it was, he managed to catch me off-guard a second time. Yesterday, he brought me another coffee and we spent an hour sitting and talking by the soccer field watching the EU team train. We didn't speak about anything major, but it was nice. He also took it as a chance to hype me up about camping in the bush. It made me a little nervous, although I'm sure he was joking about most of it.

After that, I was fully prepared to see him today.

Everyone else arrived yesterday, so I wasn't surprised to see a completely set up campsite. To ensure I could come over the weekend, I had to swap my Saturday shift with a Friday one. The others didn't have that problem and Justin told me they were heading here on Friday afternoon for an extra night.

There were five tents set up in a circle, plus a swag, which I learned at the camping store was a one-person mini tent that you couldn't even sit up in. It didn't look very comfortable. There was a river about fifty metres away and I could hear the hum of a loud engine.

"Where is everyone?" I asked curiously. It was a small village without residents.

"They're out on the water." He checked his watch. "They'll be back in soon. I had them drop me off earlier so I could be here to meet you."

"Aww," Sascha cooed. "So sweet."

That was something at least. I shivered imagining what it would have been like to arrive at an abandoned camp. The Mick Taylor nightmares would be horrendous.

Dale led us to a small orange tent. "Alright, ladies, this one's yours. It's a two-person, and the air mattress is already blown up." He left us to sort out our space and went to start the fire. It was already cold and the temperature would drop even further tonight.

"This is sort of cosy," I said as we sat on the double mattress and unrolled our sleeping bags. The mattress barely fit inside the tent, and we had to squish our bags into one corner so there was space to slide out the zippered door. We had no qualms sharing a bed, plus the proximity would provide extra warmth.

"It's sort of fun," she added perkily. "Oh, do you think we'll make s'mores tonight?"

I shook my head. "Doubt it. Isn't than a North American thing?"

Sascha shrugged. "You're asking the wrong person."

When we were satisfied with the comfort of our new accommodations, we slipped out of the tent. I zipped it up and turned just in time to see a Jeep towing a boat drive by the camp. I didn't know any of the guys sitting in the boat, but I did recognise Darcy and her friend Emily. Great.

"Ellie. Snakes!"

I yelped and jumped away from the tent. "What? Where?" My heart almost beat out of my chest as I spun on the spot looking for them.

She started laughing. "I meant zip the tent up properly or the snakes will get in."

My shoulders slumped in relief as Sascha lent down to fix the zipper. "Do not yell the word snake when there's no snake!" I growled.

"You know," another voice started. I jumped and spun around. "If you ever do see a snake, don't make any sharp or sudden movements." It was Justin, and he was laughing.

My annoyance quickly faded because he was standing there in board shorts and a life jacket. And the jacket was open. And I could see his naked chest beneath it. And it was gorgeous. At least, what I could see of it was.

I contained my shock at how good he looked in this odd outfit and turned on the attitude. "This is your fault."

His laugh deepened. "My fault? How's that?"

"Well, if you didn't tell me lies about snakes and funnel webs and I forget what else, then perhaps I wouldn't have had that reaction."

He disagreed. "Yes, you would. And I didn't tell you any lies. It was all true."

Well, that may be so, but I wasn't going to admit it now.

"You girls hungry?" he asked once the chuckles subsided. "We're about to cook a late lunch."

"I'm famished," Sascha announced. I'd almost forgotten she was there.

Justin left and I watched him walk away. He ended up at the Jeep that towed the boat. He took the life jacket off on the way and gave me a really nice view of his back.

Sascha shoved me in the shoulder. "When you're done drooling, should we go and sit by the fire?" she asked with a telling grin.

I rolled my eyes but joined her. Three embarrassing moments in about three minutes. That must be a record.

Camping turned out to be as chill as I expected. While no one went fishing, there were plenty of other activities keeping everyone occupied. The guys from the boat I didn't know were the old friends of Dale and Darcy's brother. Their names were Seone and Lewis, and they started a cricket game after lunch. Some of the guys played cards on the picnic table, and Darcy decided she wanted to whip up some cocktails, which was kind of fun. I even enjoyed sitting around drinking the vodka and guava juice concoction and gossiping with the girls, including Emily.

The time passed quickly and soon enough everyone was sitting around the fire trying to keep warm. That's also when the stories about Daniel started. Sascha informed me earlier about how he died five years ago—an overdose. I didn't get much more that, and I wasn't sure I wanted to know, but it was why we were here.

Dale and Darcy camped annually because this was one of Daniel's favourite places.

Everyone spoke about how light-hearted and funny Daniel was, and how he was one of the most ambitious people they knew. It made me wonder though, why someone who was supposedly so happy would take a lethal amount of whatever it was he took. Was Daniel an addict? Or did he do it for another reason?

That thought stirred up some other memories and I removed myself from the main group. Sascha watched me walk by and I sent her a small smile to let her know I was fine. I sat on the picnic table just outside the ring of camp chairs circling the fire. It was close enough for me to hear the conversation but far enough that I could get a little privacy.

That privacy didn't last long, but I didn't mind Justin joining me. He was watching me from across the fire, and after getting up to grab another beer from the esky, he walked over to sit with me.

"Need a refill of whatever that is?" he asked, pointing to the cup in my hand. It was the guava vodka drink. He sat down on the tabletop and an awkward tension filled the few inches between us.

"I'm all good," I told him and took a sip. My cup was still full.

"So you're over here hiding from the snakes then?" he asked, trying to make a joke. It was a half-hearted attempt. He could sense my mood. "Do you want to talk about it?"

I shrugged. "I don't know. I didn't think such happy stories could be so depressing."

We sat in silence for a little while. Justin was gazing at the fire, but it was clear his mind was somewhere else.

When he spoke, it wasn't what I expected. "I was the one who found him," he admitted, looking away from the fire to the bottle in his hands.

"Daniel?" I whispered.

Justin nodded. "It was here. Another mate and I came camping with Dale's whole family. No one noticed Dan disappear the night before. In the morning, I took the dog down to the bank to run around and he was there."

I was in disbelief and didn't know what to say. I reached over and placed a hand on his arm. "That's horrible. I'm sorry."

He looked down at my hand, but I didn't pull away. "Everyone thought he drowned until they found the drugs in his system."

"Isn't it traumatising to come back here every year?" I couldn't even imagine what it was like to see what he saw.

He sighed. "It was the first couple of times. I'm okay with it now. Coming here, spending weekends wakeboarding and hanging out, was his favourite thing to do."

I still didn't know what to say, so we sat in silence again. I was the next to speak, and I told him something very few people knew.

"When I was fifteen," I began quietly, "I tried to find my birth mother." Justin turned to look at me, but he didn't say anything, so I continued. "I was going through this nobody loves me phase, and I had a lot of anger back then, so Dad helped me find her."

"Did you ever get to meet her?"

I let out the deep breath I was holding in. "No. Eventually the agency tracked her down, but it was too late. She passed ten years earlier. Her name was Grace and she had me at seventeen. I'm the same age now that she was when she died of an overdose. She was a heroin addict." My eyes were starting to water so I looked up at the dark sky, willing them to dry up. They did. I never spoke about this part of my life, and this was why.

When I looked back at Justin, he was watching me curiously, or maybe it was with pity. He hesitated before asking his next question. "What about your birth father?"

I shook my head. "He doesn't exist. His name isn't on my birth certificate."

Justin's eyes widened. "Wow. I don't... I just..." He was at a loss for words. It seemed we both had that problem tonight. "I'm going to hug you now," he eventually said. "If that's not what you want then, you know, push me off the table or throw your drink in my face or something."

His words brought small smiles to both our faces. I thought we could each use a little comfort so I didn't protest when he put his arm around me. I even leaned into his one-armed hug. And then we sat there, staring at the fire, both lost in our own memories.

"Sitting alone again?" Justin questioned as he plonked down on the camp chair next to mine. It was well past midnight and the fire was starting fade.

"Not intentionally this time." I gave a half smile to let him know I was okay now.

"Almost everyone's in bed," he stated. "Not tired?" Darcy and Emily retired to their own tent ten minutes ago, as did one of the other guys. It was just Seone, Justin and me left by the fire. Seone was almost asleep in his camp chair.

I glanced back at my tent. "Well, if bed was an option right now, I'd probably be there." Justin raised a brow in confusion. "Sascha's in there, with Dale," I confirmed, trying to hide my grievance.

"Oh," was all he said.

"So, I'm out of options until they resurface. And I'm not sure I want to sleep on that mattress now anyway." That was the truth, and it made him laugh.

I shrugged. What could I do?

"Okay, here are our options," he began. He stood up and started pacing in front of me like he was contemplating a serious problem. "Option one; you wait and then sleep in the tent with Sass. That could be a while though. They might fall asleep. Option two; you can sleep in Dale's swag." He paused to think about that for a moment. "Personally, I'd avoid that one. He's spewed in there more than once in the past. Plus he might try to crawl back in there at some point."

Gross. No thanks.

"The third option?" I asked, knowing I definitely wasn't sleeping in the swag.

"You sleep in my tent and I bunk in the Jeep. I've got a spare sleeping bag so it's not a problem."

I think I was more shocked by this offer than the idea of Dale trying to curl up beside me in his swag. "I can't let you do that."

"Well, I'm not letting you be uncomfortable in the car." He crossed his arms as if that was the final say.

I thought about our situation for a minute, and then made an offer I never imagined I'd make to Justin Hart. "Or," I began slowly, standing up to show him I was serious. "We can both sleep in your tent and neither of us has to be uncomfortable." I held my breath, waiting for his reaction.

If he had one, he was good at hiding it. "Are you sure you're okay with that?" he questioned carefully.

I nodded, hoping my next words sounded confident and not awkward. "You have a spare sleeping bag, right? It's basically our own little bed each, just on the same air mattress."

"Makes sense," he agreed. "Well, okay, if you're ready for bed, you jump in there and I'll go grab that sleeping bag."

This could end up being a horrible decision, but I couldn't let him sleep in his car. Everything would be fine. Hopefully.

When we were both zipped up inside his dark tent, he asked, "did you want to sleep head to toe?"

I giggled nervously. "We're not five, Justin, we don't have cooties."

"Fair call." He slipped inside his sleeping bag. "Oh, did you need something to sleep in?" He looked pointedly at my jeans.

"Um, no it's okay." Was he offering me his clothes? I had a spare bag in the car. The problem with that was the keys to said car were in the tent with Sascha. "I'll just unbutton them or something."

Once I was zipped up inside my own sleeping bag, I decided jeans really weren't comfortable to sleep in. I reached down to wriggle them off inside the bag. Justin wouldn't see a thing. When I pulled them out, he was staring at me with wide eyes.

"Problem solved?" he asked in a tone a of voice I'd never heard from him. He sounded unsure of himself.

"I'm good," I chirped. "Perfectly comfortable. Goodnight."

"Goodnight, Ellie Bean," he whispered.

I was far from perfectly comfortable, turned away from him and right on the edge of the mattress. But I was fairly calm considering I was spending the night in the same bed as Justin Hart.

CHAPTER 7

I jerked awake to the sound of scratching on the tent wall. When I opened my eyes, I saw nothing but the navy blue of a sleeping bag. It wasn't mine. I was curled in a tight ball inside my sleeping bag and was surprised to find myself huddling into Justin's side.

My shivering stirred him, but I didn't move away.

"Morning," he mumbled in a husky voice.

"G-good morning," I stuttered.

He moved around beside me but didn't look up. "You alright?" he asked with concern.

"It's freezing!"

Justin moved again, taking his warmth away from my face. "You unzipped yourself. You're all twisted." He reached over me to fix my sleeping bag and zip it up. Then he played with the top of the bag and wrapped it around me head.

"You're a burrito now. Better?" he asked.

I was still shivering. "Not really."

He chuckled softly. "Maybe you shouldn't have taken off your pants."

I still refused to look up, hoping that burying my face in fabric would defrost it. That didn't mean I wasn't very aware of the hand Justin kept on my shoulder, trying to warm me up with friction.

"Why do people choose to do this?" It wasn't making sense to me. Especially in winter.

He chuckled again. "Oh, come on, it's not that bad."

The sounds of rustling outside the tent disturbed the serenity inside. I rolled onto my back and away from Justin when I head Sascha's voice. She sounded worried as she asked someone if they knew where I was.

An amused Justin said, "you should probably call out to let her know you're fine."

I shook my head and rubbed my eyes. "Nope. After last night, she can stress for a few minutes." It was mean, but I was still a little grumpy with her.

Justin rustled in his sleeping bag and I glanced over my shoulder at him. He was lying on his back with both hands behind his head, hair tousled from sleep and looking adorable. The only thing I could imagine that could make him look better, if that was even possible, was if he was shirtless.

We didn't move as our gazes locked and I wondered what it would feel like to run my hands through his messy hair.

That was an unexpected thought, and I was relieved to hear Dale's voice interrupt after a few moments too many. "She's in with Justin."

"What?!" Sascha balked in surprise. "You're kidding!"

I missed the rest of their conversation as I hurried to unzip myself. She would no doubt want details, not that there were any, and the sooner I got out there the quicker I could settle her down.

"Don't forget to put your pants back on," Justin reminded me, sounding strained.

I blushed. I'd almost crawled out of the sleeping bag in my underwear. That would give him quite the view, and I knew I would never recover from such a blunder.

Smiling awkwardly, I grabbed my jeans from the corner of the tent where I had thrown them last night and wriggled them on inside the sleeping bag. Justin kept that amused expression but was tactful enough not to watch my struggle.

When I was fully clothed, but still freezing, I opened the door to the tent and met Sascha's curious gaze. She was waiting for me only a few metres away, and she was definitely curious.

"You don't get to say a word," I frowned as I stepped out of the tent. Only she and Justin were close enough to hear me, but I wasn't oblivious to the looks being sent my way from across the fire pit. Emily was clearly annoyed, and Darcy's expression was a mystery.

"So not fair," she whined.

"So is having your bed commandeered."

She winced ruefully. "Yeah, but I'm not sorry about that." Her shame vanished and was replaced by a giddy grin.

How could I stay mad at her when she'd clearly experienced a pivotal moment in her life last night? I took her hand and pulled her away, knowing Justin shouldn't be privy to this conversation. "How was it?" I urged, laying on the enthusiasm to make up for my grumpy demeanour.

Sascha actually put her fist to her mouth and bit down.

"That good, huh?" I snickered.

She shook out her arms. Definitely good then. "I just... I'm so glad we waited. I think it made everything that much more... intense." It had been two months since they first went out, and two weeks since declaring they were in a relationship. For Sascha, who usually jumped into these things without much thought, this experience must be monumental. I wondered what it felt like to build up such intensity and then be completely satisfied when it finally happened.

I listened to her gush for a little while longer, wrapping my arms around myself trying to stop the shivering. I really needed another jumper.

When Dale came over and wrapped his arms around Sascha's waist, he piqued my interest. "Sorry I stole your accommodations," he apologised with sincerity, but it quickly turned to cockiness. "Looks like you found an alternative though."

"Out of necessity," I reaffirmed. There was no other reason for my sleeping in Justin's tent.

He shook his head with amusement. "I mean, you achieved something last night that many have worked hard for but have continuously failed at." I had a protest on the tip of my tongue, but he continued before I could remind him nothing had happened between me and Justin. "Plenty have been there, but none have had the pleasure of sleeping in his bed."

What was that supposed to mean? Plenty have been there? That didn't surprise me. Justin was hot and very charismatic. I'd seen his attraction in action. But what about no one having the pleasure of sleeping in his bed? What did Dale mean? Was he speaking literally or figuratively?

I was about to ask as much when the man in question stepped up behind me. He was close, so close I could feel the physical tension building between my back and his chest, even though no part of us touched. He also smelled extra good in the morning.

Sascha visibly tried to supress her smile. Dale had no such considerations and smirked outright at his mate. I sucked in a deep breath.

"Breakfast anyone?" Justin asked, clearly picking up on the tone of our conversation.

Dale made a face at Justin and then pulled Sascha away.

When they were out of earshot, I turned to face Justin, hoping I didn't show how mortified I was currently feeling. Neither of us stepped back. "Please tell me there's coffee," I mumbled.

Justin shrugged. "No macadamia latte's today, but I do make a mean instant coffee if you're up for it," he chuckled.

"I'll take any sort of caffeine right now, as long as it's hot." It will have do.

"Why don't you go and get changed, put a few more layers on, and I'll make you one," he offered.

I wasn't saying no to that. "Thank you," I told him, watching my feet with fake interest. It took more courage to look him directly in the eye as I said my next words. "And thanks for giving me a place to sleep last night."

He smiled his beautiful smile, the one that made girls weak at the knees. "Anytime."

I left him then to find a warmer outfit. Thankfully, Sascha and Dale had cleaned up after themselves and my bag didn't look like it had suffered any trauma overnight. I grabbed a fresh set of clothes and took them to the toilet block to change, knowing it would be easier than attempting it in the tent.

The public toilet and shower block was shared by the other campsites on the property. It wasn't unhygienic, but it also wasn't the classiest bathroom I'd been in. It did its job just fine though.

While I changed, my mind lingered on Dale's words. Many had been there, but none had the pleasure of sleeping in his bed. Surely this was different. There was nothing sexual about my visit to his bed. It was just sleeping.

When I made it back to our site, Justin had a coffee ready for me. Even though it was instant, I guzzled it down like it was fresh water on a hot summer's day. I'm certain Justin thought I had a caffeine addiction when I asked how I could make another one. He was entertained by my antics and helped me refill my mug.

The day officially started when the boys donned their board-shorts and wakeboards and backed the boat into the water. There was a few hours before we had to head home and they were all keen to make the most of it. In my opinion, they were absolutely bonkers. No one in their right mind would willingly get in the frigid winter water.

I stood down on the bank and touched said water with one toe. Nope! There was no chance I'd put more of my body in. That posed another problem, one Sascha found herself facing as she stood next to me. How were we supposed to get into the boat? It wasn't far from the shore, but perhaps we should have thought this through.

Darcy, Emily and Seone were already in the boat, having already been in it when it entered the water. That was the smart thing to do. Lewis simply walked into the water up to his waist like the temperature meant nothing and pulled himself onto the back step. Is that what we were supposed to do?

I looked down at myself and my jeans. They wouldn't roll up passed my shins.

"Never fear, Dale and Justin are here!" came Dale's heroic voice from behind us. He swept Sascha into his arms and carried her to the boat, sacrificing himself to the cold river. Sascha squeaked when he pretended to drop her.

Justin stepped up next to me. "You ready?" he asked, already amused by the look of horror that was no doubt on my face.

Was I ready to get on the boat? Sure. Was I ready to be held in Justin's arms? My heart started thumping just thinking about it.

"Well it's now or never," I mumbled under my breath.

"Don't look so afraid," he laughed. "I swear I'm a gentleman."

I had no doubts about that, but gentleman or no, when he picked me up and held me close to his chest, he was the cause of my body flushing with warmth. I wrapped my arms around his neck feeling very exposed. When he walked us into the water, I even tried climbing further up his chest to avoid touching it in any way.

It was an instant loss when he placed me gently on the end of the boat, like I'd been plunged into the freezing depths of the water. I was blushing again, and that made me feel as embarrassed as I did this morning when everyone saw me crawl out of Justin's tent.

I tried keeping my distance from him then, which wasn't hard because he sat in the observer's seat for most of the adventure.

The water was freezing, and the wind was a close match. Sascha and I sat at the back of the boat so some of the chill was blocked by the windscreen. It didn't help much and we huddled together under Dale's dry towel. He was driving the boat and we all watched as Seone and Lewis braved the water.

Wakeboarding was an extreme sport, and even novices like these guys looked incredible doing it. They jumped the waves protruding from the back of the boat with ease. I wondered how much strength it took to hold onto the rope like that. It looked like a lot of work.

When Dale and Justin switched places with the others, my eyes were glued to them from the moment they jumped into the water. Sascha was now in the observer's seat, having had a quick lesson from Dale on all the hand signals she needed to know. Lewis was driving the boat and he made sure to keep looking back in case Sascha missed anything.

I had to admit, regardless of the temperature and freezing water that hit him from all directions, Justin looked hot. There was something highly appealing about the board shorts and windswept hair. It reminded me of his first appearance yesterday, and that unclipped life jacket. Now that was a sight I wouldn't mind seeing again.

I only pulled my eyes away when Darcy came to sit beside me. "How are you going?" she asked, pulling the sleeves of her matching green sweats over her hands. He hair was up in a messy ponytail and she looked pretty in the mid-morning sun. Apparently she could also wakeboard but wasn't crazy enough to get in the water today.

"I think my nose has frostbite, but otherwise good," I laughed.

"Hot tip, moisturise as soon as we get back," she smiled, and then looked out at Dale and Justin. When she returned her attention to me, she seemed a little awkward. "So listen, I don't want to sound bitchy or anything, but I feel like I need to say this."

I sat upright, completely surprised by her tone. Was I about to get some sort of lecture?

Darcy continued after a long pause. "Justin is like a brother to me. He's been there for me and Dale and my family through the hardest time of our lives, and he's the most supportive and caring person I've ever met. I really don't want to see him get hurt."

Why would he be hurt? Was she implying that I would hurt him? We were just friends, and even then, we barely knew each other. I shook my head. "I have no intention of that." Why would she assume I'd hurt him?

"I don't think you would ever intend it. Does anyone decent ever mean to hurt those they care about?" She held her hands to her chin, lost in thought. "I'm just going to get this out and over with. I like you," she admitted looking back up at me. "And I know he does too. But Justin doesn't let himself get attached too often. He's been through a lot and it's hard for him. When he does let himself feel, he goes all in. He feels everything so deeply, and when he ends up hurt, it's not pretty. He deserves better than that."

That was new information. What was I supposed to say to that? I looked around. No one else could hear our conversation over the boat's engine.

"I'm sorry," Darcy apologised, looking sincere. "I don't want to freak you out or anything. I know you guys have a history, and I don't pretend to know details about that, but I just felt like I needed to say something. I see how he acts around you."

"No, that's fair," I told her as steadily as I could. "I understand."

She reached over and squeezed my hand before turning her gaze back to the boys on the water.

The lump in my throat was growing. I never expected to be on the receiving end of such a speech, and from someone as close to Justin as Darcy.

First, Justin liked me. Whether it was just at a friend level or something more, that was unclear. Either way, it did send thrills through me, which made it all the more confusing. Second, he rarely let people in, but apparently I was one of the lucky few. And third, I had to wonder if I was inadvertently hurting him already, and did my presence really have such an influence on him?

Darcy's words were stuck in my head, and for the next few days, they were all I could think about.

CHAPTER 8

My head was a minefield. There were so many things going on in there and I tried my hardest to dodge them all. Sometimes I was successful, other times I triggered a string of emotions I wasn't ready to feel. Guilt. Uncertainty. Confusion. Giddiness. Then more guilt. It was never ending.

Seeing Sawyer at work four days after the camping trip was a heavy misstep and I struggled to keep my thoughts and feelings at bay.

On Sunday, when Sascha and I finally reached an area with phone reception on our way home, there was a message from Sawyer. It was nothing unusual or intense. He simply asked how my trip was and made a little joke about my lack of camping experience. But as I sat there staring it, I couldn't figure out how to respond. I eventually did, but only with a generic message saying it was good and that I didn't get eaten by any drop bears.

I eventually accepted that I felt guilty. I had no idea why. Nothing happened with Justin, and Sawyer and I weren't together. There was no reason for me to feel guilty, at least that's what I told myself. Avoiding him made it easier for some reason. Now that he was here in front of me, though, I could hardly continue using that strategy.

We were in the office working on the rosters. Sawyer sat in front of the computer and I propped myself on the edge of the desk. "When does Maria go on maternity leave?" he asked.

"Not for another six weeks. Have you found her replacement yet?"

Sawyer nodded. "I've got two regular casuals looking for more shifts. They're going to share her regular hours. Do you want to keep your Thursday mornings?"

"Yeah, it works well with my afternoon classes," I agreed. "And only put me on the Wednesday and Saturday shifts."

He turned to me. "Are you sure? That's less than normal."

I looked down at my feet. He would find out soon anyway. "Yeah, I spoke about it with Dad. You'll be hearing about it in your meeting this afternoon."

"You're dropping manager responsibilities?" he guessed. It was hard to tell if he was surprised or disappointed. I simply nodded in way of response. "Does that mean you've made a decision about doing your other course?" Working so closely with my dad and myself, Sawyer knew all about it.

"No," I muttered, still not looking up. "I'm just going to focus on school and these classes. I've given myself until the end of the semester to make a decision." Which would I choose? Working full time in the family business or study for a degree that would lead me into another field, one that had helped me so much in my life.

Sawyer knew what both choices meant to me, and how hard it was for me to choose between them. My decision could also have an impact on his career. If I stayed, we would work side by side. If I stood down, he'd be doing it solo. I wasn't sure which he preferred more.

"Hey," he reached over to tap my foot with his, concern lacing his voice. I was still lost in thought and not engaging. "Are you busy tomorrow night?"

When I looked up at him, he seemed hopeful. I felt a little bad bringing him down. We had barely seen each other since my classes began. "I'm going to the Uni Bar with Sass again. It's a thing now, I think. Dale's band plays every fortnight."

Sawyer turned back to the computer screen, pressing his lips together. Was he annoyed? "How is Sass going with her new boy toy?"

As if talking about her was a summoning spell, Sascha walked through the door. She was here to join Tiana on the front desk for this afternoon's check-in shift. Her timing always amazed me.

"Let me tell you all about his toy," she announced with exaggeration. Sascha leant against the other side of Sawyer's desk.

Sawyer shook his head. "So you finally did it then? Did this happen in the creepy woods on your camping trip?"

Sascha crossed her arms. "Ah, no! It was in our tent actually, and it was magical."

I glared over at her and gestured back and forth between us. "Emphasis on our tent."

Sawyer misread it and pushed his chair back to better see us both. "Wait! Did you two finally have your threesome?" he questioned in mock outrage. "And you did it without me? I've been trying to make this happen for years. What does this guy have, a golden dick or something?"

Sascha and I both laughed as we slapped him on the shoulders at the same time.

"Ouch!" He faked a pained tone as he rubbed both his shoulders.

"You deserve it for being creepy," I said.

He shrugged, faking ignorance. "A guy can dream." The threesome thing was a running joke we had. Neither Sascha nor I took any real offence to it. He wasn't serious. Sawyer's curiosity took over again. "So Sass, if you were banging Dale in your tent, the one you were supposed to share with Elle, and there was no threesome, then where did you end up?" He directed that question to me.

Sascha jumped in before I could respond. "Oh," she chuckled. "She found new accommodations easily enough."

I stood up and walked to the other side of the room, not wanting Sawyer to see the glare I sent in Sascha's direction. He did not need to know I slept in Justin Hart's tent. Being my dad's prodigy and hearing all about our family history, Sawyer knew exactly who Justin was. I had no idea how he would react if he knew. Would he be mad? Would he tell Dad? I was not interested in finding out.

"There was spare space in one of the other tents," I stated, forcing my face back to neutral as Sawyer spun around in the chair.

Sascha took the hint and returned the attention to her. "Um, we were talking about my boyfriend's golden dick, remember? Let me tell you—"

"Nope!" Sawyer interrupted with a look of disgust. "Not interested in gossiping about your insatiable need for the D."

Sascha hmphed. "Fine, let's talk about something else then. Oh, I know!" She jumped up in excitement. "The hospitality award night thingy is next Friday night, isn't it?"

Sawyer and I both nodded.

"Do you have your outfits yet? You'd look damn sexy in a tux." She gave him a chef's kiss.

I laughed. While the event wasn't the ballgown type, we still needed to dress up. Twenty-Nine on Queen wasn't nominated for any awards this year and Dad was more than happy for Sawyer and me to attend in his place. I'd never been before and was excited. Sawyer had been once before and took it as a good chance to network. It was also a charity dinner, so a lot of high flyers in the industry would be present.

"No tux, but I am wearing a bow tie."

Sascha growled. "That's hot. You guys going out after?"

Sawyer shrugged. "Haven't thought much about it yet."

He turned to me expectantly, and I suddenly found myself very interested in a notification that flashed on my phone, which on the desk behind him.

I reached around him to grab my it and spoke as casually as I could. "I don't know what to expect at this event. We will have to see what happens on the night."

"Okay, well if things finish early, I'm headed out with Dale. Not sure where, but it's Emily's birthday, so probably more than one club."

Emily? Even though we'd had some civil moments on the camping trip, I didn't feel the need to join her birthday celebrations.

Sawyer picked up on my hesitation. It was probably written all over my face. "Who's Emily?"

"Sascha's boyfriend's twin sister's best friend," I offered with certainty.

He didn't seem to follow. "Right, well, if the night is young, maybe we could make it." It was an empty offer. "We'll see how the night goes," he reiterated and then put on a fake whiny voice. "But you've had her three weekends in a row now, Sass. Next weekend is my turn." Sawyer began an argument he knew he couldn't win.

"Sorry pal, best friends take priority." She stood up to make her point known.

Sawyer did the same. "You see her all the time, I'm having Elle withdrawals."

And so they continued fighting over me in their usual bantering way as if I wasn't standing right next to them.

I took the chance to check my phone. There was a message from Justin asking if I had time for a quick coffee before class.

I hesitated for a few seconds. I hadn't seen Justin since Sunday. After overthinking Darcy's little warning, or whatever it was, I made the decision to avoid him on Tuesday. It meant I didn't get my coffee at the campus café that day, which was devastating. Macadamia lattes were a critical part of my diet. But I had calmed down a little and felt ready to see him again. Don't get me wrong, I headed Darcy's advice, but I also found myself thinking about these mini coffee excursions Justin and I shared. They were becoming routine, and I actually enjoyed them.

But they also didn't mean anything. I barely knew Justin, which meant we were barely friends. Darcy had jumped the gun.

I glanced at my watch. There would be enough time if I left now. I tapped out a quick reply to let him know I'd meet him at the café in half an hour. The EU campus wasn't far from here and I had my car today.

"I'm going now," I announced, stuffing my phone into my bag. Sawyer and Sascha stopped their trivial argument to say goodbye.

Sascha hugged me fiercely. "No driving to classes tomorrow," she demanded. As if I could forget with her reminding me every day. "You're drinking with me this time."

I rolled my eyes. "I promise."

Friday was one of two days we shared on Campus. Tuesday was our other day, but our schedules conflicted because Sascha studied education and her classes ran on different days. Now that I didn't have to work so much, maybe we'd see each other more. Fridays would be our most eventful of the week, so long as Sascha and Dale stayed strong. She was adamant that we go to all his shows. This Friday, he wasn't just playing with Dream of Darcy at the Uni Bar, he was also doing a DJ set afterwards.

I hugged Sawyer as well, feeling a little awkward as he leant down to kiss me gently on the cheek. He lingered a little, holding me in the embrace. This was normal for us, so why did I feel a heaviness in the pit of my stomach when it took him so long to let go?

As I left, I felt that heaviness concede to something else. Not knowing what it was, I tried to suppress it and focus on driving. It didn't work. My mind returned to its battlefield. I kept telling myself I had no reason to be guilty, so why was I feeling this way? These emotions were foreign to me, so was it actually guilt, or was it something else entirely? Either way, it was undeniably frustrating.

When I strolled into the campus café, Justin was nowhere in sight. I'd beaten him here. This gave me an opportunity. Justin always surprised me with coffee, and now it was my turn. I'd memorised his order, just as he did mine, and joined the line at the counter feeling very pleased with myself.

I was one customer away from ordering when his woodsy scent snuck up on me. Without turning, I glanced to my left at the shiny glass of the cake display. Sure thing, there he was, with only one person separating us. I couldn't make out his features in the glass, but I could tell it was him by his blurred reflection. I'd been in this position many times before. It was one way I use to look at Hot Café Guy without actually looking at him. If he saw me now, he showed no acknowledgment.

I pretended not to notice him as I stepped up to the counter. I ordered and paid for my usual macadamia latte as well as a large cappuccino with a double shot of expresso for him. When I moved confidently to the waiting area, Justin followed.

"Now, I'm hoping that cappuccino is for me, otherwise I'm going to look like a bit of a tool," he remarked as he came to stand beside me.

I smirked. "Actually, it's for this guy I'm meeting up with. He's a bit of a loner so I thought I'd take some pity on him." I kept my tone casual as I referenced the first time we had coffee together. He sat with me, apparently, because I looked lonely. I was starting to wonder if that was the case at all.

"Sounds like a bloke who might need it," he shrugged, seeming disappointed. "I guess I'll leave you to it then." Justin took two steps and I quickly grabbed his wrist. I knew he was playing around, but I felt a sudden fear pulse through me and reacted.

I rolled my eyes to cover up my mini panic. "I guess you can have it if you so desperately need it."

He chuckled and held a hand to his chest. "I'm desperate? I'm pretty sure you drink more coffee than I do."

"I may buy more," I admitted, knowing it was true, "but you drink double shots."

He went to respond but pursed his lips after reconsidering. "Well, doesn't that make us even?"

It was my turn to giggle. "Not a chance. I bet you drink energy drinks as well. Those things are loaded with caffeine, among other things."

"No, no," he argued. "We're discussing coffee here, not caffeine."

The barista rang the bell on the counter and called my name. "Saved by the bell," I laughed, suggesting he was the one being saved. In reality, the bell was relief for me. He wasn't wrong.

We collected our coffees and started toward the exit. "Should we continue this argument by the soccer field?" he suggested with an air of amusement. "If I recall correctly, you really enjoyed that last week."

I held my empty hand up in defence. "Hey, if they're playing skins versus shirts, it's not my fault if my eyes wander." I wasn't even paying that much attention to them. They just happened to be there when I looked away from Justin, which I did often so that I wasn't caught staring at him. Not that he needed to know that.

He eyed me knowingly and with a smirk. "Oh, I'm no stranger to your wandering eye," he declared confidently.

It took me a moment, but as soon as I figured out what he meant, my entire body flushed. Not just my cheeks. Everything! I felt warm all over and I'm sure my face turned a bright beet red. Was he referring to the few times I allowed myself to ogle him shirtless on our camping trip? It was rare and from a distance, but I was sure I'd been subtle about it.

Justin chuckled at my reaction but thankfully let it go. "Come on then, you'll miss the show if we don't get there soon." He urged me forward with a wave of his hand.

He noticed? He always seemed to catch me staring, but not once had I seen him watching me. And he found it amusing!

Could this be any more mortifying?

CHAPTER 9

"**W**et pussies! Yew!" Emily screamed as she raised her hands above her head and gave a little shimmy.

No, she wasn't drunk. In fact, she hadn't even finished her first drink. The night was just beginning, and apparently, a tray full of wet pussy shots was the trigger that got her started.

"Thanks Isaac," she cooed to the guy who placed the shots in front of us.

Isaac, who smiled widely behind his beard, nodded to the guy next to him. "Thank Benji," he said. "He's feeling generous tonight."

Benji looked almost exactly the same as Isaac. They were both brunette with hipster length beards and wore plaid shirts. Where Isaac wore a drooping beanie, Benji opted for a single, small hoop earring as an accessory.

Who were these guys? I glanced sideways at Sascha hoping she'd have some insight, but she seemed just as confused as I was.

Emily noticed our look and interjected. "Oh, sorry," she apologised, raising her voice to be heard over Dream of Darcy playing on the stage nearby. "Sass and Ellie, this is Isaac and Benji. Isaac is Darcy's boyfriend."

Was it just me or did I hear an air of annoyance lace her tone? Wasn't she just thanking him? And since when did Darcy have a boyfriend?!

If Sascha was surprised, she wasn't showing it. Granted, she'd been hanging around Dale's friends for weeks before dragging me along. It had only been two since my first adventure to Uni Bar. But to have not heard about Darcy having a boyfriend in that time, on top of an overnight trip? Was that normal?

Benji leaned his elbows on the bar table and pointed a finger at Sascha. "Now, you I've seen here before. Sass with the attitude to match." She shrugged one shoulder, not denying the assumption. Benji turned his attention, and his finger, to me. "But you, you're new." He held his hand out for a shake.

I took it and introduced myself. "Ellie."

He held onto my hand longer than appropriate and looked me directly in the eye. "Well, Ellie, can I offer you a wet pussy?"

I couldn't hold it in and snorted.

Sascha cracked it and even Emily had a giggle. I put my free hand over my mouth to suppress my own. "I'm sorry," I said, trying to straighten my face. Wow! How did he manage that with such a straight face? "Has that line ever gotten you into bed?"

"Bed?" he questioned, eyebrows furrowing in mock confusion. "You dirty girl! I was simply offering you a drink." Benji finally let go of my hand to push forward the wet pussy shots on the table. "But if it's another kind you're after, I'd be happy to oblige."

My giggle finally escaped. Under the table, I felt a tap on my leg. Glancing down discreetly, I saw Emily's hand making a no way, don't do it sign, one usually made at neck level. What was that about? Whatever it was, if Emily of all people was sending me negative signs, she must be serious. So, I humoured her.

"Thank you for the shot." I made my tone very clear as I turned back to him. He seemed to get the message.

"Your loss, gorgeous," he conceded and straightened up. Isaac clapped him on the shoulder, clearly amused by his mate's rejection.

"Shall we, ladies?" Isaac offered the shots to us again and we each took one.

We held the small glasses to our lips and Emily counted down from three. The vodka burned going down my throat and my head shook involuntarily. I wasn't a great fan of shots, having had one too many on more than one occasion. But this was vodka, not tequila. I had a tumultuous relationship with tequila.

"Woo!" cheered Emily. "I love a wet pussy!"

I wasn't too distracted by the burning to miss the scoff and glare that Isaac gave her. Was there something else I didn't know?

Sascha picked up on the drama as well and engaged Isaac in conversation. "So, Isaac, how long have you and Darcy been together?"

He never looked away from his girlfriend, who was killing it on stage, when he answered. "About two years now. How long have you and Dale been going out?"

Sascha smiled, "about two weeks." She continued with her small talk, and I did everything I could to avoid Benji. He kept smiling at me. When he thought I was looking at him, he even winked. That was when I decided chatting with Emily was the better option.

But her better option was to down her vodka cranberry in one go.

"Something you need to talk about?" I asked carefully.

Emily let out the breath she was holding in. "Nope!" she said, popping the p. "I want another drink. Do you want another one?"

I gestured to my full glass. I'd only taken a few sips.

"Right, well hurry up then." She picked up my glass and handed it to me expectantly. I took a few sips and then put it down. I wasn't drunk enough to scull an entire drink. I wasn't even tipsy. Emily wasn't satisfied with that and stole the drink to down it herself. "Let's dance!"

She took my hand and pulled me from my stool. I had no idea what was going on with her but was quick enough to grab Sascha's wrist and pull her along. I could not deal with whichever Emily this was. She usually ignored me and now she wanted to drink and dance together? Something was definitely going on. Don't get me wrong, I wasn't complaining. It was kind of refreshing, her not glaring at me.

Emily led us to the front of the dance floor. There were already a few people there moving with the music. Darcy waved to us from her place at centre stage and kept up her energetic performance.

I stole a glance at Justin as I smiled back at her. His eyes were closed but he didn't miss a beat. He wore a tank that exposed he arms and shoulders, as well as the top of his shining chest and that elusive tattoo. With bottom lip pulled between his teeth, he was looking really good.

"So, what's the go with Isaac?" Sascha asked, pulling my attention away from Justin. "You don't like him?"

We continued dancing as Emily rolled her eyes. "He's a dick. She deserves so much better."

Thankfully, the music was too loud for Darcy to overhear. Did she know her best friend and boyfriend disliked each other?

"What about Benji?" I yelled over the sound. I remembered her reaction from earlier. "You don't like him either?"

This time, Emily laughed. "Also a dick, and he puts it in everything. Trust me, you don't want to go there."

I wasn't planning on it, but her words piqued my curiosity. "Have you been there?"

She laughed again. "Once," she admitted with a sour expression.

"And?" Sascha prompted.

"Let's just say his ego makes up for his..." she pushed her pointer fingers close together, implying what could only be his length. Sascha and I giggled. That made perfect sense. Emily touched my arm. "Nothing like Justin, hey?"

That pulled me up straight. "What?"

Now she looked confused. "In the tent? You guys didn't?"

I shook my head. No words were needed to prove that Justin and I had not done anything in that tent. I'm sure my shocked expression said it all.

"Oh, well, trust me," she continued with a wink. "You won't be disappointed." She then used her pointer fingers to show just how... fulfilling he apparently could be.

Her words sparked a heat in my chest. How did she know that?

Sascha was the one who formed the words. "Wait, have you guys?" she asked. Was she surprised or curious? I know I was suddenly desperate to find out.

Emily didn't say no. Instead, she showed us with a tongue in her cheek exactly how she knew.

Sascha's eyes bulged. "You gave him a blowie?" she giggled.

My expression must have shown my astonishment. "Don't worry," Emily told me, placing a hand on my shoulder and looking sincere. That was almost as surprising as knowing she and Justin had a history. "It was last year and we were both blind drunk. You have nothing to worry about."

What? Why would I be worried? I forced a smile, not sure why it wasn't coming naturally.

We stopped dancing and turned towards the stage. All eyes were on Justin as we stood there gawking at the drummer. The looks of appreciation on Sascha and Emily's faces showed they were imagining his manhood. But all I could see was Emily on her knees, and Justin's smirk as he let her pleasure him.

That's when the drummer himself turned in our direction. We instantly went back to dancing, hoping he didn't notice us staring at him. The heat in my chest was burning strongly and I was relieved when Darcy stepped down from the stage with her microphone to join our little group. It was a welcomed distraction.

Unlike Benji, who suddenly appeared, wiggling his hips in the centre of our circle. Now that I knew a certain something about Benji, I found it difficult to keep a straight face around him. Every wink, smirk, and hip thrust had me giggling. I'm sure he was taking it the wrong way, too, because he kept trying to dance with me.

Eventually, I couldn't deal anymore, and asked if anyone wanted a shot. Benji, thankfully, wasn't interested in wet pussies—the vodka kind at least—and went back to the table.

And that's how the night went. We danced a little, enjoyed the music, had another drink, and then did it all over again. Benji liked to join us on the dance floor, but I managed to keep away from him by dancing with Sascha.

When we sat back at the table as the band finished up on stage, I wedged myself between Sascha and Emily with the hopes they'd provide a barrier. Justin, Darcy and Ryan joined us a short while later and more drinks arrived.

Justin sat next to me when Sascha left to see Dale at the side of the stage. He now wore a leather jacket. How annoying. I couldn't see his tattoo anymore. What was it? Ugh!

And how did he smell so good after an hour of sweating on stage?

"There's been a lot of giggling tonight," he said, raising a brow and looking between me and Emily. "Something I should know about?" Was he worried that we'd become friends? Would he care if he knew that I knew that he and Emily had fooled around?

My cheeks instantly warmed. He'd caught us staring at him earlier. Maybe he did know that I knew. Emily didn't seem at all fazed by this.

"Ellie was just telling me about the stunning dress she's wearing to some fancy party next week," she said with an innocent smile.

Thank God. What would he say if he knew we were talking about how big he was?

"Oh yeah? What's the fancy party for?" He looked to me for the answer.

It hadn't occurred to me until this moment that he should know all about it. "It's the HM Awards," I admitted carefully.

His face revealed that he did indeed know about the awards night. "You're going, too? Is your dad's hotel a finalist?"

I shook my head. "Not this year." My mind was stuck on 'too'. "Are you going? Surely one of your dad's resorts is nominated."

"Yeah, the one on the Gold Coast is. I'll be there, too." Justin nodded, still looking surprised. "Is your father taking you?"

I froze. No, my father wasn't taking me. Sawyer was. And that meant Justin and Sawyer were going to be in the same place, at the same time. And I would be there, right in the middle. I swallowed the lump forming in my throat and spoke in a small voice. "No, no, Dad's not going this year. The executive manager will be there, though."

I couldn't bring myself to say Sawyer's name.

"Well, it looks like I'll be lucky enough to see this stunning dress of yours." Justin's eyes scanned my body as he sipped his beer. And then he licked his lips.

Oh, that was hot.

But oh, I shouldn't be thinking that.

My chest flushed and the room was suddenly very warm. I grabbed my drink—it was mostly ice, but there was vodka and lemonade in there as well—and downed it in two gulps.

I was very aware of Justin watching me, and it was about time I caught him staring. I just wished it was at a less embarrassing time.

He wanted to see me in the dress.

It was a nice dress.

I needed another drink.

In the background, Emily giggled again. This was totally her fault. "We should dance," I told her as I pulled her off her stool. "Dale's starting."

I tried very hard to ignore Justin's eyes. I could feel them watching me as I walked away from him.

Was I being rude? I didn't want to be rude. But I also needed to get out of there before I said something stupid.

As our little group grew on the dance floor, I let myself enjoy the moment. Sascha came to dance with us, as did Benji. Then came Darcy and Isaac, who seemed to forget other people existed around them. Gross.

The only person who didn't join us was Justin.

It took everything within me not to look around for him. Why didn't he want to dance with us? Was it because I was rude to him?

Eventually I had to use the ladies room and I left them all on the dance floor. Sitting in the cubicle was always an adventure when alcohol was involved. The four blue walls swirled in front of me. Or was I swaying? I rested my head in my hands and sat there for a few minutes.

I was so tipsy.

No, I was double tipsy!

I shouldn't have had four wet pussy shots. They didn't sound too potent, but they were secretly deadly, especially when taken in a short period of time.

The damn wet pussies!

After cleaning up, I left the bathroom wondering if I should have another one. They were pretty good.

I was so lost in my mind that I ran into a guy near the exit. It took me a moment to recognise Benji, but when I did, I had something to say.

"You're onto something with this wet pussy thing you know."

He took a step forward and smirked. "Oh yeah, how's that?"

I leaned back against the nearby wall. "I didn't know I liked wet pussies before tonight."

"Is that so?" he laughed deeply. "You want another one?"

"Are you talking about a shot or something else?"

"That's up to you."

Emily's earlier warning was somewhere in the back of my mind, but I couldn't help the giggle that escaped. He was so persistent.

Before I could respond, Justin appeared behind Benji, interrupting my train of thought. "Oh hey." He was so much taller than Benji, and so much hotter. That smile made me weak at the knees. And his hair was a little out of place. So hot.

"Hey, there you are," he said, coming to stand beside me. He placed his arm on the wall above my head and turned to Benji. "Hey, man." Then I watched his hand as it came up towards my face and tucked some loose strands behind my ear.

Justin was touching me! How did he leave tingles like that?

I can't remember how Benji responded because I was no longer paying attention to him. Justin was so close I could smell that sweet cologne. Or was it just him? And his chest was right in front of my face. If I pushed open his jacket, would I be able to see his tattoo? I really wanted to see his tattoo.

When he looked back down at me, he asked, "are you okay?"

I poked him in the chest. "You just cock-blocked your mate."

His eyes flicked down to my hand. "Oh, is that what that was? I thought of it more as saving you."

"Saving me? I don't need saving. I have everything under control." I stood up straight to prove my point, but that was a mistake. I swayed a little and grabbed hold of him to keep myself steady.

My hands were on his hips. I couldn't tear my eyes away from where they grasped at his shirt. What would happen if I just ducked a hand underneath and...

"You're so drunk," he chuckled.

"No," I argued, looking back up at him. Justin wore that all-knowing smirk. He thought he knew everything. "I'm just double tipsy."

He laughed outright this time. "If that's what you want to call it, sure."

"I had a lot of wet pussies tonight."

"I know."

He was looking at me funny. Why was he looking at me like that? And why hadn't I put my hands under his shirt yet?

That smirk of his was out in full force. What would it be like to touch them? They looked really good. What if I kissed them? No, I couldn't do that. That would be bad.

"We're headed back to the house soon. I think Sass is coming. Will you be joining us?"

I sucked in a deep breath. Go back to Justin's house? That was as bad an idea as kissing him. But if Sascha was there, nothing bad would happen, would it?

"I don't know if I should," I finally admitted. Bad. Bad, bad bad.

"I can also drive you home," he offered sombrely. "If that's what you want."

Did I want to go home? I shrugged. Party at Justin's house or go home? Maybe he had vodka and could make more wet pussies.

Justin put an arm around my shoulders and led me away. "Tell you what. Let's get you a tall glass of water and you can think about it while you sober up a little. Okay?"

I leaned into him and nodded. "Okay."

Chapter 10

A loud bang woke me the next morning, and oh, how it felt like something had slammed into my skull. I squeezed my eyes tighter than they already were and buried my head under the pillow. It was so loud!

That's when I finally noticed the scent that always sent me into a tailspin. Justin's intoxicating woodiness enveloped me with the pillow, and I froze, eyes bulging as the night before come back to me in a mixture of fuzzy memories.

Wet pussies. Mixers. Vodka. More wet pussies. Justin. His arm around me. His scent as he held me close. Stairs falling out beneath me and him sweeping me into his arms on the way up.

My heart thumped. That was all I could remember. What happened next? I was in a bed that smelled like Justin Hart! Was he in the bed with me?

It took a lot of courage to lift the pillow the tiniest fraction and use one eye to peek at my surroundings. The other side of the bed was empty, and I let out a sigh of relief. Removing the pillow, I sat up and threw the covers off. My head spun at the fast movement, but I had to be certain.

Another sigh of relief. All my clothes were still on. My skinny jeans were tight, except the button, which was popped, and my bra was still on. Out of the corner of my eye, I spotted my shoes near the closed door.

Looking around curiously, other items in the room told me it was definitely Justin's. Not only did it smell like him, but I recognised the backpack he took to classes. There was an acoustic guitar resting against a very full bookshelf along one wall, a computer desk with two screens that looked like it was out of some crime-stoppers movie, and a photo on the nightstand beside me. He was in it.

I reached for the frame, curious about the young girl he carried on his back. My racing heart dropped the moment I recognised her. It was Claire, his little sister. It had to be. I'd met her once, as a newborn, and it was shortly after that meeting that I refused to spend time with Caroline. Back then, all I could think was that she finally had the daughter she wanted. She didn't need me anymore. Not long after that, she was officially removed as my adoptive mother.

I traced a finger around the edge of the wooden frame. Justin and Claire looked happy. He was smiling and she was laughing, her long brunette hair falling over his shoulder. They were on a beach. It was beautiful. They were beautiful. I quickly returned the picture to its place on his bedside table. No, I couldn't let those feelings take over. Not right now. Not when I was in Justin's bedroom, in his house.

Thankfully, I knew he didn't live with his dad, Claire and Caroline. He had his own place—which technically belonged to his father—that he shared with Dale and Darcy. They'd moved in with him when they all started university. Their parents lived on the central coast and this was much closer to campus. Sascha had also told me that they'd become a little more lenient and accepting of their children's career desires after their brother died. But that was another story altogether.

I got out of bed and looked around. Justin must be somewhere in the house. What was I supposed to do? I'd never slept in a someone else's bed overnight before. Well, except Sascha's and my cousins, but those didn't count. I quickly made the bed, pulling the soft navy sheets up and fluffing the pillows. That was the right thing to do, wasn't it?

One of the two other doors in the room stood slightly ajar. It was a bathroom. With relief, I stepped in to use the toilet. Waterproof makeup was my godsend in this situation. Most of my foundation was gone and I cringed at the fact it had rubbed off on Justin's pillow, but my eye liner and mascara were barely smudged. I used water to neaten myself up and rinse my mouth out. I wasn't game enough to use the toothpaste of mouthwash resting on the basin. That would be weird, right?

Satisfied that I looked as presentable as I could make myself, I open his bedroom door and stepped into the hall. I held my shoes in my hand, not wanting the heels to clack on the wooden floor and wake anyone who might be sleeping. If Dale lived here, then Sascha would be here somewhere as well. At least, I hoped she was. It gave me a little more comfort and confidence knowing that I wasn't completely alone in a foreign house.

There were two other doors on this level and a staircase that told me I was on the second. I could walk up or down. Knowing that, as well as recognising the style of the balustrade and window trimmings, I knew I stood in a terrace house. It was similar to my own house.

A soft clanking sound came from the lower level and I quietly ventured downstairs. I walked through the front foyer, into the living room, and almost tripped over my own feet. Justin was there, sleeping on the couch, and looking completely at peace. He lied on his back, one arm resting behind his head and foot hanging off the end of the couch. What would have happened if I woke up in the bed next to him?

I tousled with whether or not I should wake him. How else was I going to sort out this situation? I didn't have a car here. Sascha had to be around somewhere. What would I do if she wasn't?

The clanking sound continued and I followed it into the kitchen, leaving Justin to his dreams. I felt kind of bad that he slept on the couch. He should have just left me there so he could sleep in his bed.

Darcy was the one making so much noise. As I walked in, she spotted me and pushed a bottle of water and pack of aspirin across the benchtop. "Morning sunshine."

"Ugh," I croaked, speaking for the first time today. She was in matching flannel pyjamas and wore her hair up in a neat ponytail. What I would give to use a hairbrush right now. I ran my fingers through my hair again, hoping I didn't look like too much of a mess. "Thanks. How did you escape this torture?" I took the pills gratefully and swallowed half the water bottle in a few gulps, not realising how thirsty I was until this moment.

Darcy laughed half-heartedly. "I wasn't downing shots like you and Em all night."

I groaned, lowering my head to the cool bench. "I have real regrets," I mumbled.

When she didn't respond, I looked back up at her. For someone who hadn't been drinking, her eyes were fairly red.

"Are you okay?"

Darcy sniffed and avoided my gaze. "I'm fine."

"You don't seem fine," I observed. "Are you sure you don't want to talk about it?"

She shook her head. "It was just a fight with Isaac. Nothing out of the ordinary. I'll be fine." She turned away, but it was obvious she was wiping her eyes on her sleeves. In a quick change of topic, she continued. "Do you want a coffee?"

I took her lead, not wanting to push her to talk about something that was obviously still fresh. "Yes please." I needed the coffee!

Darcy busied herself at the coffee machine. It was an expensive one that ground beans and had a frothing wand. I was both surprised and pleased. They drank real coffee here, none of that instant stuff. I wondered if Justin was the one who wanted the big, fancy machine. He was a coffee addict after all.

I waited patiently as Darcy worked. This was a lovely terrace house. It had clearly been renovated and was styled with a mix of modern and eclectic items. If a stranger walked in, they probably wouldn't pick that three young musicians lived here.

When Darcy returned to the island bench, she placed two mugs in front of me. At my questioning expression, she nodded toward the living room and said, "one is for Sir Justin in there."

My brows rose. "Sir Justin?"

"Mhmm. His armour gets shinier by the day," she smiled with an air of satisfaction.

Was she suggesting that he was a knight in shining armour? Sure, he saved me from Benji's ridiculous flirting last night, but I would have been fine. And sure, it was chivalrous, depending on whether you liked that thing or not. But it was completely unnecessary.

Ignoring that dig, or whatever her intention was, I took both mugs and went to the living room. Thankfully, Justin was already awaking up. I didn't have to poke him or anything. He sat up in the middle of the couch and rubbed his eyes with the back of his hands.

"Morning," he croaked when he saw me standing there gawking like an idiot. "Is one of those for me?"

I stepped forward and held a mug out to him, trying very hard to ignore how adorable he looked with ruffled hair and a wrinkled shirt.

He shifted over on the couch and threw the blanket he slept with into a nearby armchair. "Take a seat." He patted the cushion next to him.

Hesitantly, I sat down. I'd woken up surrounded by his scent on his sheets, but somehow sitting next to him made it more intense. How was it possible that my headache seemed to lessen almost instantly? The pills didn't work that quickly.

After sipping our coffees in silence for a few moments, I was the first to speak. "You really didn't need to sleep on the couch."

He shrugged. "You were gone before we even made it back here. Sascha thought it was best."

Best to stay here in Justin's bed? I'd have to ask her about that later.

"You still didn't need to sleep on the couch. You could have left me here and slept in your own bed."

Justin shook his head, the corner of his lips turning up slightly. "I wasn't letting you sleep on the couch."

I rolled my eyes. Knight in shining armour indeed. "Well then you should have slept in the bed too."

He raised on brow in surprise. "Without your permission?"

My chest was feeling warm again. Why did it always do that around him? "It's not like we haven't slept in the same bed before," I countered. The memory of that night frequently came back to me and was as vivid as ever.

His grin widened. "That was different. It was your idea, and our other options weren't as comfy as this couch." Darcy was right. With every word that left his mouth, his armour got shinier.

"Okay, fine," I accepted defeat. I wasn't going to win this argument. "Did Sascha stay here as well?" Oh, I hoped she did. I hadn't seen any sign of her this morning.

Justin nodded. I was almost positive that she did, but it was a relief to have it confirmed. "She's probably still locked up in Dale's room. I rarely see her when she's here."

"Ew," I mumbled. A closed door could only mean one thing with a new couple who couldn't keep their hands off each other.

Justin's head bobbed again, this time he gave me the pleasure of hearing his deep, soft, laugh. "She'll be down eventually."

"Thanks for making sure I found a safe place to stay," I said, looking down at my half-full mug. I wasn't his responsibility. "I was pretty wasted last night."

He laughed again. "I believe the term is double tipsy."

I couldn't help my smile. "Ah, yes, my intellect was showing with that one."

"Hey, you were double tipsy, and it was cute, so it's fine." Drunk and cute? Did those things usually go together? Justin's face quickly fell from amused to serious and I felt my mood plummet with it. "But now that you're not drunk anymore, there is something I need to talk to you about." He reached for my mug and placed it on the coffee table beside his own, then he turned his body towards me, arm resting on the back of the couch.

Okay, whatever it was, his approach was enough to start my panicking. He started talking again, not giving me time to spiral in a sea of possibilities that were ready to flood my mind.

"The AHM Awards," he began, not meeting my eyes. "I don't presume to know your feelings or your thoughts, but I feel like I should be telling you this, that you should know."

He paused then, and I had to urge him on with my hand. What was so important that he needed to get all serious like this? Did he know about Sawyer? And why did that thought bring the guilt back to the surface? My headache suddenly made itself known again. Whatever balm he unknowingly provided had disappeared.

"Well, because my dad will be there, and he's up for an award, Caroline is also going." He looked at me then, searching my face for some kind of sign. I'm not sure what it portrayed because I'm not sure what I was thinking. I just froze. "She'll be there. I thought you should know, but maybe that wasn't my place. I'm sorry. I didn't mean to bring anything up." His voice was starting to show panic.

"No, it's okay," I reassured him when I finally found my words. "Thank you for telling me." A whole new realm of possible awkward moments just popped into my mind. Not only did I need to worry about Justin and Sawyer at the same party, but now Caroline would be there too. I wasn't sure if I could handle seeing her. I could back out, but that would also result in disaster. Another thought occurred to me then.

My dad went to these awards annually. Did he have to see Caroline? Did she go every year as well? And why had he never told me? Did he deal with this on his own all the time?

"You okay?" Justin asked in a wary tone.

I shook my head, but smiled carefully. "I'm fine. I promise."

Luckily, Sascha decided to make an appearance at that moment and I didn't need to deepen the lie. I swear it was a sixth sense of hers. She had the perfect timing in every awkward situation.

"Morning Boss Lady!" she chirped as she skipped into the room.

My eyes widened. "Oh damn!"

"What?" she giggled, taking my cup from the table and sipping my coffee.

"I don't have my uniform!" I looked down at my watch. Our shift started in an hour. How could I forget about work? There was no time to drive back to my place and get it. Not that I had a car.

Sascha laughed again. "Sometimes you're slow in the morning. Boss's daughter, remember? Just get another one out of the store-room." I sighed in relief. I didn't even think of that, not that it was an ideal fix, but it would do and I would pay for it. "And quit panicking, I've got my car and we're only about 20 minutes away."

Thank goodness. I don't know what I was thinking. I never did this type of thing. I was always punctual and never caught in a situation without knowing the consequences, or how I could get out of it. And I had a hangover to boot! "Okay, well let's go."

Sascha handed the coffee to me. "Just give me two minutes." She backed out of the room.

"It better actually be two minutes," I yelled after her. We could not be late. When I turned back to Justin, who had stayed silent for the entire exchange, he looked amused. "Okay, so we're going now. Work and all. Thank you again for everything."

He gave me his genuine smile, the one that sent my heart fluttering. "You're welcome. I'll walk you out."

Justin lead me to the front door and opened it, letting the sun stream into the house. I stepped out onto the front porch to wait for Sascha. Justin stayed on the threshold, leaning against the doorframe with his coffee mug. He sipped it slowly and I couldn't help admiring him. His clothes were wrinkly, his usually well-kept hair was sticking out in all directions, and he had small bags under his eyes, yet somehow, he made it all look... sexy.

Sascha and Dale appeared in the foyer behind him and I was happy to know we'd be on the road any minute now. And then they started making out.

Justin turned to face me with a groan. He was still leaning against the frame, but his movement somehow brought him closer. Looking into his eyes, it was easy to forget what was going on right behind him. He was staring at me in that odd way again. What was he thinking? I wished I could ask, but that would be too forward.

When he spoke, it was in a low voice. "Are you so addicted to coffee that you'd resort to petty theft?"

"What?" I asked, completely confused. He looked pointedly at the mug in my hands and smirked. "Oh, right, this is yours," I blushed. I held it out to him, but not before downing the rest of my precious coffee.

That made him laugh. I was hearing a lot of it this morning, and it was nice. "Tell you what, you're welcome back for a coffee any time," he smiled.

"How come I never got that invitation?" another voice came.

I jumped, not having heard anyone approach. It was Emily. She winked at me knowingly and I blushed again. She probably thought something had happened between Justin and I. This was the second time she'd caught me with him in the morning. We'd made some progress last night, and I had to admit, I kind of liked her. I'd misjudged her in the beginning and now knew she had no real interest in Justin. Not that that should bother me either way.

"Is Darcy in her room?" she asked, turning serious. She must know about Darcy's fight with Isaac and had come to console her best friend.

"Last I saw, she was in the kitchen," I told her.

"Thanks," she smiled.

Justin stepped out onto the porch to let her pass. She was a confident person, and I had to laugh when she barged her way through Dale and Sascha, breaking up their make out session.

"Hey," I called to them. "Do not even think about roleplaying the horny teenagers again. It's time to go!"

Sascha spun around and stuck her tongue out. "Yes, mum."

Dale waved as we left the porch and I said goodbye to Justin. I walked down the path wondering if he was there watching me. Not that he should be, but would he? When I closed the gate to his small front yard, I allowed myself to look back. Sure enough, he stood by the door, both our mugs in his hands. And he was still smiling.

I turned away, lips forming a smile of their own. It was the kind of smile you couldn't hold back, and that confused me even more.

CHaPTer 11

"Darling, you look lovely," Dad said as he watched me twirl around in the living room. I was careful to spin on the balls of my feet so I didn't trip over my heels. They were golden and shiny and were a perfect match to my emerald silk dress.

"Yes she does," Sawyer agreed. I spun to face him, surprised by his presence. I didn't hear him come in. The look he gave me was devilish, and if he wasn't careful, he'd rouse Dad's suspicions. Even so, I couldn't help but smile at him.

"You look pretty dapper yourself," I said, hoping the mutual compliments would quash any questions. It was also true. Sawyer wore suits to work all the time, but they were nothing like the three piece he was wearing now.

"I feel a bit like I'm picking you up for the Year 12 formal," he laughed and straightened his cuffs.

Dad cleared his throat. "If that's the case, then I better lay down some ground rules." I froze. Oh no! "Be sure to wear your coats outside. Use the valet service, don't park my car in some second-rate parking lot. There will be trouble if you scratch it. And have my daughter home anytime she likes." I rolled my eyes but was secretly relieved he'd made a joke out of things. "Oh and if you dance, be careful of Mrs Gulliver. She can get a little handsy."

Sawyer laughed outright. "Yes, Sir. I'll have your car back in perfect condition."

"Good man."

I stood between them with my hands raised. I must be chopped liver because apparently the car took precedence. "Good to know I'm more important than the Audi." They both laughed this time.

When the moment passed, Dad turned serious. "Are you sure you still want to go? Because if you don't, I've got a suit right upstairs."

I didn't need an explanation to know why he asked. We'd spent multiple dinners this week discussing tonight's event and who was attending. I never admitted how I knew Caroline would be there, but I caved and asked him if he saw her every year. I had to know why he never told me. Naturally, it was his fatherly instinct to protect me. I'd kicked up a big stink as a child any time seeing her was even mentioned. So, he never brought it up.

That, of course, made me feel extra guilty. He was dealing with this all on his own. He said it was fine, and that he was over all that happened. He'd moved on. But had he really? Over the years he dated a few people, but he'd never had a serious girlfriend. It had been more than twelve years and he never found a significant other.

He never told me because he didn't want to cause me pain. Instead, he shouldered it all himself. Was that my fault?

Even though I was petrified of seeing Caroline and potentially talking to her, I couldn't let Dad do this again. Now that I knew, I needed to step up.

"I'm sure Dad, I'll be fine." I had to be.

He stepped forward and took my hands. "If at any point you want to leave, you just leave. Don't feel like you need to stay. It's not a big deal."

I squeezed his hands and put on my most genuine smile. "I'll be fine," I reiterated, hoping I sounded sincere.

He didn't seem convinced, but let it go and gave me a kiss on the cheek. "Well then, it's time to go. Have you got everything?"

I looked around and found my clutch resting on the armchair. "I just need to grab my coat," I said and left them in the living room to retrieve it from my closet. I did a final check in the mirror, making sure there were no panty lines showing beneath the skin-tight dress. I wasn't one to toot my own horn or anything, but I was pleased with how I looked tonight. The dress was stunning.

On my way back downstairs, I caught a snippet of their conversation and stopped at the top where I couldn't be seen. "Just watch her," my dad said. "She will put on a tough face, and she won't tell you if she's overwhelmed. She'll try to deal with it on her own."

When Sawyer responded, he sounded worried. "She's a bit like her old man in that way. I promise I'll look after her."

I intentionally made excess noise with my heels on the stairs, to let them know I was coming. As expected, they stepped back, pretending they hadn't been speaking.

"Are you ready to go?" Sawyer asked. His voice still sounded concerned. Now I would have to tiptoe around him as well. As if tonight wasn't going to be difficult enough.

Was I ready? Not in the slightest. Was it time to go? There was no more putting it off. "Yep, let's go."

Dad walked us to the car. We didn't have much of a driveway and it was in the garage. Sawyer parked his road bike as close to the side fence as he could get it. As hot as he looked riding that thing, it was impractical for events such as tonight's. He was nervous to drive Dad's car, but it was the best alternative. Plus, I was not getting on the back of his bike in this dress.

The further we drove into the city, the more prominent my nerves became. I was going to see Caroline. I stayed quiet in the car as I thought about what she'd be like. Did she look the same? Would she have the same haircut? It had been over ten years since I'd seen her. Surely, she looked different now. Would I recognise her instantly?

While I worried about her looking like a different person, one question kept pestering me. Was she happier now? Dad and I clearly weren't enough for her, but did Michael, Claire and Justin fill that void?

Sawyer kept glancing my way in concern. My silence was likely worrying him, but I wasn't in the mood to talk. I was lost in my own mind.

When we arrived, he took Dad's advice and used the valet service. He pulled up to the convention centre and was out of the car and at my door almost instantly. I thanked him with a nervous smile.

The moment was getting closer by the second.

We visited the cloakroom, and I carefully placed the ticket inside my clutch.

The centre was bustling with people preparing to enter the AHM Awards, all dressed to the nines in expensive suits and cocktail dresses. Some even held champagne flutes brought around by waitstaff meandering through the crowd.

I kept my eyes down. Perhaps if I didn't look up, I wouldn't see her, and she wouldn't see me. It was a fruitless tactic. I couldn't avoid her forever.

"Are you doing alright?" Sawyer asked as we stood in line to find our table number. He was worried again, that much was obvious by the tone of his voice. He rubbed a hand down my arm and I finally looked up. "Do you really want to do this? Because we go home."

"No," I told him, shaking my head defiantly. "This is something I need to do." Whether I was ready to see Caroline or not, I had to do this tonight.

I couldn't avoid her forever.

Sawyer took both my hands in his. "Whatever you need, I'm here, okay?"

I nodded. I knew he meant well but I could never dump all this on him. "Look, it's almost our turn."

We stepped up to the concierge and received our table number. I was relieved to find out it was located at the back of the room. Twenty-nine on Queen wasn't nominated for any awards this year, so we weren't considered important company. Justin's father's hotel was nominated, which meant they would all be sitting closer to the front.

We took our seats at the empty round table and waited for the ceremony to start. I looked around the room with the hopes of glimpsing Caroline. Perhaps seeing her from afar would make it easier later, but there were so many people here I had to wonder if she'd even notice my presence.

It didn't take long for me to spot her. My earlier worries about not recognising her were absurd. She looked the same, if not healthier. Tanned skin and long brunette hair. Tonight, it was styled neatly at the base of her neck, and it complimented her burgundy dress perfectly. She was beautiful and I shouldn't have expected anything less.

Then I noticed the men standing with her. Michael, her husband and Dad's ex-friend, and Justin. He confidently spoke to the group surrounding him near the front of the room. That smile of his was so charming on a regular day. Tonight, in his designer suit, it captivated those around him.

That's when I remembered my other concerns for tonight and turned my attention back to my table. An older couple had just sat down and Sawyer was introducing us. "My name is Sawyer McKinnon, and this is Elizabeth Newcombe."

"Newcombe?" The lady questioned as she shook my hand. "Any relation to Richard Newcombe?"

I nodded. "Richard is my father."

"Oh, how fabulous. Looks run in the family, I see," she winked. "Is he here tonight?" The woman looked around expectantly.

I tried hard to portray a polite smile rather than an amused one. Under the table, I slapped Sawyer on the thigh. He wasn't even trying.

"No, he's not here."

"What a shame, he does always indulge me with a dance at the end of the night." She pressed a wrinkled and heavily jewelled hand to her chest and smiled. "Oh forgive me, I haven't introduced myself. I am Juliet Gulliver, and this is my husband, Emmett." She rested a hand on the shoulder of the man beside her. He'd already taken his seat.

He winked. "Forgive my wife, she's a little eccentric."

"Eccentric? Darling, I prefer the term endearing."

Mr Gulliver chucked and kissed his wife's cheek. I let my amused smile free. They were cute. I also got the impression that Dad's warning about dancing with Mrs Gulliver was well-placed. Like her husband, I found her to be eccentric, and I'd only spoken to her for a minute.

Sawyer offered to pour her a glass of wine from the bucket in the middle of the table. He did the same for Mr Gulliver and for me.

"Do you want the red or the white?" he asked me with a gentle voice.

"White, please."

As he poured my glass, Mrs Gulliver spoke again, this time with a suggestive tone. "Are you two a couple? You make a very handsome couple."

I was quick to correct her. "Oh no, we're not—"

Sawyer cleared his throat and sat back.

"Oh, I'm sorry. It's not my business." She took a sip of her wine and looked Sawyer over as if he was definitely her business.

I did the same, but instead of looking him over, I glanced sideways to gauge his reaction. His smile was still there, but it looked strained. I felt a little uncomfortable listening to the woman and couldn't imagine what he was feeling right now. Thankfully, more people arrived at our table and introductions took over.

I was grateful when the ceremony began and waitstaff came around with our dinner. Conversation was limited as everyone ate, drank, and listened to the host introduce each award.

Unsurprisingly, Justin's dad won the resort category. On stage, he thanked his team—from the executives to the floor employees—and his family. He mentioned Caroline and Justin specifically.

Beside me, Sawyer made a noise deep in his throat. What did that mean? I was hesitant to ask in case it opened up a conversation I didn't want the rest of the table to hear. I didn't like to relive my past, so I had no intention of explaining anything to them. Plus, Mrs Gulliver seemed like a bit of a gossip.

Once the ceremony was over and dessert had been served, people started to mingle. That was when the bar opened as well. Thank goodness. During dinner service, we were restricted to table wine. If you were lucky enough to catch a waiter, you could order something from the bar, but I didn't see much of that happening. I didn't hate wine, but there were other drinks I preferred.

"I just saw an old friend from Uni," Sawyer announced. We were standing with Mr and Mrs Gulliver and they were reminiscing about a recent holiday to Fiji. Sawyer turned on his most charming smile. "Please excuse us."

Mrs Gulliver looked disappointed. "Promise you'll save me a dance," she cooed.

Sawyer didn't respond with words, instead choosing to avoid answering by giving her another tight smile. He took my hand and pulled me away at a polite pace.

When we were safely out of earshot, he said. "My God, that woman hits all the wrong nerves, doesn't she?"

I laughed and wriggled my eyebrows at him. "Feeling her deep down, are you?"

Sawyer shivered. "Keep me away from the dance floor later."

"What about now?" Mr and Mrs Gulliver were making their way through the tables and were heading in the direction of the small dancefloor in the corner. A band had just started playing some well-known classics. I had no idea what type of band they were, but they didn't sing, and they had a cellist.

"Well, it's a good thing I really did see an old mate. I'm a little busy and Mrs G will have to find another victim."

I laughed at his antics. He was being a little dramatic, but I always enjoyed this side of him. He started walking again and I realised he was still holding my hand. I pulled it out and placed it on his shoulder. "Do you want anything from the bar?" I asked. "I'm sick of wine and desperate for a lemon drop."

"Sure, whisky straight please."

With his order, I left him to approach his friend and headed for the bar. The line was already long and I was in for a wait. They were making all sorts of cocktails tonight and the bartenders were being put to work.

I found myself eavesdropping on a conversation between two potentially desperate housewives. The blonde one in the very tight dress was bragging, quite explicitly, about her masseuse's gentle hands, and the redhead wasn't shy in asking if she could borrow him for a session.

"How do you think this will end?" a deep voice asked beside me. I jumped, not expecting to be caught eavesdropping. "Cat fight in the carpark?"

The tailored suit did a lot for Justin, or maybe for me. Either way, with his hands in his pockets and that all-knowing smirk in its rightful place, he was looking fine.

I pretended to mull over his words as I watched the women. "Threesome in the cloakroom," I countered.

His eyebrows rose in surprise. "Okay, yeah, I see it," he nodded in agreement. Then he did something completely unexpected. He lent down and kissed me on the cheek. "Hey."

There was nothing sensual about it, although I felt the heat from his lips tingle all the way from my cheek to my fingertips.

"Hey," I breathed when I could finally form the words.

He glanced down at his feet for a moment, like he was preparing himself for something. When he looked back up, he didn't hide his wandering eyes. "You are stunning," he said confidently.

My blush was instant and I couldn't hide my smile. I knew I looked good in this dress, it was gorgeous, but I hadn't expected such a straightforward compliment. "Well, thank you. You look quite stunning yourself," I admitted. He really did.

"I know," he said, straightening the collar of his jacket.

"Careful now, cockiness could land you a position in the cloakroom."

He held my gaze with intense eyes. "You offering?"

That wasn't my intention at all, but now that he'd put it out there, I'd be lying if I said it didn't cross my mind. I couldn't let him see that though, so rolled my eyes and lightly slapped his arm.

"If you're in line for some wet pussy shots, I wouldn't want to prevent you from reliving a good night," he said with amusement. I felt the need to slap his arm again. "But can I steal you away for a minute?"

"Why?" I questioned cautiously. Where was he going to take me? "The cloakroom's already spoken for, sorry pal."

That made him laugh. Justin placed a hand on my lower back and started leading me away from the bar. "Do you hear that?" he asked.

"Hear what?"

"The song. Don't you remember?"

I listened carefully to the band but couldn't pick the song they were playing. It was currently instrumental.

I shook my head. "I don't know what I'm supposed to remember." Did he play it at a gig?

"Come on, I'll jog your memory." I was acutely aware of his warm hand on the bare skin of my back, and how it distracted me from his true intentions.

Justin was leading me to the dancefloor.

Chapter 12

I almost pulled away from Justin as he led me through tables, but curiosity encouraged me to keep going. I let him take me to the dancefloor. What memory was he talking about?

I felt nervous under the scrutiny of eyes. Were they watching us? Would they judge us for dancing at an event like this? There really weren't many couples on the dancefloor. Mr and Mrs Gulliver were tearing it up, arm in arm and having the time of their lives. There were two other couples, but they weren't nearly as lively. All of them were at least fifty years old and clearly had enough life experience not to care what others thought of them.

I had reservations, even when Justin took my hand and gently pulled me to his chest. A sharp intake of breath opened me to his delicious scent. Being this close, it was more intense than I'd ever experienced.

"I'm a little hurt that you don't remember," he said with a frown as we swayed side to side. "You do know what song this is, don't you?"

He let go of my waist to slowly spin me around. When I came back to his chest and rested my hand on his shoulder again, I was smiling. I recognised the song the moment I let myself listen to it closely. It was an instrumental of Stevie Wonder's Isn't She Lovely. "Of course I know it. My question is, why should I know it?"

Justin gave a small chuckle. "Again, I'm hurt that you find me so unmemorable. Think back about twelve years. Same song, similar but very different circumstances."

I did as he asked, and as he twirled me again, the memory came to me. "The wedding?" It was usually a memory I actively blocked, but letting it in now, I remembered. At his dad's wedding to Caroline, we danced together to this same song, that time with lyrics.

"If I recall," he continued, "you weren't very keen on me back then."

I wasn't very keen on anything that happened back then. "Who says I'm keen on you now?" I asked, raising a brow and trying to look serious.

Justin chuckled again. "Well you can look at me this time, and you're not frowning. I must not be as repulsive."

"Nine-year-old boys have cooties," I shrugged. While I was smiling on the outside, my insides were in chaos. I couldn't believe he remembered that moment, or the fact that I'd spent the entire dance glaring at him. I didn't know whether my blush was from embarrassment at my past behaviour, or from the fact that he noticed me even when we were kids.

"And now?" he pressed, holding my gaze. There was nothing innocent about the way he looked at me now and my blush deepened. I could feel my chest warm. And the tingles his gentle hand left on my skin? They intensified to a point where I could feel his touch in every nerve of my body.

A tap on Justin's shoulder broke the intensity flaring between us. I wasn't sure if I should be thankful or not, but Mr and Mrs

Gulliver's timely interruption prevented me from answering. "May we have this dance?" Mr Gulliver asked in his most haughty voice.

Justin's arms dropped from my hand and waist. I tried sending him a silent message—don't do it—but he was no longer looking at me. "Sure," he politely agreed. And then Mrs Gulliver grabbed his hand and they were dancing.

"Don't worry, Dear," Mr Gulliver said. I turned to him and took his hand. He'd been patiently waiting as I watched Justin get swooped away. "My wife is a little out there, but she's all talk and no action. She's harmless."

I smiled at him, but inside, I was still worried. Was she harmless? Surely, if he was this blasé about his wife's behaviour, she couldn't be too bad.

Mr Gulliver and I danced to Michael Bublé and he asked how my father was doing. As it turned out, dancing with the Gullivers could work in our favour. They were travel bloggers, and apparently quite well-known. They'd also stayed at my dad's hotel over the summer. I would have to look them up later to see that review. I never knew there'd been one.

Thinking about my dad brought other things back to mind. Justin had this uncanny way of making me forget about the world around me and all its problems. With him gone, thoughts of Dad, Caroline, and even Sawyer creeped back in.

I quickly glanced around the large room. I found Justin's dad swiftly enough, but no Caroline. I also couldn't spot Sawyer in the place I'd left him or with the friend he'd been talking to. I was supposed to be getting him a drink, but instead, I'd ended up dancing with Justin.

As the song ended, so did our dancing. Mr Gulliver and Justin shook hands and Mrs Gulliver pulled me in for a hug. "I like this one, he's a spunk," she whispered in my ear. As we parted, she winked at me, and I pressed my lips together to hold in my giggle.

"What's so funny?" Justin asked as we slowly walked away.

I shook my head. If I said it, I would definitely laugh.

"That woman likes to get up close and personal. She put her hand inside my jacket!"

I pressed my hand to my mouth.

"What? I'm not saying I hated it," he shrugged with a smug expression.

This time, I let it out. "Well, she does think you're a spunk," I laughed.

"What does that mean?"

My turn to shrug. "I have no idea," I said. Yet somehow, I had to agree with Mrs Gulliver.

"Maybe we can puzzle it out over a cocktail," Justin suggested as he put his arm around me again. He was leading me to the bar, where I was supposed to be getting Sawyer a drink.

"Actually," I began, pulling away from him. "I need to visit the ladies room."

"Are you okay?" he asked in concern.

I nodded. "Yeah, I'm fine."

Justin didn't question me again and I walked back across the dancefloor toward the bathroom doors.

It was a luxury space, as far as bathrooms went. The cubicles were behind another door. I didn't need them and instead walked to the middle of the room where there was a round sofa made of white velvet. I sat and took a few deep breaths.

I was an idiot. Dancing with Justin was not the best idea. Of course, I couldn't deny how good it felt at the time, but now that I was away from him, I felt something heavy forming deep in my chest. Then there was Sawyer to think about as well. Had he seen? What would he say? It shouldn't matter because we were just friends, but I had a feeling in the pit of my stomach, and it wasn't a good one.

"Elizabeth?"

I stood up when I heard her voice. I didn't hear the door to the second room open, but there was Caroline, watching me with a curious expression. She walked across the room to wash her hands and I couldn't take my eyes off her. Just as I'd observed earlier tonight, she was beautiful.

I was rooted to the spot as she watched me through the mirror. When she finished drying her hands, she turned back to me with a tight smile. "How are you?" she asked with caution as if she was approaching a baby bird who'd fallen from its nest.

It took a few moments to find my voice, but when it came, I put as much strength as I could muster into it. "I'm well, thank you. Yourself?"

She smiled again. "I'm also well, thank you." And then we stood in silence, neither one of use knowing what to say.

I'd imagined this moment countless times over the years, particularly in the last week. I had plenty to say, but now that the situation presented itself, I was speechless. And I couldn't stop looking at her. She had a few more wrinkles around the eyes than the last time I saw her. I suppose a decade of life lived could do that to a person. Even though she looked a little older, she somehow seemed younger. Was that because she now lived the life she always wanted?

Caroline broke the silence. "I saw you and Justin dancing earlier. I didn't realise you two were friends."

I nodded. "We study the same course at Uni."

There was a feeling in my chest. Satisfaction? Or perhaps dis-appointment that she knew very little about my life? Not that I should blame her. I was the one who cut off all ties.

"Richard must be happy you're learning the family business."

The mention of my dad's name triggered a different feeling. I looked away from her. She had no right to talk about my father, not after what she did to him. Some familiar feelings, the ones from my childhood that I'd buried long ago, came rushing to the surface.

"Actually, Dad is supportive of all my interests. He's happy as long as I'm happy," I said firmly, even though I couldn't be sure of his happiness. What I did know was that I wasn't the cause of all his pain over the years. She was.

"I should get back out there," I said, taking a step back.

"Ellie, wait," Caroline started. She pressed her hands together and held them in front of her mouth for a moment. "I realise that I have little right to know this, but growing up, were you okay? Were you happy?" The look in her eyes told me she was sincere, but she we right, she didn't deserve to know.

I was going to tell her the truth regardless. We were alone, but even if we weren't, I don't think I would hold back. I took two deep breaths to calm myself, and then I let loose the speech I'd been preparing all week. "I actually spent the end of primary school in the counsellor's office."

Caroline looked like she wanted to say something, but I cut off her attempts and continued. I had to say it all now before I chickened out.

"I was lucky, though, because I had a father who loved me unconditionally and did everything he could to help me. And he still tries every day to make sure I'm the happy one, even at his own expense. So was I okay growing up? No. I don't even know if I'm happy now. But I am stronger, and I'm the one who gets to decide my life."

Tears were threatening to escape by the end of my heated speech, but I refused to let them free. She did not get to see me cry.

"I'm so sorry," she whispered, looking like she might shed a tear herself.

I started backing up again. When I was halfway out the door, I looked back. "I'm not."

I walked straight passed the dancefloor and weaved through the tables and suits. I'd just told off Caroline and now I wanted to forget it. My outburst hadn't worked. All the emotions that had been welling inside me were still there, and they felt heavier than before. So, it was time to go.

When I reached our table, Sawyer wasn't there. He was my ride and my way out. Luckily Mrs Gulliver was there sucking down a bright pink cocktail. "Have you seen Sawyer?" I asked carefully, hoping that I sounded confident.

She was either oblivious or drunk because she didn't pick up on my shaking voice. "He went to the bar, Darling. I think he's buying me another cosmo."

I thanked her with a tight smile, grabbed my purse, and turned in the direction of the bar. Unfortunately, when I got there, my escape plan was faced with another barrier.

Sawyer was there. So was Justin. They were both leaning on the edge of the bar with their backs to me. And they were talking. I stopped a few feet away. Could this night get any worse? What were they talking about?

Sawyer's voice was the first I heard, and it was full of contempt. "It takes a big man to live off daddy."

"What's that supposed to mean?" Justin asked, standing up straight.

Sawyer did the same. "Some of us have to work for our positions, we don't all get to be some spoon fed, private school lad with a trust fund that kicks some poor sod out of his office just because he can."

Justin turned to face him with a look I'd never seen before. "Mate, you've got no idea what you're talking about. And at least I'm not climbing the ladder by sleeping with the boss's daughter."

I spoke up before either one of them could throw a real punch, because that's where it looked like they were headed. "You're both arseholes."

They turned to face me at the same time. One looked guilty, the other angry. I shook my head, turned, and walked toward the door. They were just another reason I needed to get out of this stupid party.

CHAPTER 13

S tupid, stupid, stupid!

Caroline. Sawyer. Justin. They were all so incredibly frustrating, but none of them was stupid. That title fell to me. I was naïve to think any part of this night would go without drama. And I was stupid to believe I'd get through it without incident. In fact, there'd been multiple.

I had to get out of there before my overwhelmed mind combusted. Now I wandered aimlessly around Sydney Harbour in my thin, silk dress, letting the cool of the winter night sooth my raging emotions.

There were plenty of partygoers out tonight, stumbling from one club to another before lockout. The women all wore tight or short dresses. The alcohol coursing through their veins likely kept them warm. I crossed my arms and rubbed them, hoping to steal away some of the chill with friction.

I was riling from my conversation with Caroline. Not that it was a conversation, for the most part; it was more me telling her off for a lifetime of undeserved pain. I wasn't sure if she deserved it or not, regardless of her regret and empathy. She broke my dad's heart and there was no forgiving that.

Then there was Justin and Sawyer. Deep down I knew they wouldn't get along. That's why I'd been so worried about them being in the same place tonight. But again, I'd been stupid to let this even happen. I knew it would blow up somehow.

My phone buzzed relentlessly in my purse, but I left it there, still needing time to calm down. It was probably Sawyer. We'd arrived together tonight, and I'd just taken off. He'd be worried. But I couldn't get the look on his face out of my mind. He was mad, and he needed time to calm down as well.

"Ellie!"

I turned at the call of my name and Justin approached at a slow jog.

I kept walking, not sure I could deal with him either.

"Ellie, wait a minute." He stepped up beside me and I stopped to face him. "You're mad," he stated, eyes glancing over me as I tightened my arms across my chest. Yes, I was mad, and I had every right to be.

He started unbuttoning his suit jacket. "What are you doing?" I asked, even though I knew exactly what he was doing. Despite his choice of words in his argument with Sawyer, he was usually a gentleman.

Justin shook off his jacket. "You've got goosebumps," he said, not taking his eyes off me.

I shrugged, even though he was right and my goosebumps had goosebumps. "But you'll be cold."

That amused him. "I've got long sleeves, I'll be fine," he said, wrapping his jacket around my shoulders and pulling the collar up under my neck. I held onto it and wondered if taking a sniff would be too creepy. Was it weird that I enjoyed his scent wrapping around me more than the actual warmth the jacket provided?

An awkward silence ensued as we watched groups around us pass by joking and laughing with ease. Last weekend, we'd been with a group of friends having a good time just like that. Now we stood here uncomfortably, and I was afraid to open my mouth for fear of what I'd say.

After what seemed like forever, but was only a minute or so, Justin broke the silence. "I'm sorry," he apologised, eyes as sincere as his tone.

I had to look away. The anger still simmered, as it should, and I knew looking at him would just soothe those feelings. I had to stay mad, at least for a little while. "You should be," I murmured, looking down at my feet. They were slowly turning purple in the chilly air.

Justin took a step closer and spoke in a low voice. "I know I have no excuse for what I said."

Screw it! I looked up him, hoping my demeanour made up for my small stature. He was far taller, but I had a point to make. "You implied Sawyer only slept with me to climb the corporate ladder. That that's all I'm worth."

"That was not my intention at all, and you know that." His shoulders slumped right in front of me, and his eyes seemed desperate. Good! He knew he'd done wrong.

Then, just as quickly as my own emotions changed, his tone switched from apologetic to irritated. "You could have said you had a boyfriend."

I shook my head, looking away again. "Sawyer isn't my boyfriend."

"He sure acts like it," he stated in disbelief. I had to wonder what Sawyer had told him before I arrived. Justin knew we'd slept together, but to what extent did Sawyer reveal our arrangement?

"That's not an excuse for what you said."

"I know that." His shoulders sunk further but he shook his head, the irritation obvious. "I just let him get under my skin."

I kept my eyes trained on a guy giving a girl a piggyback ride along the water's edge as I replied. At least they were having fun tonight. "You still said it."

Justin took another step closer and placed a warm finger under my chin. He tipped my face up gently so I had to look at him for his next words. "And I really am sorry." Looking into his eyes, I knew my earlier fears were accurate. He could soothe me in a single moment. It was some weird superpower of his. "I'm an arsehole," he grinned.

I couldn't help the smile. "Yeah, you are."

We stood like that for another moment. How could this night go so wrong? And after everything, how could we end up like this, standing together in a near-embrace as if nothing had happened?

Justin broke the silence of our moment. "You're buzzing," he said, taking his warmth from my face.

We were so close that my hand, the one holding onto my purse, was pressed between us. He could feel the vibration of my phone through the fabric.

I reluctantly took a step back. It had been going off for a while. When I took it out to check my notifications, I saw three missed calls and five messages from Sawyer. He may have been angry, but he was always concerned. He wanted to know where I'd gone, and I was reminded that I'd come here with him tonight. I glanced up at Justin, who watched me with glistening eyes, before I tapped out a single message to tell Sawyer that I was clearing my head and I was fine.

Putting my phone back in my purse, I pushed the guilt down. I just needed a little while longer. "Can we walk for a little while?"

Justin gave me his lazy smile and nodded. We set off at a dawdle around the harbour without a word.

Despite the chill, it was a beautiful night. The sky was clear and the water was sparkling with the lights of the city surrounding it. We walked all the way to the Sydney Opera House where the Opera Bar, beneath the sails of the historic building, was pumping.

We walked to the furthest entrance, away from the loud music and the most enthusiastic drinkers, to sit on the concrete bench overlooking the Harbour Bridge.

Not having spoken since we started walking, I had a lot of time to think and calm down about other events of the night.

"I saw Caroline," I admitted quietly, looking over the water.

Justin turned his body so that we were facing each other. He spoke carefully when he asked, "What happened?"

"I sort of yelled at her in the bathroom." At least I could speak calmly when I thought about it now. Inside, I cringed at my behaviour. Regardless of my feelings, yelling at someone in a public bathroom, whoever they were, wasn't a nice thing to do. Oh, how I hoped no one had overheard. Looking back on things now, I was embarrassed enough.

"It must have been difficult for you." The wind blew as he spoke, and I pulled the jacket tighter to my chest. Justin placed an arm around me and rubbed my back gently, using the friction to help warm me.

I was so distracted by his touch that I almost forget what I was going to say. "I was just so angry. I think she cried." I'd seen the tears in her eyes. At the time, I didn't think my words were all that harsh, but looking back, I could see the expression on her face. I'd hurt her. Maybe she deserved it, maybe she didn't. I had no idea anymore.

"I don't think she'd blame you," Justin said. It was like he could read my mind, like he knew exactly what I'd been thinking. It was another superpower of his. He just had this innate ability to understand me. Or maybe he was just observant, and I was terrible at hiding my feelings.

"Has she ever said anything to you about..." I didn't know how to finish my question, but again, he seemed to understand.

He shook his head gently. "Not really, but I imagine she has a lot of regret. I think she still has a photo album of you from when you were little."

I didn't know what to think about that. It was surprising, yet it made sense. My dad kept an old album of family photos that were once proudly displayed in our home. They now sat in the back of a cupboard in his office. I'd come home one morning after a sleepover at Sascha's to find him passed out on the couch, half a bottle of scotch on the coffee table next to the open album. Back then, I had the urge to tear up those photos, or burn them, but couldn't bring myself to touch them. Dad kept them for a reason, and I couldn't take them away from him.

I looked out over the water. It was so still and calm, a stark contrast to the feelings welling inside me. "There's been too many years of hurt. And then there's Dad as well. I don't know if I can ever let it go."

"No one says you have to," Justin said, still wary of his words. "You can't change the past and you don't have to pretend things never happened, but do you think it might be easier for you if you tried?" It was difficult to be sure, but I thought I heard a spark of hope in his voice.

I turned back to him. "Forgive but not forget?"

He shrugged. "Something like that."

"I don't know." The mere thought of forgiving Caroline felt like blasphemy. Maybe I wasn't ready to deal with this. "I think I'm still too worked up. Can we talk about something else?"

More silence, and thankfully, it wasn't awkward. My mind was overloaded, and I couldn't think of other things to say. Justin seemed to be in a world of his own too, but eventually offered a new course of conversation.

His attempt at warming me up with friction paused as he moved in closer. Our legs pressed together, and I could feel his warmth, even through two layers of fabric. He leant down, causing our cheeks to touch, as well. I relished the searing pleasure his left against my cold skin. "Have I mentioned how stunning you are?"

When he pulled back, he didn't go far. His ability to make me forget all the bad things going on was still astounding. "You might have mentioned it," I said, almost breathlessly.

The intensity in his eyes was enthralling. "You always look good, Ellie-bean."

"Stop," I giggled, pushing his chest. He didn't budge.

"Take the compliment," he smirked.

I rolled my eyes, but inside, my heart was doing that thing it liked to do whenever Justin was around. I'd gotten used to it now and barely noticed, but apparently times like this were exceptions. "Thank you," I said, not really knowing how to reply. He was being forward, like he wasn't worried about what I'd think. I wondered what it felt like to be that confident. "Did I mention how good you look as well?"

He shrugged, and it seemed to bring him closer. "You might have mentioned it." His smirk grew.

"The new haircut suits you, by the way." I felt a little shy admitting it, but he really did look good. The shorter sides and longer top accentuated his already dazzling cheekbones. He was nice to look at.

"Oh yeah, you like it?" He licked his lips as he pushed a hand through his hair. I couldn't look away.

"Maybe." Then I did something completely unexpected. I reached up and pushed back some fly away strands that had come loose.

When I realised what I was doing and pulled away, Justin grabbed my wrist and held it between us. My pounding heart felt like it might jump right out of my chest. Was he going to kiss me? Did he want to? Did I want to?

We weren't given the chance to find out. A push on my back forced me out of the moment and I spun to see a guy throwing his guts up over the barrier, aiming for the water.

I jumped further into Justin's arms. "Ugh, that's disgusting," I gagged, scuttling across his lap to get as far away from the horrible stench as I could.

Justin turned with me on his lap to put his body between me and the intruder. "Are you alright?"

A few metres away, some drunken guys were laughing at their mate. One offered us an apology for his friend as he came forward to pat the guy's back.

"I'd be better if we got away from that filth," I frowned.

Justin placed his hands on my waist and helped me up. "Come on, we should walk back anyway." He draped his jacket back over my shoulders. It had fallen off when I jumped onto him.

As we walked away, I pulled my phone out. I'd been ignoring it, but now that my mind was clear of the intense fog brought on by Justin's proximity, I recalled its incessant buzzing.

There was a single message from my dad, and I opened it first. Sawyer must have called him because he wanted to know where I was. I sent a reply letting him know I would be home soon.

Then I checked Sawyer's messages. He expressed similar worries, but when I saw the final one, which had come less than five minutes ago, all the others revealing his concern for my whereabouts, became redundant.

'Looks like you've got things sorted. See you at work next week.'

I glanced around the bar and at the walkway above. He'd been here but was nowhere to be found now. I let out a deep sigh.

"Is everything okay?" Justin asked.

"Yes. No. I don't know," I rambled. Sawyer's message was a stark reminder of the night. "I should go."

I was a horrible person.

Justin must have sensed the change in me, because his demeanour suddenly turned stony and not at all like the warmth he'd given moments ago. "Do you need a ride home?" he asked in that gentlemanly way of his.

I couldn't bring myself to look at him. "That would be very helpful, thank you. I just have to get my coat." In my haste to escape, I'd forgotten it was in the cloakroom at the convention centre.

In my peripheral, I saw him nod once. "Okay, let's get you warmed up."

This entire night was a disaster, and I had a feeling things were going to get a whole lot messier.

CHAPTER 14

Making the decision to keep clear of Sawyer and Justin for a few days was smart, it was needed, but I never imagined it would make me feel so alone.

I'd arrived home after the AHM Awards to find my father waiting up for me. In his haste to find me, Sawyer had called him. Dad wasn't particularly pleased that I'd taken off and abandoned Sawyer. He assumed I'd been upset because of Caroline, which was true, but what surprised me the most was that he had no idea I'd been with Justin Hart.

Sawyer managed to leave out that little detail, and I didn't know whether to feel relieved or concerned. Why didn't Sawyer tell him? I hadn't heard a word from him since his last passive-aggressive message, and I didn't contact him either. It was clear he didn't want to talk to me and obviously needed some time to cool down.

I was also grateful for that time. I couldn't stop thinking about the look on his face when I interrupted him and Justin at the bar. Had it been anger? Or hurt? The more I thought about it, the more my memory of the moment blurred.

And speaking of Justin, I hadn't seen or spoken to him either. After he dropped me home with an awkward and strained goodbye,

I couldn't bring myself to message him. When I wasn't thinking about how upset Sawyer was and what would happen when we finally spoke, my mind wandered back to all the moments Justin and I shared. They'd been so intense at the time that I forgot the world around us still turned.

Maybe that's why when Tuesday came around, I organised a meeting with my group for our shared assignment at the time I usually had coffee with Justin. I couldn't bring myself to face him. One minute he was all sweet and giving me his jacket, and the next he was saying goodbye without even looking at me.

It was all very confusing. So, I kept to myself for a few days. I didn't even talk to Sascha, who was busy with her own life anyway. Unfortunately, my self-imposed solace had to come to end when it was time to start my Wednesday shift at the hotel.

I hesitated outside the office door, my hand on the doorknob as I took a few deep breaths. Just one more moment.

When I opened the door, Sawyer was sitting at his desk, his back to me as he typed on the computer. He turned slightly at my entrance but continued what he was doing. I put my bag down and leant against the other table, waiting until he was ready.

Sawyer eventually stopped typing and slowly spun to face me. We sat there looking at each other for a little while. I couldn't read his face. Whatever he was feeling, he wasn't revealing anything.

"You didn't tell Dad," I said, breaking the tension.

He looked down at his lap. "About what?"

"You know what I'm talking about." My father didn't know a single thing about Justin or the time I spent with him. I needed to know why.

When Sawyer's eyes finally met mine, his jaw was set. "I didn't want to break his heart."

The lump forming in my throat felt thick. Would my dad be as devastated as Sawyer implied? He was always the supportive and encouraging type of parent. Granted, I'd never actively kept anything from him, or hung out with the son of the people who betrayed him. There was obviously a reason I hadn't told him. Maybe this was it. Maybe it would break his heart.

That was the last thing I wanted to do.

Sawyer ran a hand over his stubbled chin as he stood up, turning his back to me. "So, this is where you've been for the past month? You've been blowing me off to hang out with him."

I shook my head. "That's not true. I've mostly been hanging out with Sascha and her boyfriend. Justin just happens to be Dale's best mate." It wasn't a lie. Most of the time, Sascha was there. And yes, I had coffee with Justin, but we weren't always alone. Others frequently joined us. "Plus, we're doing the same course at Uni."

My reasons didn't sway him. Sawyer finally faced me, and this time, he didn't hide his feelings. "Have you slept with him?"

"What?!" Between my open mouth and raised eyebrows, I'm sure I looked ridiculous. Possibly guilty, which was absurd because I'd done no such thing. "No, of course not. Why would you ask that?"

I mean, I could see why his mind would go down that path, but he knew me better than that. He knew that if anything happened with anyone else, I'd tell him straight away. It was part of our deal, or arrangement, whatever it was.

He looked down again, taking a breath before he spoke. "The other week, you showed up to work without your uniform in the clothes you wore out the night before. You said you and Sass stayed at her boyfriend's place. Is that true?"

"Yes." I had to tell him the truth.

He still didn't seem convinced. "And the part of the story you forgot to mention?"

"Justin and Dale live together," I admitted before quickly elaborating. "Nothing happened, I slept on my own."

"But you've kissed him." There was no question in his words.

I shook my head again, denying his assumption. "No, I haven't."

Sawyer let out a huff as he shook his head and looked to the roof. "You sure? Because you two looked pretty damn cosy on Saturday night."

My heart rate was starting to pick up. I needed him to see. I needed him to understand. "I'm sure. I haven't seen or spoken to him since then, either."

"That's something at least," he murmured. He then turned away again and asked a question that made my heart skip. "Do you have feelings for him?"

My grip tightened on the edge of the table I leaned against. How could I possibly answer that?

"I just met him." That was the truth. I barely knew Justin. Feelings weren't a part of it. They couldn't be, could they? "Well, as an adult. I met him a few times when we were kids."

Sawyer didn't respond. He paced back and forth across the office, lost in his own mind. What was he thinking? Did he hate me? I wasn't sure I could deal with him hating me.

I stood up and took a step forward. "Why are you so mad?" I asked softly, feeling stupid.

He looked at me as if I'd said something ridiculous. Which, I guess, it was. He was still angry about Saturday night and Justin. He wasn't going to get over it so quickly.

Except he didn't look angry anymore.

Sawyer moved towards me with hands spread wide as if his words were the most obvious thing in the world. "Why do you think, Elle? You've been spending all this time with another guy when I thought we had our own thing going on."

That didn't make any sense. "You were the one who said you wanted to keep it casual," I rambled.

"I guess I've changed my mind," he said in a low voice as he started moving toward me. "Before that first night, I watched you go out with guys and drop them whenever things even started to look like they might get serious. You were turning your back before the poor blokes could show any real interest in you."

I backed up against the desk again. There was nowhere else to go. "What are you saying?"

"Do you really need me to spell it out for you?" Sawyer was inches away. He leant further in, resting his hands on the desk either side of me. "It may have started out as a physical thing after one drunken encounter, but can you honestly look me in the eye and say you don't feel anything else for me?"

His proximity pressed our bodies together. I could feel his warmth and my heart was picking up an unsteady rhythm as I took in his handsome face. Sawyer was the man I lusted after for years. I'd pined for him, and it was like dreams coming true when he finally noticed me. For a long time, he was all I wanted. We weren't in a relationship, but it had been enough for me. Now that he was admitting he wanted more, I couldn't deny how he made me feel.

I bit down on my bottom lip and took a deep breath. "You know I can't."

Sawyer's eyes closed slowly as he took a steadying breath of his own. He brought his hands up from the desk to rest under my chin. I knew it was coming. The warmth of his fingertips felt so familiar. But the kiss, that was new.

Sawyer and I had locked lips countless times in the past few months, but they were usually lust-filled, hot and furious in the throws of passion. This time, as Sawyer pressed his lips gently to mine, it was a completely different feeling. There was so much emotion as our lips moved together that I had to reach up and hold onto his wrists to brace myself.

I eventually broke the kiss, licking my lips but not moving away from him. "That's not fair," I whispered, slightly out of breath as he rested his forehead on mine. It had been so gentle, yet so intense. I didn't know what to feel.

Sawyer rubbed a thumb over my flushed cheek. "Why, because I have an advantage?"

I closed my eyes, already knowing my next words had no ground to stand on. "It's not a game. I'm not a prize."

"Isn't it?" he countered. "You've got two men ready to gi—"

The office door swung open and our bodies jerked in response. It was my natural instinct to pull away from Sawyer, like I'd done so many times before, but he didn't let me go. He stood still, gazing at me with sparkling eyes as if someone didn't just walk in on us, as if I was the only thing that mattered in this moment.

"Oh, I'm so sorry," stammered the new girl on the front desk. I couldn't remember her name, but I was grateful she was the one to intrude and not someone like my father. "I didn't mean to interrupt. I mean, barge in. I should have knocked. I'm sorry."

"Can we help you with something?" Sawyer asked calmly without turning to look at her.

"There's just a guy out here denying he used the minibar and refusing payment, and he wants to see the manager," she rambled nervously. She clearly never expected to walk in on the bosses making out.

"I'll be right there," said Sawyer, not taking his gaze off me.

The girl mumbled a thanks and disappeared, closing the door behind her.

We stood pressed up against each other for a few more moments, me still catching my breath and Sawyer assessing every part of my expression, before he let go.

"I realise you need some time to figure things out," he said gently, taking a few backward steps towards the door. "You're still so young. I won't force anything. I won't even kiss you again until you're sure I'm what you want."

A million thoughts and possibilities were running through my mind. How was I supposed to figure that out? I had no idea what I wanted. My words were lost and I crossed my arms to stop them from shaking.

"And I want you to know that I'm here, right now, if you want me." He was halfway out of the room but turned slightly to say his last words. "But I can't wait around forever."

Then he walked out, leaving the door wide open and me more confused than ever.

CHAPTER 15

I 'm not sure my mind was capable of working through all the events and emotions thrust upon it in the last week. Sawyer's admission on Wednesday had me reeling. He wanted more than friendship, but I had to wonder if he actually felt that way or if Justin's appearance in my life was the cause. Perhaps he only thought he wanted more because it seemed like somebody else did.

According to Sawyer and his jealousy, there was someone else interested in me, but as I sat alone in the campus café on Thursday, I began to think he was wrong.

I spent my lunch break scheduling the following week in my date book. All the important events, like work and assignment due dates, were listed already, but I enjoyed organizing my days by the hour. It ensured I had enough time for studying, breaks, even cooking. I liked knowing what was ahead.

I was working on time blocking when I flicked back to check my class schedule. That's when I noticed I had 'coffee with Justin' pencilled in for today. I rolled my eyes, took an eraser, and rubbed it out. It was a silly thing to do. It's not as if these coffee meetings were agreed upon. They just happened.

Justin still hadn't spoken to me. To be fair, I didn't have the guts to message him either. So perhaps all these pent-up emotions were my own doing. Every spare moment I had in the last month went to thinking about men.

I needed a distraction.

Who better to provide one than my lovely best friend? We hadn't spent time together for a while. Work didn't count. Neither did the camping trip or nights at the Uni Bar. We were always with other people then.

Sascha and I needed a girl's day.

I managed to get hold of her that night and was pleased that she agreed. It had been so long since we'd hung out, just the two of us, so we made plans for the coming Saturday. We were working together in the morning and decided to spend the rest of the day doing things we use to love.

By the time Saturday rolled around, my thoughts of Sawyer and Justin had slowed. Only a little, but at least it was something. Thankfully, Sawyer had the day off, so I didn't need to dodge awkward questions if Sascha noticed any unusual tension.

We went for lunch, but instead of going to a restaurant like usual, we did something we hadn't done since we were in school.

"These are still the best chips in the world!" Sascha exclaimed before popping one in her mouth. She almost spat it out, her lips opening slightly to blow out the steam from the hot potato.

"And you're still the most impatient seagull in the world," I laughed. She'd done it countless times before and clearly hadn't learned her lesson.

"It's not my fault," she whined. "I can't wait. They're too good."

"At least wait until we find a spot to sit. Let them cool a little."

Her shoulders slumped. "Fine. Let's go out to the dock."

"Which one?"

"Coney Island," she confirmed and turned in the right direction.

We were at Luna Park, a frequent haunt of our early teen years. Hot chips, slushies, and gravity defying amusement rides were all things Sascha loved.

We found a spare bench by the edge of the water, overlooking the harbour in the warmth of the mid-afternoon sun. There were a lot people walking about--couples, teens, and young families--all enjoying a fun-filled day at Sydney's most famous amusement park.

"I'm so glad we did this," Sascha admitted before digging into her chips.

"We've both been busy." That was the truth. School, work, boyfriends, and not-boyfriends. They took up a lot of time. "And speaking of busy," I continued slyly. "How's Dale?"

As expected, she perked up immediately. "Hot as sin!"

"Things are going well then?"

She nodded with glistening eyes. "He's amazing. I've never known any guy like him." By that, I'm sure she meant a good guy, one who treated her the way she deserves.

"I'm so happy for you. So do you think he's it, the one?"

I wasn't sure I believed in it, but she always did. Her track record wasn't great. She'd announced several of her previous boyfriends as 'The One', but I'd never seen her like this. She was giddy at the mere mention of Dale's name. Usually, she had a string of complaints or annoyances whenever we talked boyfriends. Not this time.

Sascha looked down at her lap, smiling to herself. "I know it hasn't been that long, but I can actually see myself doing life with him, you know?" She glanced up at me. "Do you remember when we were younger, and we use to imagine what our husbands would be like? And where we would live and how many kids we would have?"

I nodded. Of course I remembered. We often gossiped about the things in life we desired, especially after watching cheesy rom-coms where there was always a happily ever after.

"I can see all of that with Dale."

"Where will you live?" I laughed.

"A swanky Bondi beach house."

"And how many kids?"

She thought about it for a moment. "Two or three. At least one boy and one girl. A third will break ties and mediate fights." Sascha had one sister, and arguments were frequent and unrelenting. That obviously influenced this part of the dream.

"What will you both do to afford this mansion?"

Sascha held one hand up and gave me a quizzical look, as if her response was obvious. "I'll have a kickass marketing job and he'll be a famous DJ of course."

"Of course!" I laughed.

Sascha's smile was so bright that I couldn't help but smile with her. It was infectious. "Now that he's in his last semester at Uni, he's starting to take the YouTube thing more seriously. He's getting lots of views and gaining so many followers."

Dale produced house music, which wasn't really my style. He was good at it though, and he was starting to put himself out there now that he was finishing his degree. The on-campus audience loved him, and I had no doubt the rest of the world would, too.

"That's cool. Maybe you'll have your beach mansion sooner than you think."

She smiled at that. "Maybe. Oh, do you know what we should do next?" she asked, her expression devious.

"What?" That look in her eyes meant I wouldn't like it.

Sascha pointed to something behind me and I turned to look at the amusement rides nearby.

"Which one?" I asked with a frown.

I didn't like either option. The Mouse Trap was a rickety old roller coaster that felt like you'd fly right off the edge and into the harbour at one of the sharp turns. The other was the aging Ferris Wheel. Despite the circular cages with secure doors, it felt like you'd plop right into the water whenever it stopped near the top.

"Ferris Wheel," Sascha chirped. "For old time's sake. Let's go!"

She didn't give me much of a choice, grabbing our rubbish with one hand, and me with her other. Before I knew it, we'd made our way through the waterfront theme park and were waiting in line surrounded by groups of people eager for the experience. That was something I'd never understand.

"Can you believe people pay good money to dine on this thing?" I asked. It was utterly ridiculous.

"I hear it's very romantic."

"What is possibly romantic about constantly stopping and starting, spinning in a circle, and trying to keep your food on the table? Imagine if it was windy." Dreadful indeed.

"Oh, come on. Are you telling me you'd reject a guy if he asked you on a date here?"

I nodded vigorously. "Yep! He'd be done for."

"You're so full of it," she laughed.

Then it was our turn to board the death trap. We sat on either side of the circular cage, just as the operator instructed, and I gripped the seat so tight my knuckles turned white. "I can't believe you're making me do this," I grumbled as the ride started moving.

Sascha simply laughed and turned in her seat to catch the view, making our entire carriage rock. I really wished she wouldn't do that.

As luck would have it, we were the last to board, so the ride started straight away. It also meant we were the last to get off. It stopped for each carriage at the bottom, which meant ours stopped over the water several times.

And the wind blew.

The whole ordeal was torture!

"You're the meanest best friend in the world," I said as we walked out of Luna Park when the ride was over.

Sascha rolled her eyes. "You survived."

"And now my hair is a mess." I tried flattening it by running my hands through it, but the breeze just blew it out of place again. "Do you have an elastic?"

Sascha checked her wrists. "No. But I think I have a hair clip." She pulled her backpack around to her front and searched through it. "Ah huh! Hair clip." She snapped it in my face before handing it over.

"Thank you." I wrangled my hair into the claw-like clip as best I could. It was too short to tie up neatly, so it was difficult.

"You look like a moose," Sascha giggled when I was done.

I frowned. "Yes, but a very cute moose."

"Make all the boy moose go hwaaah!"

We paused for a moment and then burst out laughing. "Princess Diaries marathon tonight?" I suggested when I'd caught my breath.

"Yes!" she agreed. Then her excitement turned curious, her eyes trained on something behind me. "Justin?"

My eyes widened at his name. Was he here? How? Why? No!

Sure enough, when I slowly spun to see what Sascha already had, Justin was standing there. And he was wearing a suit. The suit was less intriguing, however, than the young girl standing beside him.

"Hello," Sascha said sweetly, realising I couldn't form words. "I'm Sascha."

The girl smiled brightly. "Hi, I'm Claire," she introduced herself confidently.

Claire. Justin's sister.

"You're Dale's girlfriend, right?" Claire asked, looking us over with curiosity. Of course she knew Dale. He was Justin's best mate.

"That's me." Sascha took my hand and pulled me forward. "And this is my friend, Ellie."

I found a smile as I tore my eyes from Justin. "H-hi, Claire."

My stuttering could only be caused by two things. The first being that Justin was watching me with an unidentifiable expression, and the other because his sister Claire was standing right in front of me.

The baby Caroline had been pregnant with when she left our family was standing right in front of me.

What was I supposed to do?

What was I supposed to say to her?

Did she know who I was?

Sascha picked up on my unease and fuelled the conversation. "You two are looking swanky. Special occasion?"

"Justin's taking me to the ballet as an early birthday present," Claire announced, bouncing with excitement. "Swan Lake."

"At the Opera House?" I asked carefully. We were on the other side of the harbour.

"We had an early dinner first."

"She got to choose the restaurant, as well," Justin added, speaking for the first time. My eyes flicked back to him, and then they were stuck again.

Sascha was on a roll this afternoon. She picked up on the tension again.

"Well, you look fabulous. Do you know what you need? A picture with the Opera House in the distance. If we stand by the fence, we could snap one at the perfect angle," she suggested.

Claire turned to Justin. "Do we have time?"

He nodded in Sascha's direction. "Go on."

When Sascha and Claire skipped off to the edge of the water, Justin moved closer.

"How old is she now," I asked, doing the quick math in my head. "Thirteen?"

Justin nodded. "In two weeks. Acts like she's on the verge of adulthood, though."

"Wow." It really had been that long.

I looked over at Claire posing in her dress. She was pretty, her hair the same dark shade as Caroline's. In fact, she had a lot of Caroline's features. If I didn't know any different, I wouldn't have pegged her and Justin as siblings. Well, half-siblings.

"Are you okay?" he asked, placing a gentle hand on my shoulder.

I didn't need to think about what he meant. The concerned tone in his voice said it all.

"Yes, I'm fine," I admitted, pleased that I was telling the truth. While seeing Claire today reminded me of Caroline, I couldn't harbour any distain toward the sweet girl. None of what happened was her fault. "You're a good brother, taking her to the ballet."

"It was the only thing she kept asking for. She's obsessed," he chuckled, glancing over at his sister. "What are you two doing out here?"

"Just having a girl's day. Sascha made me ride the Ferris Wheel." I shuddered thinking back on it.

Justin's lips turned up at the corners. "Are you afraid of heights, Ellie-bean?" The amusement in his tone was not funny.

I crossed my arms. I knew my argument well. "That thing is ancient. One day it's going to roll right into the harbour and everyone on it is going to be trapped in those horrid cages and they will all drown!"

Justin pressed his lips together, leaning down. "Mhm, definitely afraid of heights."

"Afraid of death traps!" I countered.

"There's nothing wrong with being scared of heights," he continued, that cocky smirk of his making an appearance.

"I know that. It's not my fault you don't see dying a horrible death at the bottom of the ocean as something to be worried about."

We stood there pretending to glare at each other. I couldn't hold it for long before my smile broke through. He had this innate ability to make smile, no matter the situation.

"Are you two arguing?"

I jumped at the sound of Claire's voice and took a step back. I hadn't noticed her approaching with Sascha.

"Oh!" Claire continued as if she'd realised something. "Is this the girl you keep talking about? The pretty one in the green dress?"

Justin's eye's widened at the same time mine did. "Looks like it's time to go," he said to his little sister in a tone that clearly meant she better shut up. "Got your picture? Good. We'll be late."

Claire rolled her eyes and I had to hold my hand over my mouth to hide my growing smile. "Wimp," she mumbled confidently. Then she turned to me and Sascha. "It was really nice to meet you. Maybe I'll see you again soon."

"I hope so," Sascha grinned.

"Have a good time at the ballet," I said, hoping my voice sounded normal. "And happy birthday."

"Thanks."

Justin started to walk backwards and nodded to say goodbye. "Sass. Ellie." His eyes lingered on me a little longer, then he turned and offered his arm to Claire.

The girl you keep talking about.

What did Claire mean by that? Had Justin been talking about me? To his little sister of all people? That didn't make sense. I hadn't seen or spoken to him in a week. He clearly wasn't thinking about me, so why would he talk about me?

My mind couldn't help but wonder if he did think about me. It gave me butterflies to imagine him daydreaming about me the way I fantasised about him. But that also couldn't be right. Guys didn't do that, not in the same way.

When Justin and Claire were out of sight, Sascha spoke. "Now that you're done checking out Justin's hot ass, are you finally going to tell me what happened last weekend?"

I glanced sideways at her. She knew I'd been avoiding it and had been lenient with me. But it was time.

"Let's get a bottle of rosé on the way home," I suggested.

"That good, huh?"

I shrugged. "Let's make it a bottle of vodka."

CHAPTER 16

Out of the blue. That's usually how Justin appeared in front of me. When I least expected him, he was there, calling me Ellie-bean or bringing me coffee. It occurred so often recently that it wasn't so out of the blue anymore.

After running into him on Saturday, I was expecting Justin to appear again today. We may not have said much, or implied that we would have coffee, but I just knew.

And I was right.

Justin placed a fresh coffee in front of me before taking the seat opposite. I didn't glance up, knowing a smile would break free as soon as I looked at him. Instead, I pretended to focus on my reading.

"Not speaking to me today, Ellie-bean?" he asked in an amused tone.

I gave a light shrug, my insides fluttering.

"I guess I'll take this back then," he said, faking disappointment as he lifted my coffee.

I placed a hand on top of the disposable cup. "Don't you dare."

I was right again. The grin that spread across my lips the moment I looked up at him was uncontainable.

His seemed to do the same. "Knew you couldn't resist me."

"You or the coffee?" I countered with confidence.

He leant forward a little. "You tell me."

I kept eye contact as I brought the cup to my lips and tasted the delicious brew. Macadamia, of course. "Mm, it is the best coffee on campus. How could I possibly resist it?"

Justin closed his eyes and shook his head. "You wound me, Ellie-bean. Here I am, thinking my name in your diary meant something."

My cheeks warmed immediately, and I reached for my open date book where his name was pencilled in for coffee again. I slammed it shut and tidied my belongings. I'd spread my books and laptop across the table while I was studying, apparently laying all my business out for him to see.

I didn't respond because in truth, I didn't know what to say.

Yes, I daydream about you so much I end up writing your name all over the place?

While I write your name in my book, I imagine what your naked chest looks like?

No way was I admitting anything.

Instead, I pulled my textbook closer and tried to refocus my attention.

In the reshuffle of my belongings, my laptop screen caught Justin's eye. "What kind of music are you into?" he asked, eyeing the streaming service curiously.

I glanced up at him and shrugged. "I don't know, songs that sound good?"

He pulled a set of headphones from his backpack. "Mind if I listen?"

"You want to listen to my playlists?"

"Music interests say a lot about a person."

I had to wonder if that was true and decided I wanted to find out. Maybe Justin had some insider information, being a musician and all. I pushed my laptop toward him as way of permission for him to analyse me through my favourite songs.

He plugged his headphones in and started scrolling immediately. His eagerness suddenly made me feel nervous. Some of those songs were embarrassing.

I tried to push those thoughts from my mind by looking back down at my text. It was about the impacts of innovative and sustainable designs on new hospitality venues. Considering the subject matter, the reading was rather dry.

It was so uninteresting that I found myself glancing up at Justin every few moments. If he noticed, he didn't let on. He seemed so engrossed in the music, nodding along occasionally as he clicked through the tracks.

I'd finished my coffee by the time he removed his headphones. "Hmm." He brought a fist to his chin, pulling a nonchalant thinker pose.

I took the bait. "What's your verdict?"

He took a final swig from his coffee before answering. "You're a very complicated woman, Elizabeth Newcombe."

Not what I was expecting. I imagined him saying I was weird or angsty. But complicated? "How so?"

"You surprise me," he went on, pointing at the screen. "There's a lot of alternative and soft rock here. Paramore. Coldplay. Parachute. Obscure bands. Bands no one has heard from in years. Artists that even I haven't heard of, and that's saying something."

It wasn't surprising that he would have a wide repertoire of preferences.

"And what does that say about me?"

He rubbed his chin in thought. I couldn't help notice the stubble on his usually clean-shaven jaw. It added little ruggedness to his already tall, dark and handsome façade.

"Well, it makes perfect sense actually. You're an empathetic person. It makes sense that you'd like songs that tell stories. Struggle to triumph. Usually something to do with romance. That sort of thing."

I shook my head. "I don't get it."

"Some research says that music preferences are linked to personality types."

"So, you're saying you can read into my soul based on the music I listen to?"

Justin laughed. "Not quite. But there are links between the two."

Interesting. "So, what's my personality type?"

"I'm no expert," he said, sitting back.

Was he trying to avoid answering? I kind of wanted to know what he thought about me.

"No, no," I chastised. "You started this. Please, continue."

He seemed hesitant. "No way."

"Why not?" I argued.

Justin shook his head. "It's a trap."

I rolled my eyes. "How about in three words?"

He considered that for a moment. Then, he leant forward on the table, arms crossed, eyes entrancing.

"Passionate," he said softly.

Okay, that was good. Was that because I liked a lot of songs about romance?

The corners of Justin's lips curved up. "Altruistic," he continued.

That opinion couldn't be based on the music I listened to, surely.

"And..." I prompted when his pause went for too long.

"And fascinating," he finished, leaning back in his chair with a smug expression.

Fascinating? That was unexpected. "Like weird fascinating or you want to study me type fascinating?" I asked.

His eyebrows rose. "I didn't realise fascinating meant weird. And if you wanted me to study you," he continued, eyes looking me up and down, "all you had to do was ask."

I rolled my eyes but couldn't contain my ridiculous grin. I grabbed one of my pencils and flicked it at him.

Justin dodged it, ducking to the side, and it hit the guy sitting behind him in the back of the neck.

I'm sure my eyes widened so far in horror that they bulged right out their sockets.

I threw a pencil at a stranger!

Somehow, Justin kept his cool. He turned around, picked up the pencil, and apologised to the guy who was giving us a dirty look.

When Justin faced me again, he laughed. "Well, I hope that taught you a lesson. Don't throw sharp things at nice people."

I was still mortified but managed a quick comeback. "A nice person wouldn't have let a stranger take the blow."

"Who said I was the nice one?" he murmured; eyes boring into mine.

I couldn't look away. His intensity was captivating.

Justin eventually looked away and returned his attention to the playlists on my computer. "What's this one about?"

The playlist he pointed to was titled Wedding Songs, and for some reason, I blushed. "Sascha's sister is getting married in a few weeks."

Justin nodded, realising the connection now. "I heard."

"It's going to be big and fancy, and the band gave us a list of songs to choose from," I rambled, still unsure why me cheeks were pink.

"Dale's going," he added.

"I heard," I said, mirroring his words. Sascha had mentioned it once or twice, or ten times, over the weekend. She was excited, but also very nervous for her entire family to meet her new boyfriend. But his attendance posed another problem, one I hadn't realised until this moment. "What does that mean for the rest of you? The wedding is the same night as one of your gigs."

Justin already had an answer. "Darcy's going acoustic for the night. I'll be there to support her."

That would be nice for her. I had to wonder, though, how Justin could support her. I knew very little about music, except how to listen to it. But I also knew a singer and a drummer on stage together wouldn't sound very good.

Just as I was about to ask, a notification popped up on my screen. It was time to head to my next class.

"Wait," Justin began with a confused expression. "You have a schedule in your diary, but also on your computer?" He pointed to both on the table.

I shrugged. "I don't always have my diary, and I don't always have my laptop. This way I won't miss anything." Plus, I loved the aesthetic in my handwritten diary. The calendar on my computer was simply functional. "I like to keep organised."

Justin still seemed confused. "You do realise you have something that's with you all the time? Your phone can do all of that."

"I'm aware," I agreed, feeling a little hot. Maybe I shouldn't mention that my laptop and phone were already synced. "But I just like it this way, okay."

He held his hands up in mock surrender. "Okay," he said, smiling in amusement. "I'll walk you to your next class."

Justin waited patiently as I packed up my belongings, then he walked with me out of the café and across campus to my next lecture.

We walked silently for a while, and I found myself thinking back on his words and what he thought about me.

Passionate, altruistic, and fascinating.

Why did he think so highly of me? I was a nice person, sure, but I also had a lot of issues. He saw those as well, right? He was just being kind, I was sure of it, but I needed to be certain.

"So, earlier," I started carefully. "You learned all of that about me from a few songs?"

Justin smiled as he shook his head. He slowed his pace a little and I was grateful for the extra few minutes that would bring us. "No, I'm observant is all. I got all that from you. Your music preferences are just... confirmation."

"Oh." In my mind, being observant really meant he was paying extra attention to me. My cheeks warmed again, and I secretly liked the idea of him watching me.

His genuine smile turned to a smirk. "But then you have every Jonas Brothers album in existence, and I start to wonder..." He put his hand up and shook it side to side, implying my taste is music was a little shaky.

I felt the sudden need to defend myself. "I went through a phase, okay."

Justin put his hands in his pockets and shrugged. "Right, a phase. Sure."

"It's true," I said defensively, even though that phase was still relevant.

This just seemed to amuse him further. "What's your favourite Jonas Brother's song?"

That was a difficult question to answer. "Pre-breakup or post-reunion?"

"I didn't realise there was a difference," he laughed.

How could he not know this? They were like a new band now. In fact, I would bet a lot of their new fans didn't even realise they had this entire history. "Their sound is completely different!"

"Okay," he continued, trying to sound sincere. He didn't. "I'm familiar with their new stuff. They're always on the radio. What's your favourite pre-breakup song?"

"I can only choose one?"

He confirmed it with a nod.

That wasn't even possible. I took a few moments to think it over, and it was so hard. "I think it would have to be When You Look Me in the Eyes. Oh, but then there's Burnin' Up and Love Bug. And don't get me started on their last album before they broke up. It was so underrated. There are some absolute gems on that one, not including the tracks from their Disney show."

With every word, he grew more and more entertained. "So, they hailed from Disney? That explains a lot." When I didn't respond with anything except for raised brows, he continued. "What? They all fall off the wagon eventually."

I crossed my arms, even though it was kind of true. "So judgy."

"Hey, I'm all for passionate obsessions," he defended himself. There was that word again, passionate. Somehow, I knew liking a band wasn't what he actually meant by that.

I rolled my eyes, trying to play it cool, and realised where we were. The fork in the path that led us to different buildings for our classes. It was usually where we parted ways, but Justin kept walking in the direction of my lecture hall. I was surprised but didn't say anything. I was enjoying our conversation and didn't want it to end just yet.

Unfortunately, due to our slow pace, the hallway was packed with students ready to enter the lecture. I usually arrived early so that I was at the front of the crowd, which also meant a good seat.

"Come this way," Justin suggested, placing a warm hand on the small of my back to turn me in the right direction. He led me to a skinny stairwell down the hall. "Barely anyone uses this entrance."

He gestured for me to walk up and followed when I did. I'd never entered this lecture hall from the back before, but I had a feeling I would be using it more often now.

I was focused on my feet when I felt Justin's hand press gently against my hip. He pushed a little, coming up behind me and pulling me against the wall just as a group of students came barrelling down. The previous lecture must have finished.

When they passed, Justin didn't move back. He was one step down, bringing us to the same height, and he was standing a little closer than expected when I turned to face him.

He was so close. It reminded me of our time together at the other night. The dancing. The chat by the Opera House. We almost kissed then. Would he try again now?

I was out of luck. Another group of students broke the tension as they passed, and Justin cleared his throat.

"So, are you coming to the gig on Friday?" he asked in a low voice.

I nodded shyly. "I think Sascha would drag me there by the ear if I didn't."

That made him laugh. "She's a little scary that way."

My turn to nod. Sascha could be scary when she wanted to be.

Justin's amusement fell from his face, which suddenly turned serious. Why the change? There could only be one reason. We'd avoided it until now, but I knew he had questions, about Saturday night, and about Sawyer. It had been over a week and a half since then, but I still wasn't ready to answer them.

He opened his mouth ready to say something, but I beat him to it.

"I should probably find a seat," I said, throwing a thumb over my shoulder and moving up a step.

Was that disappointment in his eyes? "Right. I should probably get to class, too."

Why did my heart suddenly feel so heavy?

He turned to walk back down the stairs but gave me one last glance. "Coffee on Thursday?" he suggested.

I smiled. "Sounds good."

"I'll put it on my schedule," he mocked, smirk returning to his lips.

CHAPTER 17

Empty shot glasses with remnants of vodka and peach schnapps covered the table and judging by the state Sascha and Emily this early in the night, it was a good thing I didn't succumb to peer pressure. They were borderline drunk, and Dale hadn't even started his set yet.

Dream of Darcy had just finished and were packing up the small stage in the back corner of Uni Bar. Well, the guys were packing up. Darcy had found her way to our table and was engaged in an animated discussion about ugly bridesmaid dresses with Sascha, who was sharing her disdain about her sister's upcoming wedding.

"I'm telling you, the only good thing about this dress is the colour!" Sascha whined.

Emily shook her head. "Bridesmaid dresses aren't supposed to be too pretty. Nothing should take the attention away from the bride."

"I disagree," Darcy said firmly, taking a sip from Emily's drink. "A bride is a bride. They have the attention regardless. The whole day is about them, right? I think you must be very insecure if you're worried about someone looking prettier than you. Plus, you have those photos and memories for the rest of your life!"

Sascha jumped back in. "I don't think she's insecure, I think she just has bad taste."

"Oh, come on," I added, "Your dress isn't that ugly." She was exaggerating.

"That's because you know you'd look good in it."

I rolled my eyes.

"You look good in everything," Sascha continued before turning back to Darcy and Emily. "Did you see the gorgeous dress she wore the other week, to that award night thing? She was..." Sascha finished her sentence with a chef's kiss.

"No!" they said in unison.

Emily placed her drink on the table, a little too enthusiastically, and turned on me. "Have you got a picture?"

"Actually, not really," I admitted after thinking about it for a second. I was a little too preoccupied that night to think about taking pictures.

Sascha, unfortunately, had no filter when she was drinking. "What about that selfie with Sawyer?"

"Sawyer?" asked Darcy loudly. "Who's Sawyer?"

I shrugged, acutely aware that Justin was in the room. I glanced toward the stage. He was busy doing something with his drums, and even though I knew he wasn't paying attention to us, and he definitely couldn't hear our conversation, it felt weird talking about Sawyer while he was here. I briefly flashed back to the awards night, the night I wore the dress in question, and remembered their argument. They really didn't like each other.

When I turned back to the girls, they were waiting eagerly. "He's just the manager at work," I told them innocently.

Sascha almost spat out her drink, but thankfully Darcy and Emily didn't notice her reaction. It wasn't a lie, exactly. Sawyer was a manager. I just didn't see the necessity in telling the whole story.

"What colour was your dress?" Emily prodded. "Pictures please!"

Reluctantly, I pulled out my phone and searched through the gallery. Sawyer had taken the picture outside the Entertainment Centre before the night, and all the drama, began. It only showed the top half of the dress, but you could see the waistline enough to get a good idea of the fit.

"Wow!" Emily exclaimed, holding my phone close to her face.

"The dress or the guy?" Darcy added, approval in her tone as she took the phone from her friend. Sawyer had his arm around my waist and we both smiled at the camera. I couldn't disagree with Darcy. He did look good.

Sascha was desperately trying to hold in a laugh, and I shot her a look of disapproval. This was neither the time nor the place to bring up Sawyer drama.

"It's a beautiful dress," I said, hoping to keep the attention away from Sawyer.

Emily nodded. "Your boobs look great. I love the material."

I reached for my phone, hoping to move things along. Sascha, finally able to control herself, jumped back into the conversation. "See! If this was the dress I had to wear, I'd have no complaints. I just look so flat chested in my one."

"Have you tried it on with chicken fillets or a strapless push up?" Darcy asked.

"No, do you think that will work?"

Darcy shrugged. "Try it. All cleavage is good cleavage."

"What's this about cleavage?" a new voice asked.

I turned to see Benji and Isaac approach the table. They'd been here a while but didn't come to say hello, instead choosing to sit at the back of the crowd to watch the show. Now, they brought gifts in the form of shots and chasers.

Emily responded to Benji with tight lips and attitude. "It's nothing you'll get to concern yourself with."

That made him smile. "The night is young, Gorgeous."

"Oh yeah?" she challenged in a sarcastic tone. "What's your game tonight?"

Benji winked at her before nodding at Sascha. "Sassy." Then he turned to me. "Sassy's friend. Can I offer you a wet pussy?"

He placed a shot in front of me as an invitation. I gave him a sweet smile in return. "I think we've been here before."

His grin widened. "I'm keen to change the outcome if you are."

I sighed and pushed the tiny glass back toward him. "Thanks, but I'm staying dry tonight."

He kept his confidence when he replied. "That's a shame." He then downed the shot, keeping eye contact with me.

I broke it and looked anywhere else, eager to avoid any attention from him. That's when I noticed Isaac and Darcy making out. Emily, who was still sitting next to me followed my gaze. She pressed her lips together and rolled her eyes.

Yes, this was far more interesting than engaging with Benji. It wasn't the first time I noticed the tension between Emily and Isaac, and I'd be lying if I said I didn't want to know what was going on.

Unfortunately, without asking directly, I didn't think I would ever find out. While Emily and I were friendly towards each other, we weren't at that stage.

The entire table fell into awkward silence. Sascha left, most likely to find Dale. It only got worse when Justin approached. He confidently inserted himself at the round table between me and Emily but paused when he picked up on the tension.

"Having fun?" he asked, unsure of what he'd walked into. His eyes panned across everyone before resting on me.

His question didn't seem important, not when heat filled my chest and scrambled every coherent thought I had. He was standing so close that our arms pressed against each other. I didn't move back, but I did have to wonder why he squeezed in where he did. There was plenty of space on the other side of the table. There was even an empty stool. But he chose to stand on my side of the table, the one up against the wall where there was very little space to move.

Emily responded, seeming grateful for the distraction. "We were just talking about how hot Ellie looked in this stunning green dress."

Justin smirked, glancing back down at me "Ah, I know the one."

I blushed as he subtly looked me up and down, his body turning toward me.

"That was a nice dress," he admitted with a tone of approval. His words brought back a memory from that night. He'd paid me a compliment and it had sent thrills through me, just as his gaze did now.

"That's right," Darcy said. "You went to that hotel award thingy too." I hadn't noticed her resurface, but she now stood wrapped in Isaac's arms, attention back on the group. She also seemed a little suspicious as she looked between me and Justin, hopefully not making any connections that weren't there. Emily wasn't afraid to think with her expression and seemed pleased with this information. Benji turned away to look at the stage.

Thankfully, Dale's voice filled the room just then, and I was glad he put an end to the discussion.

As Dale spoke and everyone listened, Justin's hand found its way to my hip. I was wearing a crop top and skirt set, and the feel of his warm hand against my exposed skin sent another thrill through me. Not to mention his chest pressed against my back as he attempted to shuffle between my stool and the wall.

It took a lot of self-restraint not to lean back into him.

He leant down over my shoulder, hand still gentle on my waist. "Are you drinking tonight?" he asked in low tone.

I glanced up at him and swallowed in the hope of regaining my words. He was closer than I thought, and he didn't pull back, not even when the tip of my nose grazed his cheek. To anyone else, we'd look very intimate, like we were about to kiss. The thought did cross my mind. No one was paying attention to us, and it would be so easy.

But I didn't. I couldn't do that.

"Not tonight," I managed to say quietly. It was a miracle any sound came out at all.

"Okay." Justin gave me a small smile and lingered for a moment before gently squeezing my hip as he moved passed.

I watched his back as he walked away, trying to steady my heart and my breathing. We'd barely touched since that night, but I never forgot the intensity I felt when we danced. I also couldn't help wonder if he replayed it in his mind the way I did. Over and over again.

I'd been acutely aware of his body every time we'd met since that night, conscious of the impending awkwardness if we got too close again. I thought he was on the same page; he'd steered clear of physical contact as much as I did. But maybe I was wrong to be so worried about that. Justin didn't hesitate at all tonight. In fact, he was undeniably confident.

I was stuck in my head, thinking about the what ifs of this scenario, so much so, that I'd missed the beginning of Dale's set and had ignored everyone around me. I only resurfaced when Justin reappeared by my side.

He placed a green bottle and glass of ice with a lime wedge in front of me. Sparkling water. It was my go-to when I wasn't drinking alcohol.

I smiled at the nice gesture.

Justin pulled up a stool beside me. I hadn't noticed Emily moved to the other side of the table to sit with Sascha, who had returned.

I sat awkwardly, suddenly unsure of what I should be doing with my hands. And how was I supposed to place my legs on this stool? There was definitely something wrong with me. I was usually... normal whenever we hung out.

Justin didn't seem to have the same overthinking problem. He picked up the conversation as if it was the easiest thing in the world.

"How did your meeting go yesterday?"

It took a moment to remember what he was talking about. "Yeah, good actually," I nodded, thinking back on the meeting with my course coordinator for my social studies units. "There's a few things I can do if I want some more experience now."

"Can you bring forward your placement to the summer?"

I shook my head. "Unfortunately, no. Apparently there's an assignment to do alongside the placement, so the unit needs to be running for it to count. I'll have to wait for next semester."

Justin took a sip of his beer before responding. "That sucks."

"A little, but I can still do some volunteer work. The coordinator gave me a list of youth programs always looking for volunteers, especially during school holidays."

"That's great!"

It was great, but the way his leg brushed against mine under the table was even better. "I have to do some more research on them, but I'm already leaning toward one in Western Sydney. The academic and social programs for the kids look amazing."

"Do you have to do anything before you can volunteer?"

"Yeah, I'll need to get a Working With Children Check done, but that shouldn't take too long. Hopefully they really are after some more volunteers and take me on."

Justin's shoulders turned toward me, and it somehow pushed his leg more firmly against mine. "I'm sure they will, especially someone as passionate as you."

His eyes were particularly blue tonight. How could they sparkle in such low lighting? And why was he looking at me like that?

The strange desire to kiss him came back. I don't think he'd reject me, but it really wasn't a smart thing to do.

"Come and dance with me, pretty please?" Emily interrupted with a desperate tone, thankfully taking away my choice. "I can't go out there alone with them."

By them, she meant Isaac, Darcy and Benji, who were already sauntering towards the front of the dancefloor.

"Why not?" I asked, hoping she'd give me a real clue.

She pressed her lips together and raised her brows. "Do you really need me to point it out?"

"Yes." Yes, I really wanted to know what was going on there.

Emily crossed her arms. "Benji's trolling and it's gross."

That wasn't the answer I hoped for, but it made sense. "If I go out there, he'll come after me," I whined.

Emily turned on Justin, who was in the middle of sipping his beer. "Not if Sexy Drummer Man here comes with."

Sexy Drummer Man placed his glass on the table and raised his hands, showing us his palms. "Hey now, what if he starts dancing with me?"

I smiled widely, remembering something he once said to me. "If I recall correctly, you don't hate that kind of thing," I teased.

He faked a frown. "History doesn't lie," he admitted with a shrug.

"Great!" Emily said, taking hold of my hand. She pulled me around the table to grab Sascha's as well. "Let's go!"

That's how we all ended up dancing in a small circle as Dale played his tracks. It's also when my conflicted feelings really flared up. While Justin dancing with us worked to keep Benji at bay, it really sent my mind and body into overdrive.

The music was loud at the front of the dancefloor, and the low lighting made everyone look surreal. Or maybe it just seemed that way because I was trying to focus on everyone but Justin. I felt awkward dancing near him, like I wasn't sure what to do with my body. This had never really been a problem before, but every time our eyes met across the small circle, I sort of faltered in my step. I felt rigid.

Emily, subtle as she was, didn't think that was good enough. She twirled in front of me, took hold of my hands, and we danced a little. Then she spun me around and winked before letting me go. Suddenly, she was in my spot, and I was dancing right in front of Justin.

I knew exactly what she was doing, and I let her.

His confidence was mesmerising, and once again, I was very aware of his proximity, especially as we seemed to move closer and closer with every step. My whole body felt warm, and it had nothing to do with the amount of people dancing around us.

It was all Justin.

The intensity in his eyes.

How a single touch, as his hands found my waist and brushed against my bare skin, electrified that warmth.

Everyone else disappeared.

When we'd danced before, it was overwhelming. But this... this was all-consuming. We swayed together with the music. I had no idea what song was playing, but the beat was perfect.

Justin pulled me in closer and I leant back into his chest, relishing the way his confident hands ran smoothly up my side and across my navel. Everywhere we touched, I tingled.

It was getting hard to breathe, and when he reached up to push my hair away from my neck, and his fingers moved gently across my skin, I thought I might lose it altogether. But that was nothing compared to when his face came down next to mine and I felt his breath brush against my ear.

Just a small turn. That's all it would take, and it would be so easy.

We must have been in sync because the tingles from my waist followed his hand to my jaw, where he gently turned my chin towards him.

Looking into those blue eyes, I wondered if he was as affected as I was.

A few centimetres. That's all there was between us. One small movement away.

What would it be like to kiss him?

I never got the chance to find out.

I jerked out of our trance when ice-cold liquid hit my skin. I spun out of Justin's arms to see where it came from. A girl stood beside us at the edge of the dancefloor with her hand over her mouth as she shook her head. Behind her, a few girls, clearly her friends, were trying to hold in laughs.

I couldn't hear what she said over the loud music, but it seemed like an apology, so I shook my head and gave her a small smile to let her know I was fine.

But I wasn't fine. My chest moved up and down quickly as it tried to steady my breathing. And my heart and head were both racing in overdrive.

Turning back to face Justin, I noticed his forearm was also dripping with alcohol. I looked down at my white skirt. Red liquid was soaking through to my skin, and the iciness made me shiver.

Justin leant down to speak in my ear.

"Are you okay?" he asked. He was sort of yelling, but I could barely hear him.

I nodded, knowing no sound would come out of my mouth, even if I tried. I made a weird gesture to my skirt, shrugged, and pointed in the direction of the bathroom. He seemed to understand and gave me a nod.

I could feel his eyes watching me as I walked away. That did nothing to curb the nerves.

When I made it to the bathroom, I found that my hands were slightly shaking. I turned on the faucet, wanting to splash some water on my arms, which were feeling a little sensitive. Every droplet felt like it was setting my skin alight.

The door opened and Emily walked in. "You okay?" she asked, coming to stand by me at the counter.

Was I okay? No! I was freaking out!

I'd almost kissed Justin. How could I let myself get into that situation? It was wrong in so many ways.

I cleared my throat, hoping words would come out. "Y-yeah," I stuttered, gesturing to my sopping skirt. "Someone just spilled their drink on me."

"I saw." She made a face, one that seemed to imply it wasn't an accident.

I shook my head. "I'm sure she was just clumsy."

Now Emily smiled. "Mmm. It couldn't have anything to do with you and Justin getting all hot and heavy on the dance floor. Bitches play hard."

That was ridiculous and made no logical sense. She was drunk. She didn't know what she was saying.

I humoured her. "It was probably good I got covered in cranberry juice then."

"Why?" Emily challenged, pulling herself up onto the counter. She almost stumbled and fell off. Unfazed, she continued, "It's obvious you like him. The chemistry between you two was fogging up my contacts."

"It's a bad idea," I continued, shaking my head. A very, very bad idea. Why was she so interested in what happened between me and Justin? "I'm not sure we're compatible."

"There's only one way to find out," she shrugged. Then her perkiness seemed to fade. She looked down to her lap where she was playing with her manicure. "Believe me, you want to take your chance while you can."

"Are you okay?" I asked, suddenly realising that maybe she didn't come in here to check on me. She seemed sad.

Emily gave a rigid smile. "I'm just having a shitty night."

"Do you want to talk about it?" Maybe she needed to. I suddenly felt guilty. I'd been obsessing all night and ignoring everyone around me. That was selfish. But I also had to wonder if she was upset about Justin, not that that made sense. She was the one who'd pushed me towards him.

She shook her head, jumped down from the counter, and perked up again. "No, it's okay. I just need another drink. You coming?"

I nodded as she pushed the bathroom door open. "I'll be out in a minute." I needed to get my thoughts in order and calm down first.

Emily smiled faintly and walked out.

Out to where Justin was no doubt waiting for me.

CHAPTER 18

"Come inside, I'm just about to jump in the shower," Sascha commanded, hanging up the call before I could respond.

I stared down at my phone in disbelief. She was supposed to be ready. That was the deal we made last night before I bailed on her at Uni Bar.

After failing to calm myself down and then walking out of the bathroom to see the girls who'd laughed when their friend spilled their drink on me flirting with Justin, I said a few quick goodbyes and left. It was cowardly, but I didn't have the courage to deal with what happened between us at the time; I was in way over my head.

I wasn't sure I had the courage now either, but it seemed I didn't have a choice.

I looked through my car window at Justin's terrace house. I was currently parked across the road waiting for Sascha, who spent the night with Dale. Apparently, Saturday mornings at this house were becoming a regular thing. At least I wasn't waking up in someone else's bed today.

A thought wandered through my mind. If I'd given in, or if we weren't interrupted, would I have woken up in this house? Did I want to wake up here?

I shook my head, trying to rid my mind of the procrastination. I had to face him. Maybe he wouldn't say anything. Maybe it was just a heat of the moment thing and he'd forgotten all about our almost kiss. Maybe he was still sleeping, and I wouldn't have to see him at all. Yes, that was likely. It was only 8am on a Saturday morning.

Taking a deep breath, I got out of the car, locked it, and crossed the road to the small, paved garden. I walked with feigned confidence up the short pathway and didn't hesitate when I knocked on the door.

It was only a short wait before someone opened the door. Darcy smiled when she saw me, but it seemed strained. She held her phone to her ear and was listening to whoever was on the other end.

Darcy waved me in and pointed towards the living room. I followed her direction and caught part of her conversation as she closed the door. "Em, please don't be like that."

Her tone was intriguing, but I didn't get a chance to hear anything else. As I stepped into the living room, I froze. Justin was there, and not only was he awake, but he was hanging upside down on the couch with a guitar in his hands.

He smiled when he saw me. "Morning."

"What are you doing?" I giggled, stepping further into the room. My nerves seemed to vanish when I saw him. Maybe it was the peculiar position I found him in.

Justin sat upright and placed the guitar on an armchair. "Just practising for Darcy's gig." He had to mean the gig that was the same night as the wedding.

"You play the guitar, too?" I asked in surprise. Drums and guitar? "Let me guess, you can sing as well."

He shrugged and gave a sheepish grin. "I also play the tambourine."

"Impressive," I laughed. And it really was. Of course he could play multiple instruments and sing. I shouldn't have expected anything less.

We lulled into an awkward silence, and I waited for the inevitable. Maybe I should start. Things would be on my terms, then. But what was I supposed to say?

Justin beat me to it. "Do you have time for a coffee?" he asked, standing up.

I released a heavy breath in relief. I had a few more moments to figure it out. "If Sass only just got in the shower, then sure," I smiled.

"Great," he said and walked to the kitchen. I followed and sat down on one of the stools at the counter.

I'd seen Justin make coffee before, but it was still mesmerising. Well, maybe he was just mesmerising, and his coffee-making skills were a bonus. He looked good in the morning, with his plaid pyjama pants and plain white shirt. He usually wore darker colours, and he always looked good in them, but there was something about the white that made him look... different.

To distract myself from ogling too much, I asked about his music. "So, seeing as you play all these instruments and apparently can sing, have you ever thought about making it a career?" For someone so talented, he seemed so humble. He was so focused on his business degree and working for his father's company, I had to wonder about his priorities.

"When I was younger, I thought about it," he admitted, opening the fridge to retrieve the milk. "Is full-cream okay?" he asked, holding up the bottle. "We don't have light or skim."

I nodded. "That's fine. So, you're not interested in doing the Dale-Darcy thing and making something out of it? You seem to have the talent."

He shrugged again; his humble side still prominent. "Plenty of people can play instruments and sing, but I'm happy just doing it casually. For fun."

We stopped talking for a moment as he frothed the milk. When it was finished, he poured it into the mugs and handed me one. He quickly wiped down the machine and then led the way back to the living room where he sat down on the couch, leaving a space for me.

I took the seat next to him without hesitation, crossing one leg over the other. I was wearing my uniform and my pencil skirt, while made of stretchy material, was still somewhat restrictive. We sat in silence for a while, sipping our coffee. It was nice; he did a good job making it. My mug was half empty by the time I said something.

I'm not sure what made me ask. Maybe it was our proximity, or the way his chest faced me as he sat with his arm across the back of the couch, one leg curled in front of him, the other hanging off the edge. It was right in front of my face, peeking out from the V-neck of his shirt. I'd wanted to know for a while, and I felt strangely confident for some reason.

"What's your tattoo?" I asked, avoiding looking down at where it hid by placing my mug on the coffee table.

When I turned back, he was watching me, the corner of his lips twitching upwards.

"It's my mum," he said softly.

I must have looked confused because he started pulling at the edge of the neckline, trying to show a little more of his tattoo.

When that didn't work, he grabbed the hem and pulled it up to his shoulder.

That showed me more of the tattoo, plus other things. I swallowed discreetly, keeping my eyes focused on the ink, trying to avoid staring at the other wonders of his body, like the soft lines of his abs and the enticing curves of his chest. It was a lovely, and completely unexpected floral pattern, done beautifully in black and white, fading in all the right places.

Apparently, only showing part of his tattoo wasn't enough. When he struggled to pull the hem up high enough to show the ink disappearing beneath the fabric at his shoulder, he reached behind his back with one hand and tugged the shirt off in one swift move.

Now he was half naked, and completely ogle-worthy, and I had a really hard time keeping a giddy smile from surfacing.

And then, because I was feeling unusually confident, or perhaps because I'd gone completely mental and wasn't thinking straight, I reached up to trace the beautiful petals.

Justin shivered beneath my fingertips, and I pulled back, looking up at him in shock. "Sorry," I apologised, completely mortified. I couldn't believe I did that.

Sensing my panic, he gave me a genuine smile, but that just made it worse. "It's fine."

Was it, though? Because I didn't feel fine.

After a short bout of awkward silence, he continued. "It's not what you expected, right?"

I shook my head, not sure what I was expecting. "It's a surprise," I admitted, looking up from the tattoo. "But it makes sense."

"Yeah?"

I nodded. "I think I remember your mum's name. It was Lilian, wasn't it?"

Justin seemed thoughtful, and a little sad. "It was."

I reached up to trace some of the leaves on his chest, up to the edge of his collarbone and to his shoulder. He shivered again, as if he wasn't expecting my touch, but I didn't pull away this time, even though I could feel my heart rate going crazy. I was touching Justin's naked chest!

"Hence the bouquet of lilies."

He glanced down at his tattoo, an air of fondness in his tone. "She liked lilies, white ones, and it's sort of like writing her name without actually writing it."

Losing a parent so young wasn't easy. I could empathise, sort of. We experienced different types of loss, but pain was pain, and the absence hurts.

My hand found its way to his knee in comfort. I looked up at him, hoping my words were enough. "I think it's beautiful."

He looked me over with those gorgeous blue eyes, like he was searching for something, his expression unreadable. Then he reached up to tuck some hair behind my ear, which was pointless seeing as it was pinned back off my face perfectly. The tingles I felt where our skin met were also kind of perfect.

It was difficult to keep eye contact with him. His eyes were so intense, I felt the need to look away, but I didn't. I couldn't.

His hand moved to rest against my jaw when he spoke softly. "You know, I've been wanting to do something for a while now, but..." he trailed off, like he was changing his mind.

Part of me knew Justin shouldn't finish that sentence, but the other part was sort of desperate to hear him say it.

"But we seem to get interrupted every time I try," he continued, a little worry seeping into his tone as he brushed a thumb gently over my cheek.

I sucked in an unsteady breath. He was talking about last night on the dance floor, with the grinding and the tension, and the almost kiss before we were covered in alcohol. There was also the time beside the harbour. We'd come close before a random intruded on the moment, and I think I wanted it then, too. Sort of like I wanted it last night, and how I wanted it now.

I'd walked in today expecting to talk to him about our almost kiss, but this wasn't going as planned. This was a stupid idea, being this close. There were so many consequences on the line here. I really shouldn't give in, but Emily's words from last night found their way to the forefront of my mind.

There's only one way to find out.

Find out what, exactly, I didn't know.

Justin was closer now, leaning in, eyes searching for my reaction. It was like he was waiting for something. I looked down just as his tongue darted out to lick his lips. The sight of such a simple, yet insanely sensual, act was enough.

I glanced back into his tentative eyes. "So stop hesitating," I whispered. And then I pressed my lips to his.

I'd imagined kissing Justin many times, but in all those torturous daydreams, I never predicted how soft his lips would be.

Surprised for only a moment, Justin smiled against my lips before kissing me back. His warm hand moved from my jaw to the back of my neck, pulling me closer as he deepened the kiss. He tasted like coffee and sweetness, and something I'd never experienced before.

In the back of my mind I knew we shouldn't be doing this, but now that the ship had sailed, I was onboard. My hands splayed across his bare chest before finding their way to the nape of his neck and into his short, ruffled hair. He smiled again, briefly breaking our rhythm as his hands moved down to my waist.

He squeezed gently and lifted me without effort, pulling me into his lap. My tight skirt rode up as I moved to straddle him, the fabric straining as my knees rested on either side of him.

Justin's eyes glistened as they looked me over, resting briefly on his hands as they brushed the top of my bare thighs and found their way back to my waist. His mouth met mine again with an eagerness that I matched. In this position, I was closer to him than ever.

I gasped into his mouth when his hips jerked, and I felt his excitement beneath me.

"Sorry," he mumbled between kisses, brazen and not slowing down.

Instinctively, I ground against him, pressing my hips firmly against his.

Justin's moan sent a new type of thrill through me as his lips broke away from mine, mouth moving to my jaw, leaving a trail of hot kisses down my neck.

"That was cheeky," he whispered, tone low and laced with something that made me feel even bolder.

So, I did it again.

CHAPTER 19

The satisfaction of hearing Justin gasp was almost more than I could handle. All barriers were down. The lines had been crossed. There was no going back now.

Justin's hands seemed to agree, as they wandered over my bare thighs, brushed gently along my ribs, and reached up to cup my face. He pressed his lips back to mine, changing our tempo and slowing down.

My mind was foggy, and I couldn't think straight, not that I wanted to. Justin had this way of making me forget the world around me, and that was usually when I was just in his presence. Now? I was completely blank, the only thing I could focus on was the way he made me feel with the smallest of touches.

Nothing else mattered.

Until a loud bang caused me jump and pull back from the kiss.

"Wow! Sorry!" came Darcy's surprised voice as Justin flipped me around, shielding me with his own body. "That's... wow..."

"Goodbye Darcy," Justin said, turning to wave her away.

When he looked back down at me, where I laid between the armrest of the couch and his naked torso, he gave me a sheepish grin. I pressed my palm against his chest, over his tattoo, and pushed gently. He took the hint and sat up, pulling me with him.

I cleared my throat as I untangled our legs and stood up. Looking around the living room, I noticed Darcy had disappeared. But that didn't matter. She had seen us doing whatever it was we were doing. A flush of embarrassment covered my body and a lump had already formed in my throat. Hastily, I pulled my skirt back down to where it should be.

"You okay?" Justin asked cautiously.

I didn't dare look at him as I started tucking in my blouse, and I didn't trust my self to speak, so I hummed and nodded.

A set of heavy footsteps sounded in the hall, and I looked up to see Isaac bound through the doorway on trail to the kitchen. "Morning," he said, looking at us curiously. I would probably do the same if I walked into such a tension-filled room to see one person half naked and the other standing timidly and avoiding eye-contact. When neither of us said anything, Isaac continued into the kitchen.

"Ellie," Justin began, standing up beside me.

I turned to him, face to chest, not sure of anything. Coherence had returned and she was weaving some very tangled webs in my mind.

Justin's slight frown and concerned eyes weren't helping either.

Familiar giggles sounded through the door and I took a step away from Justin as Sascha and Dale ran into the room, his hands catching her around the waist.

"Morning," I squeaked, hoping to sound normal. By the way Sascha's eyebrows rose as she glanced curiously between me and a shirtless Justin, I'd failed.

Justin cleared his throat and reached for his shirt, which had ended up on the floor. He pulled it over his head swiftly.

"I'll just go grab my purse," Sascha said with a wide grin, taking hold of Dale's hand and pulling him out of the room. Dale's smirk as he trailed after her reminded me of the position we'd just been in.

I hooked up with Justin in the middle of his living room, where anyone could walk in and see. And they had!

When I looked back up at him, the worry in his expression had deepened. He reached for my hand, the one hanging by my side, not the one fiddling with my collar.

"Are we okay with what..." he trailed, not finishing his sentence.

I slowly pulled my hand from his, giving him a small smile. "Y-yeah," I stammered. "But we should really get going to work. I'm covering most of Sascha's shift because she has her sister's hen's party tonight. It's going to be a really long day." I was waffling as I walked around the coffee table and to the doorway.

When I glanced back at him, I was struck by his confused expression and his dishevelled appearance. He crossed his arms over his chest and ran one of those gentle hands across his jaw, keeping his eyes on me. My response didn't seem to placate him.

Sascha came back into the room, bags in hand and looking ready to go. She gave me a slight push, effectively reading the room and helping me out of the awkwardness. "We're running late. Bye Justin," she called behind her as we reached the door.

Justin didn't say anything.

I avoided eye-contact with Sascha as we crossed the road and got into the car.

"Your hair is out of place," she stated in an all-knowing tone.

I grumbled at her, looking in the mirror to fix my hair and pin it back into place. I couldn't deal with her sass right now. "Do not say a word!"

She didn't. Instead, she just giggled.

Work proved to be exceptionally difficult that day. Not because Sascha made little remarks about this morning, or because the jobs I needed to do were difficult, but because I couldn't keep a clear mind and was highly distracted with thoughts of Justin.

There was also the fact that Sawyer, who'd greeted me with his usual charm, was just behind the office door. The guilt was weighing heavy on my shoulders.

Now that I was away from Justin and could think somewhat clearly again, I remembered the many reasons kissing him was a bad idea, and this was one of them. How would Sawyer react if he found out? He said he would wait until I made a choice between them. Was carrying on with Justin this morning me making that choice?

It couldn't be. There were too many other things to think about. Starting something with Justin meant seeing his family, and Caroline. I couldn't be in a relationship and not meet his mother. Well, stepmother. And I'd already met her. I'd spent my first few years of life with her, which brought up a whole range of other complications I didn't want to think about.

"You doing okay over there, Boss Lady?" Sascha asked from the other side of the room where she was watering the plants.

I frowned at her for calling me Boss Lady. "Everyone has checked out on time with no complaints, so yes."

She wandered back over to the counter and placed the empty watering can underneath. "You're spiralling," she said knowingly. "I can tell."

Of course she could. She had this weird intuition. Or maybe she was just good at reading people, namely me.

"I don't want to talk about it," I said, bending down to pull out a heavy draw full of room keys.

"You can't avoid it for long."

"Can't avoid what?" another voice asked.

I jumped up, groaning as I banged my knee on the bottom of the draw.

Sawyer made a face as I leaned down to clutch it. "Ouch. You good?"

I nodded, trying my best to ignore the pain. It wouldn't last long; it wasn't that bad. "I'm good."

Satisfied with my response, he continued. "Elle, I know it's not your job anymore, but can I please get your help with the rosters. Maria's taking her maternity leave early—she's been put on bed rest—and they need redoing, and I'm on hold with the contractor for the remodel, and then I have a meeting with Richard. It needs to get done, and you're really quick."

"Don't worry, I'm coming," I said, seeing the stress in his eyes.

Sascha piped up as I started toward the office. "Don't forget I leave in twenty," she called to Sawyer.

"She'll be back out by then."

I hoped Sawyer was right and it was a quick task. As we walked into the office, he sat down at his desk and picked up the phone while I sat at the computer against the other wall. I felt weird and rigid, and decided I needed to focus on something other than being alone in a room with him feeling this guilty.

I opened the software and looked carefully at the available staff who could cover Maria's shifts and cross-checked how many hours they wanted to work. While I was doing that, I completely blocked out Sawyer's voice as he spoke to the contractor on the phone.

Focusing on a controlled task with a definitive outcome was a good distraction. So good, in fact, that I didn't notice Sawyer approach until his hands landed on my shoulders. I jumped at his touch.

"Sorry," he smiled. I looked away, turning back to the screen, squirming a little. "Is everything okay?" he asked, concern in his tone.

"Sure," I said, forcing a smile. But everything was not okay!

Sawyer mistook my guilt as physical pain. "Is your knee okay?" he asked, spinning my chair around so I had no choice but to face him. "Let me see."

He squatted in front of me to examine my knee. It was a little red, but it didn't hurt. When his fingers poked gently at it, my knee gave an involuntary jerk, but it had nothing to do with me hitting it earlier.

"Honestly, it's fine," I said, trying to turn my chair around.

"Are you sure?"

I nodded earnestly, but he didn't let go. "Elle, what's going on?" He could tell something was up.

I deflected. "We just need to get this done so Sass can go."

Sawyer let go and I spun back to the screen to show him what I'd done. He seemed satisfied with my work. His hands found my shoulders again as he leaned in to get a closer look. "Knew you'd sort it out quickly."

A knock at the door made me jump again, but Sawyer didn't move this time, probably because it was Sascha at the door and she knew about our... thing. There was no reason to hide from her.

She, however, seemed taken aback. "I need to head off," she said, her usual sass absent from her tone.

I stood up and Sawyers hands dropped. "I'm coming now."

Without another word to Sawyer, I left the office and went back to the front desk. Sascha had disappeared down the hall to the staffroom, likely collecting her things. When she returned, it was with a serious expression.

She stood right next to me, one elbow resting on the counter as she spoke in a low voice. "This is going to sound harsh, but I would be a shitty friend if I didn't say it."

I turned to her, surprised that she seemed upset. She didn't wait for me to say anything.

"You need to tell him about what happened with Justin."

"I will," I mumbled, hoping this conversation wouldn't go any further.

"When?" she asked, a little irate.

I shrugged. "When I tell him."

That wasn't good enough. "Ellie, you've got two really good guys hanging on the hook here. This morning you hooked up with Justin, and now I catch you getting cosy with Sawyer in the office? What the hell?"

"Nothing was happening with Sawyer just now," I said defensively.

Sascha scoffed. "Sure didn't look that way."

I shrugged again. He was just being Sawyer. We were so comfortable around each other that he didn't think twice before touching me. That's all she saw.

"You need to tell him," she repeated, pushing off the counter and stepping away.

"I will," I told her, still defensive. "But not here in the middle of a shift when we still have hours to work together."

Sascha walked around the desk, ready to leave. "Fine, but maybe you should go to staff drinks tonight," she suggested, challenging me with raised brows.

I sighed. "Yeah, maybe."

She backed up towards the door. "See you later."

"Have fun tonight!" I called before she disappeared, feeling extra guilty now.

Sascha and I hadn't argued in a long time, not that this was much of an argument. It still made me feel like a horrible friend, though. I knew there was a reason I shouldn't have given in and kissed Justin. This was just another thing to add to the list of consequences I should have considered.

I placed my head in my hands and let out a frustrated groan. How could one action cause such a mess?

CHAPTER 20

I 'd become more familiar with the bar scene over recent weeks, but this establishment was nothing like the one at the edge of campus. I sat with a small group of employees from the hotel, taking up two of the high tables near the long, white marble bar running through the centre of the room. For now, it was a good place for a few after-work drinks, but in thirty minutes the lights would dim further and the music would start pumping, turning the casual atmosphere into a high-energy one.

I was usually gone by the time that happened.

I was usually walking out the door arm-in arm with Sawyer.

I was usually excited to go back to his place.

That wouldn't be happening tonight.

"Down in the dumps?" Tony, one of our night security guards, asked as he pulled up a stool beside me. I shuffled over to accommodate his muscular stature, my shoulder touching the wall.

"I don't know what you mean," I said, my words sounding more sarcastic than intended.

Tony hummed, following my gaze to the bar where Sawyer waited to order another drink. The crowd was growing as more and more patrons arrived for the change into a nightclub, taking advantage of happy hour before the DJ arrived.

"She's nowhere near as pretty as you," he continued slyly.

I rolled my eyes. "I don't know what you mean," I repeated, hoping he would let it go. But I did know what he was talking about. The woman outright flirting with Sawyer a mere few metres away, in her short-cut dress and ridiculous heels.

Sawyer was a nice guy, so he engaged politely. The way he was smiling at her, though, was completely unnecessary, especially when he kept glancing towards our table. Towards me.

It certainly didn't help when he made his way back, sat at the other end, and then smiled at the girl who decided to follow him two minutes later.

Tony picked up on the tension. "Did you two have a fight or something?" he asked quietly.

"What?" I squeaked.

He shrugged. "You're usually joined at the hip."

Did he know about me and Sawyer? "I don't know what you're talking about."

My response made him laugh. "Come on, Boss, you two aren't exactly subtle."

I thought that we'd been careful. We barely touched at work, and when anything did happen, I took control of the situation quickly so we wouldn't get caught. "Who else knows?" I asked, glancing around at our colleagues. They chatted happily amongst each other and I hoped no one was listening in on our conversation.

"Almost everyone," he admitted, amused by my reaction.

Great.

"So did you two have a fight?" he asked again.

I shook my head, glancing over at Sawyer. He was still smiling, and the front of his new friend's dress was as low cut as the skirt was short.

I stepped down from my stool. "Not exactly. I'm going to get some fresh air," I told Tony before shuffling out of my corner. He didn't try to stop me.

When outside, I dawdled a few metres down the path, wrestling with my own thoughts. I could feel a migraine coming on.

I was outside for only a minute when Sawyer approached, weaving his way through a crowd of guys hyping themselves up for the night.

"Hey," he said, shoving his hands in his pockets.

I gave him a curt smile. "Hey."

Sawyer wasn't one for awkward silences, usually making jokes when something felt uncomfortable. But there were no jokes tonight. "You want to talk about whatever's been on your mind today?"

"Thought you were already busy talking with lips and lashes in there," I remarked, completely surprised by my own words.

Sawyer's lips curved down. "You're jealous."

"I'm not jealous," I replied defensively. I'd never been the type.

One of his eyebrows rose, questioning me. "No?"

I had no right to feel jealous, even though thinking of him with that girl inside frustrated me. "It's just weird seeing you flirt with other girls."

"Should I not be talking to other women?" Now he really seemed serious, like he was testing me.

I shrugged, avoiding eye-contact. "I don't know. I just didn't expect to feel..."

"Jealous?" he offered.

I crossed my arms, annoyed by the insinuation. "I don't know, maybe. It's a little cold of you to do it right in front of me."

"That wasn't my intention; I was just being friendly and she's horrible at taking hints."

I knew that, of course, but still felt weird about it.

His tone was low when he continued. "And you haven't exactly been warm and fuzzy lately."

"I know," I admitted, looking down at a crack in the pavement, feeling like a hypocrite. He was right. I'd been weird with him all day.

His cool fingers reached for me, settling under my chin as he turned my attention towards him. His eyes darted across my features as if they were searching for something. "Did something happen?" he asked softly. I could hear the note of devastation in his voice already.

Because something had happened, with someone else.

It didn't matter what our arrangement was or that there was no label. The guilt I felt building all day was evidence that we were more than that, even if I couldn't admit it. "Yes," I confessed immediately. "I wasn't sure how to tell you."

His hand dropped. "When?" he asked, tone hard.

Sascha was right. He deserved better than what I was giving him. I needed to be honest as soon as possible. Maybe it wouldn't be that bad. "Just this morning."

Sawyer let out a sharp breath. "Did you sleep with him?"

I looked back up at him quickly. He'd asked me that question before. "No, it was just a kiss."

The hurt in his eyes was evident as he nodded to himself, looking down at his feet. "Okay."

I was a horrible person. It didn't matter that he said he would wait while I figured out my feelings. I shouldn't have led him on like this. Sascha was right; his hurting was all my fault. "I'm sorry, Sawyer. I didn't think this would happen."

His hands were back in his pockets, eyes avoiding me. "I did."

"What do you mean?" I asked, unsure of what he was saying. How could he possibly know that something would happen with Justin?

He sighed. "It's been different ever since he came into your life. I could feel it right away, I was just hopeful. I guess that's my own fault."

I shook my head at his admission. That was ridiculous. None of this was his fault. Certainly not my actions. I didn't mean for anything to happen with Justin. In fact, I actively held myself back. This morning was spontaneous. It just happened. It didn't mean I'd chosen him. "I don't know what I want, Sawyer."

"Even so, it was never going to be me. If it wasn't Justin, it would have been someone else." He looked down with sad eyes that told me he was right. "I'm just the easy option, the safety net."

The easy option? Did he really believe that?

How could I let things go this far? How could I let myself hurt someone so caring, so beautiful? "I'm sorry. I really didn't mean to hurt you," I mumbled, looking to the dark sky as my eyes stung.

"I know that," he whispered, reaching out for my hand. "Come here." He pulled me to his chest and wrapped his arms around me.

With dry eyes, I snuggled into his warmth, comforted even though I didn't deserve it. "How can you still be so nice to me?" How could he still care after I rejected him? And after all the time we'd spent together, he just lets it go?

His chest lifted in a heavy breath beneath me. "There's just something about you, Elle."

After a few more moments, Sawyer let go and stepped back, the disappointment in his eyes evident. "I'm going to go back inside. You coming?"

I watched him carefully, assessing how he might really feel. If I let myself follow him inside, I'd only make things worse. Plus, I was in no mood to deal with other people, especially those in really short dresses. "No, I think I'll just go home."

"Do you want me to walk you to your car?" he offered. Despite everything, he was still a gentleman. I definitely didn't deserve him.

I shook my head. "No, I'll be okay, it's just around the corner."

Sawyer nodded and started backing up. "Be safe."

I watched him walk back into the bar before leaving. I knew this was how it needed to be, even though a part of my wanted to chase after him.

Still, my heart felt heavier than it ever had before, and the drive home gave it time to wallow some more. I was unsure of what he meant by safety net, but Sawyer was right; he and I should have never been together, in any way. He was a colleague, and my father's prodigy. If it had gone on any longer, things could have been really messy, messier than they were right now.

Then there was Justin to think about. There was a whole list of reasons I didn't want to think about him and what happened on his couch this morning. My head was hurting enough already, and the pain seemed to worsen when I walked through the front door to see Dad lounging in his armchair with a glass of whisky.

I'd made a huge mistake.

"Hi Honey, you're home early," he said as I reached over the back of his chair and wrapped my arms around him.

"I just felt like a night at home," I said, squeezing a little tighter.

"Anything going on?" he asked as I let go and flopped down on the couch. He was watching the financial report on the news.

Looking into his tired face, I considered spilling everything. About Sawyer. About Justin. But there was only so much my old man could handle. So, I shook my head. "Nothing, I just have a bit of a headache."

"You work too hard," he said, standing up. "I'll get you some pain killers and a cup of tea."

"Thanks, Dad."

He reached over to ruffle my hair and hand me the television remote. "Why don't you pick a movie and I'll open a pack of Tim Tams."

"The double coated ones, please!" I called as he walked down the hall. Comfort food sounded like a good idea. I kicked off my shoes and pulled the throw rug from the back of the couch over my legs, nestling into the pillows.

Before I got too comfortable, I reached into my bag for my phone. It was blinking with a notification, just like it had been since lunch time. I hadn't opened it. I couldn't bring myself to read it. Even now, I felt guilty just looking at Justin's name on the screen.

So I locked it again without opening his message and placed it back in my bag.

CHAPTER 21

I never felt so conflicted in my life, not even as a child when I asked for Caroline to be removed as my adoptive mother. I knew exactly what I wanted then because my feelings were clear. I wished to have that same clarity now, but I struggled to make any decisions.

I couldn't talk to my dad. Sascha was grumpy with me. Sawyer wasn't an option, obviously. Besides them, I didn't have anyone else to go to for advice.

Of course, there was always Justin. We had become friends over the past couple of months, but I'd already ruined that. Talking to him about my feelings was also tricky, seeing as he was the cause of my confliction.

I'd eventually replied to his message on the weekend, but I could tell he wasn't happy with my responses, which had been few and far between. I didn't know what to say to him when he asked if we were okay, or when he tried to make me smile with our usual banter.

Things were different now, and it was my fault.

Maybe that's why I sat outside by the soccer field, even though it was overcast and chilly, instead of waiting for Justin in the café like

I did every Tuesday. I wanted to see him, and I knew we should talk, but I was also petrified of what might happen.

Naturally, fate had its own plans.

I sat alone on a bench surrounded by textbooks. I'd been studying, or at least trying to, but I'd lost concentration. My mind kept wandering back to Friday night and the intensity on the dance floor. To the following morning in Justin's living room. Then to Sawyer's disappointed expression. Did I do the right thing, or was it all a huge mistake?

I'd sunk deep into my own mind when Justin walked into my line of sight, no doubt on his way to the café. He didn't see me until the last corner on the path. He paused, and it was like the moment of truth. Would he approach or keep walking?

My heart swelled in my throat as it waited for him to decide.

I moved my books from the bench to my lap as he wandered over, the empty seat a clear offering. Justin sat down, elbows resting on his knees, eyes wandering over the happenings on the field rather than me. Neither of us spoke.

Eventually, the silence was too much. If he wouldn't look at me, I needed to hear his voice. "No coffee today?" I joked weakly, forcing a smile. Inside, my heart beat in overdrive.

He took his time responding, and when he did, he titled his head toward me but those gorgeous blues stayed away. "I wasn't sure you wanted to see me."

I fiddled with the ribbon on my diary. "That's fair." I'd been ignoring him for days, so his doubt was justified.

Justin leant back against the bench. "Seeing how awkward things have become, I think we should talk about what happened."

"You're probably right," I agreed, eyes still on the ribbon.

"Do you regret it?" he asked, a hint of worry in his tone.

"No." In the moment, I enjoyed what happened between us. It felt right then, and even though I had other thoughts about it now, I couldn't regret kissing him.

"But it's weird."

I nodded. "Kind of."

Justin finally turned to me. "Would things be better if we hadn't?"

I thought about it for a moment. If we hadn't kissed, we wouldn't be having this awkward conversation. If we hadn't kissed, I wouldn't have let Sawyer go. If we hadn't kissed, I wouldn't have known how good it felt to be in his arms. If we hadn't kissed, nothing would have changed.

"I don't know," I said, glancing down. Now that he was facing me, I couldn't look him in the eye. What was wrong with me?

"If you don't regret it, then how can you not know? It's a yes or no question." His frustration was clear.

"It's not that simple," I countered, matching his tone.

He shook his head. "How? I wanted to kiss you, so I did it. Why did you?"

"I don't know." I knew this conversation would be difficult, but it had quickly turned into the beginnings of an argument. A real one.

"You are so confusing." He stood up and started pacing, pausing every few steps to look over at me. "One minute you're hot, like really hot, and then the next your ice cold. I don't know what to think."

"You don't have to think anything."

He spread his arms in a shrug. "Then what's the point of us being here talking about this right now?"

"I don't know." It was my response to everything lately, but it was the truth. I couldn't figure out my feelings. They were spiralling out of control and I had trouble deciphering what they meant.

Yes, things between us were hot, really hot, but hooking up wasn't a miracle cure for all the underlying problems bubbling beneath the surface. If we continued on this path, wherever it was going, they would all rise. I wasn't sure how to deal with them if they did. "There's just so many things to consider."

"Like what? It's not that complicated, Ellie. You meet someone, you like them, you go for it."

Now it was my turn to stand up. "How do you do that? You have everything figured out like life is easy. You're 21 years old, you're so self-assured about everything, and you know exactly what you want to do." It wasn't fair! He seemed to do whatever he wanted without considering the consequences, and things usually worked out for him regardless of said consequences.

Justin took a step closer. "I don't have everything figured out. There was a reason I hesitated to kiss you. I didn't know how you would react. And after this, I guess I should have waited a little longer."

Would it have made a difference if he did? I'd been fantasising about kissing Justin for a while, and now that I had done it, things were different to how I imagined they would be. For starters, I never thought we would be arguing about it in public.

"Is it Sawyer?" he asked, tone softening. "I thought you and him weren't a thing."

"We're not. Sawyer and I are just friends, and maybe not even that any more." That was made clear days ago, and I still wasn't sure how I felt about it. Sawyer had been so good to me, and I'd been horrible to him.

Justin took another step closer. "Then what is it, because I'm struggling to understand?"

His proximity was notorious for scrambling my brain, but I didn't move back. "There's a lot of history and baggage between the two of us. If we take this any further than friendship, it could ruin everything." How could I even begin explaining that? Our fathers were once best friends until Caroline's betrayal tore them apart. Not to mention his sister was a constant reminder of that betrayal. I couldn't let this pain back into my father's life.

"Everyone's got baggage, Ellie. It's a part of being human."

"Not like ours. Being with you means knowing your family, and that could cause drama for too many people." It didn't matter that I technically knew them already. Relationships required effort in the family department. How could I possibly sit around a table at Christmas with Caroline? The last time I saw her, I yelled at her. We couldn't even be in the same room.

Justin's hands, warm despite the weather, slid up my arms to rest on my shoulders. "It's not about other people. It's about you and me."

I closed my eyes. If I looked into his now, I'd be done. "It's not just about you and me. It doesn't work that way."

"Maybe you're right. If we ever get to that point, it will take effort, and you have to be willing to make it." His hands dropped from my shoulders, the loss of their warmth causing me to take a step away from him. "What do you need me to do?"

I crossed my arms, holding them tight as I hugged myself. "I don't know. I'm sorry for being like this. I just have so much going on."

Justin looked away again. He was back to watching the players on the soccer field. "Look, Ellie, I'm not going to tip-toe around you any more."

I froze. "What does that mean?"

He sighed, tucking his hands into the pockets of his jeans. "It means I'm not going to treat you like a porcelain doll, like everyone else does."

His assumption was clear and my frustration returned. "I'm not fragile, no-one is tip-toeing around me."

Justin grimaced when he turned back to me. "Aren't they? Sascha did it the other day. She saw you in an awkward position and before we even had a chance to talk about it, she whisked you out of there. It's not the first time she's done that, either. I was hesitating to make a move because I was worried I'd do something you weren't ready for. I bet Sawyer did that, too."

His words struck like a glass of icy water had been tipped over me. Sascha didn't do that, did she? We were running late for work that day. And Sawyer? How could Justin possibly know anything of my relationship with Sawyer? No, he was mistaken.

"I don't know what to say right now."

"I'm not surprised." Another glass, this one as full of ice cubes, and they had nothing to do with the cold droplets sprinkling from the darkening sky.

Justin let out a heavy breath and reached for me, warm hands gently cupping my jaw. "I haven't been subtle. You know where I'm at and what I want, but I can't follow you around like a lapdog waiting for you drop a few treats. You clearly have some bigger things to work out before I'm even an option." He sighed, leaning in to brush his soft lips against my temple. "If you find your way out of here, give me a call."

He lingered for a moment, his entire being taking over my senses, but then his hands dropped and he backed away. I crossed my arms again as I watched him walk away. Instead of going to the café, he followed the path in the other direction.

When he was gone, I hugged myself tighter. My breaths were shaky and my eyes stung.

What just happened?

CHapTer 22

The rest of my week was the worst I'd had in a while. Concentrating on school and work seemed fruitless. On Wednesday, I worked with Sawyer. Things were tense between us, and not in the usual way. I didn't know how to act around him any more. He didn't know what to say either, and I had to wonder what the future of working together would be like.

Thursday was worse. I didn't expect for things between Justin and I to return to normal, but I also couldn't predict the overwhelming disappointment that flowed through me when I didn't see him. He was a no-show at the café. There was no sign of him in the commons. And the walk to class was lonely, not the usual leisurely stroll full of smiles and banter.

Justin was upset with me and I'd be lying if I said I wasn't a little mad at him. His presumptions were confusing and I spent most of my time thinking over his words. I never considered myself fragile or that people tip-toed around me. That didn't even make sense. And the lapdog treat thing? That was clear. He thought I was leading him on. Sascha implied the same thing last week. I never intended to do that, but maybe I had been.

There was a knock at my door and a sliver of light brightened the room as Dad opened it. "You missed dinner. I didn't think you were here."

I sat up, running a hand through my tousled hair. "Sorry, I've just been..."

"In here hiding?" He looked pointedly at my bed where I'd flopped down over an hour ago, on top of the blankets.

"Something like that." I looked down, a little embarrassed.

Dad crossed the room and turned on my desk lamp. The soft glow didn't quite fill the room and I was grateful he didn't turn on the ceiling light. "Do you want to talk about it?"

I shrugged, fiddling with a stray thread on the hem of my sock.

Dad wandered back to the bed and sat down on the edge. I could feel one of his pep talks coming on. "Is it about Justin?"

My heart dropped. Looking up at him, I swallowed. "How did you know?" He knew about Justin, and I wasn't the one to tell him. Was it Sawyer? Or maybe Sascha? Neither of them was happy with me right now, but I didn't think they would ever tell my father about Justin Hart.

"Caroline called. She was concerned."

If it was even possible, the churning feeling in my stomach worsened. "Oh, Dad, I'm really sorry."

His brows furrowed. "Why are you sorry?"

That was a silly question. The woman who cheated on him and left us was calling. "Because you had to talk to her. That must have been hard, and it's my fault she called."

The hurt look in his eyes said it all. At least, that's what I thought. He disagreed.

Dad reached for my hand, untangling my little finger from the loose thread. "Ellie-bean, I'm a grown man, and my history with Caroline is in the past."

A new wave of confusion washed over me. "It doesn't bother you to talk to her?"

He shrugged. "It's a little weird, but no, it doesn't bother me. Does it bother you if I talk to her?"

I never imagined he would want to talk to Caroline, not after everything she did. I know I didn't want to talk to her. I couldn't. Every time she and I crossed paths, or her name was merely mentioned, the resentment over her betrayal flared up. I hated thinking about my sweet, hurt father going through all that pain again. Should I not feel that way? Had I read everything wrong?

There was a tingling feeling rising in my throat. "I guess not. Not if you're okay with it."

"Okay, good," he nodded, letting go of my hand to clasp his together. The pep talk was on its way. "So do you want to talk about what's happened with Justin and Sawyer?"

I let out a sharp breath. He knew about Sawyer as well? Did I have any secrets?

My reaction made him smile. "I'm not blind, Ellie."

I thought Sawyer and I had been careful, but if everyone at work knew, then I suppose it made sense for my father to know as well.

My fingers found the loose thread again and I tugged on it. "I'm just thinking about things." There was a lot to consider, especially now that Caroline was in contact with my father, and that apparently, he was okay with it. Knowing this might change a few things.

"Yes," he agreed. "Alone. In the dark, while I've been pottering around downstairs wondering when you'll be home." I'd heard him walk through the front door. I'd heard the clanging of pots and pans from the kitchen. I could still hear the faint sound of the television from downstairs. "You know you can talk to me about anything. I won't judge."

It wasn't an offer, but a reminder. I knew he would always listen, and I knew he would try not to judge, but I didn't want to subject him to the reminders of the past and open old wounds. That wouldn't be fair to him.

"I do know that, and I'm sorry I've been so closed off. There's just a lot of thoughts up here." I gestured to my head. Maybe my father could help me understand a few things, like one of Justin's remarks. "Do people not tell me things or avoid doing things because they're worried I'll react badly?" Did he do this, too?

"Do you think people do that?"

I rolled my eyes. "Thanks, Dr. Hayes," I smiled, referring to a psychologist I used to see. She had a knack for answering questions with questions, and while I found it annoying at the time, her methods did seem to have a positive impact.

"Maybe we should we call Dr. Hayes," he suggested, expression turning serious again. "I know you haven't spoken to her in a while, but you seemed to bond with her when you were younger."

He wanted me to talk to someone again. Was I worrying him that much? Dr. Hayes had been incredibly helpful throughout my childhood and teen years, but I hadn't needed her in a while. The last time I saw her, years ago, I was in a good place. I was thriving at school. I had a boyfriend. I was preparing for my final exams and managing everything well.

A lot had changed since then.

"Maybe, I don't know."

Dad stood up and walked the few step to my bookshelf. He ran a hand over the assortment of coloured notebooks at the top. "How about journaling? You use to do it all the time. You've got a lot going on at the moment, so if you don't want to talk to Dr. Hayes, maybe writing things down will help you see things clearer."

He turned back to me, a small smile on his face. My father was tired. The crows feet at the corners of his eyes were deeper now, and his hair was greying.

With pursed lips and worried eyes, he reached into the front pocket of his button-up shirt. He pulled out a yellow sticky-note and looked at it hesitantly. "And if you decide you might want to talk to someone else..." He handed me the small piece of paper and started backing towards the door. "You don't have to use it. You can throw it out, burn it, or flush it down the toilet if that's what you choose. But the option to talk to her is there if that's what you need. It always has been."

It was a phone number, and below it, a name. One at the root of all my problems. Caroline.

Before he could back further out the door, I pounced off the bed and threw my arms around his waist. He reached around me and ran a soothing hand over my hair. "I love you, Daddy."

"I love you, my sweet Ellie-bean." He was smiling, I could hear it in his voice. Dad held on a few seconds more before kissing me on top of the head and letting go. "I'll put your dinner in the fridge."

With those parting words, he backed out of my bedroom, closing the door behind him. I was alone again. Alone, and with so much more to think about.

I perched myself on the edge of the bed and examined the note. Dad said the option to speak to Caroline had always been available to me. Deep down I knew that, but I think Dad stopped suggesting it after a tantrum, one of many related to Caroline.

Did she want to talk to me? I hadn't made things easy. After avoiding her at the awards night, and then yelling at her in the public bathroom, I wouldn't want to talk to me. Thinking back on that encounter, I remembered the pained look in her eyes and her expression. Perhaps it was somewhat apologetic, but in my opinion, at the time it just seemed cold.

I glanced up at the top shelf of my bookcase. The journals holding memories of woeful times, triumphant escapades, and the chaotic emotions of my childhood stared back at me. One of them held a photograph, a polaroid I refused to look at and hadn't laid eyes upon since I stuck it between the ink-sodden pages.

I reached for that very first journal. It was pink, and adorned with a unicorn sticker and a lock to keep all my secrets hidden. The security measures taken by my eight-year-old self were dismal. The key was hanging right there. I didn't even need to detach it from the latch because the string was long enough to reach the bottom of the lock.

The edge of the pages were slightly discoloured from the sun that usually beamed through my window, but the ink inside remained untouched. I ran my fingers across the pages, some words jumping out at me as I flicked through. Sad. Betrayed. Abandoned. Did I still feel those emotions now?

When I reached the last page, I paused before turning it. The edges of the polaroid picture had made an impression on the paper. I traced the square slowly, the pressure behind my eyes building, and then took the plunge.

It was an image of a happier time, a family portrait from the Christmas before Caroline left. We were all smiling, sitting in front of our tree, me nestled in my father's lap. There was also a tear through the middle of the photo, cutting Caroline's face off from ours. I'd done it during one of my angrier moments, believing she didn't deserve to be in such a happy family portrait. I also threw both pieces in the bin. I then found them a few months later in my dad's desk when I was rummaging through his drawers for a pen. He'd taped it back together. It seemed odd for him to keep this vandalised picture. I knew he had albums full, hidden away where I couldn't see them. I took it and pasted it in my journal, not really sure why at the time. Now I imagined Dad had kept it and left it there on purpose, knowing I would find it.

Before I could talk myself out of it, I reached for my phone and dialled her number. Waiting for her to pick up was excruciating. Each ring allowed more time for my sense to return. Maybe she wouldn't answer.

"Hello, Caroline Hart speaking."

I stopped breathing.

"Hello?" she repeated.

I cleared my throat, praying I could stay strong. "Hi-hi, Caroline." No such luck with the being strong thing. My words came out in a muddled squeak as I tried holding myself together.

"Elizabeth?" She was surprised, but contained herself quickly. "Elizabeth, is that you?"

"Y-yes." I choked on an unsteady breath. The pressure behind my eyes gave way and the tears I'd held onto for so long finally flowed.

"Oh, Ellie."

CHAPTER 23

I had a turbulent relationship with weddings. Most I'd been to were a good time, but the first I'd been to was traumatic.

Sascha's sister's wedding was a good time for everyone else, but I found it difficult joining in the festivities. The bride and groom, Mina and Marko, were a perfect vision of true love, or what I imagined it could look like. Even though I could sense their nerves from my place at the back of the church, I was mesmerised by the way they gazed into each other's eyes and the way they said 'I do' with absolute confidence. They were meant to be. They believed that, and so did everyone else.

Were all relationships supposed to be like this, so pure and unopposed? How did a couple even make it to this point? And if a relationship went beyond the so called honeymoon phase, how did they keep it from falling apart?

When they said 'until death do us part,' my mind instantly considered the point of all this. Was there one if nothing lasted forever?

"You're going to get wrinkles if you keep frowning like that."

I glanced up at the sound of Sascha's voice. She was a vision in her bridesmaid dress, waltzing over to the entrance of the corridor

I stood in. Her complaints about the colour and cut were completely unjustified in my opinion. The powder blue sweetheart dress suited her. She was gorgeous, and I hoped she felt that way today.

"How are you doing?" I asked, hoping to keep the attention on her. "It's a beautiful wedding." I looked pointedly at the decorations in the large reception room. Mina had good taste. The white florals hanging from the ceiling and the scattering of crystal chandeliers was exactly what I expected from her.

"I am exhausted," Sascha whined, "And I can't wait to get out of these shoes!"

"Did you bring flats?"

"I wasn't allowed," she pouted. "Bridezilla won't let me wear anything but these heels until the videographer leaves." Also not a surprise.

"That's still quite a while away."

"I'll live." Her pout turned serious. There really was no escaping her. "So, do you want to tell me what you're doing hiding over here? Is Dale being annoying? He can be a little annoying."

I shook my head. "Dale's been great. I just need a break."

"What's going on?" she prodded, concern now lacing her tone. "Is it me? I know I've been a little bitchy this past week. I'm really sorry I've been that way to you. I have no right to treat you like that."

I shook my head. "You haven't done anything. Promise." That didn't satisfy her. A non-answer was not going to cut it, so I caved. "I spoke to Caroline last night."

Sascha's perfectly glossed mouth fell open. "Excuse me? What? Why? What happened?"

With heat bubbling in my chest, I relayed the cliff notes version of my horrid week. From breaking things off with Sawyer and arguing with Justin, to my talk with Dad, calling Caroline and having a meltdown at the mere sound of her voice. It took a while for me to calm down after the tears started rolling, but when I did, Caroline was there to listen to me for what felt like the first time in my entire life. It was a long talk, nearly two hours, but I learned a lot. My world had been turned upside down in the past twenty four hours and I was still coming to terms with it.

Sascha was dumbstruck, speechless even. She didn't say a word until she was sure I'd finished. "Ellie, I'm so sorry I've been such a cow lately. Why didn't you call me after?"

I shrugged. "You've had the wedding to deal with, I didn't want to bother you. It's okay, I'm okay."

"Are you really?" She didn't seem so sure.

"I am actually. I'm not perfectly okay, but I am okay."

"So does this mean you and Caroline are speaking now? Did you sort things out?"

Not by any means. We'd spoken about my anger at her leaving, and the subsequent consequences I'd faced since. I let a lot out, and she listened quietly. Then she shared her own feelings, about the shame and guilt that had plagued her since the day she left. About the hurt she struggled through when I rejected her. We'd both suffered and were still suffering in our own ways. "Not exactly, but I think it's a start."

Concern laced Sascha's expression. She'd lent against the wall for my entire story and now stood up straight, readjusting her strapless dress. "So this all happened because Justin was a dick?"

"I think I needed to hear some of the things he said."

Sascha pursed her lips. "He could have been nicer about it."

I shrugged. Perhaps, but I didn't want to talk about him.

Sensing my discomfort, she changed the subject. "So do you really think I look okay? I wore the chicken fillets and I think it works."

Maybe Justin was right. Maybe Sascha did aide my deterrence to difficult situations and undesirable emotions.

"It definitely works," I laughed.

"Are you sure?"

"Are you kidding? Dale has been undressing you with his eyes all night. The way he's been looking at you has made me picture you naked."

Her lips formed a smug smirk. "Like what you see?"

I rolled my eyes. "Speak of the devil, here comes Mr. Perfect now."

Dale weaved his way through Sascha's mingling family members, a look of terror on his face. When he reached us, he was in panic mode. "Your grandmother keeps giving me the evil eye," he whispered, leaning in to give her a quick kiss on the lips. "Ugh, sticky."

"Sorry, I can take it off later." Sascha reached up to wipe the gloss from his mouth. "Baba will keep giving you the evil eye until you introduce yourself."

Dale fidgeted with his cuffs. He was no stranger to new people, but this was different. Meeting most of Sascha's family in one go must be daunting. "Help?"

"Okay, come on, she's really not that scary."

I had to disagree. Baba was intimidating until you got to know her. I could vouch for Dale's fears, having experienced many myself when I first met Sascha's grandparents.

Sascha glanced back at me. "Are you sure you're okay? I'm here for you."

I gave her my best everything's fine smile. "I know. Go be with your boyfriend, I'll go and get a wine."

She still seemed unsure but left with him anyway.

When they were gone, I did as I said and found my way back to my table where I poured a large glass of white wine. My eyes found Sascha and I watched as Dale stuck his hand out to shake Baba's. She looked at it as if it were the most offensive thing in the world. Then the short, old woman reached for him, pulled him down to her height, and planted a wet kiss on his unsuspecting cheek.

That's when the MC called for attention and for everyone to return to their seats for the speeches. Sascha reluctantly let go of his hand and started for the bridal table and Dale made his way back over to our little corner and sat beside me, expression taut.

I reached into my purse and pulled out a tissue. "She got you good," I laughed, gesturing to the red lipstick stain on his cheek. It was closer to his lips than expected.

"Thanks for the warning."

"Hey, so not my fault. I've never seen her do that before."

Dale scrubbed the stain and checked the tissue. "Not even with her ex's?"

The confusion on his face told me he had no idea. "Baba has never met any of her ex's."

He paused, tissue pressed firmly against his cheek. "Oh." I took a small sip of wine, giving Dale some time to process that information. His surprise was quickly replaced by smugness.

"How are you going with meeting everyone?"

"Good actually. I think my worry was misplaced. They all seem keen to meet me actually."

On cue, the rest of our table returned and took their seats. Some of them I knew, having met Sascha's cousins at family events over the years. Even so, there was a degree of separation and I was thankful to be seated with Dale and have someone familiar to talk to.

Waiters brought around the main course as the speeches commenced. I found it difficult to relate to the inside jokes and childhood stories told by the parents and best man. When it was Sascha's turn to speak, it felt natural to laugh at the events from her childhood. When we we're younger, we enjoyed gossiping about her older sister. Our sleepovers often involved laughing at and looking up to Mina, who was doing things we desperately wanted to do.

Sascha's words were entertaining to me, but their effect was insignificant compared to what Dale must have felt.

Eyes glistening with admiration, he soaked up every word she said as if it were gospel. And when she glanced over to him mid-speech, his genuine smile caused her to blush so brightly that I could see it across the room. She looked down at the paper in front of her trying to regain her focus, not that she needed to. Sascha had this speech memorised weeks ago.

My best friend was in love.

And she was loved.

They hadn't said those three, scary little words to each other — Sascha would have told me if they did — but I had no doubts.

I couldn't help wonder what it was like. Was it worth it? Love?

For Sascha and Dale, it certainly seemed to be.

"You alright?" Dale asked when the speeches concluded and we'd raised our glasses for the cutting of the cake.

"Mhmm," I mumbled, taking a long sip from my glass. I reached for the bottle across the table and refilled my wine as the bride and groom began their first dance. Not long after, the bridal party joined them on the dance floor and Dale was back to watching Sascha's every move.

"You've been really good for her," I admitted quietly.

He reluctantly tore his gaze from Sascha's glow to assess me.

"And to her," I added. I'd never seen her so happy in a relationship and it was thanks to him.

Dale chuckled.

"What?" Did I say something wrong?

He hesitated, taking time to decide if he should tell me or not. "It's funny. Justin said something similar to me the other day, that she has been really good for me."

Justin.

"Oh."

I was surprised it took so long for his name to come up. Dale was his best mate, so I'd been expecting it in one way or another. Even so, hearing it said aloud caused my heart to race faster than the aunties running to the dance floor for the Grease Megamix.

Dale's next words came laced with caution. "Are you planning on working things out any time soon?"

Crossing my arms tightly around my waist, I looked down into my lap. That was a loaded question I couldn't answer. Thankfully, Sascha's impeccable timing was my godsend once again.

Sascha brushed passed us, affectionately running a hand across Dale's shoulders, to say hello to her cousins. When she was done hugging everyone she fell into her boyfriend's lap with a sigh. "I need another drink."

"Your speech is done, you can drink as much as you like," Dale smiled, wrapping his arms around her.

"You say that now, but you're the one taking me home."

He shrugged, not worried about the consequences of getting Sascha drunk. "It's a special occasion. What do you feel like drinking?"

Sascha scanned the small selection scattered in front of us. "Table wine or beer? No thanks! Marko's parents are paying for an open bar!"

"Tequila or vodka?" Dale mused.

Her eyes sparkled with mischief. "They have rakija." She pounced to her feet as if her heels no longer hurt and started backing towards the bar. "Let's go! Ellie?"

"Sure," I agreed. I'd tried rakija a few times and enjoyed it.

"Just give us one minute," Dale pleaded, taking his phone out of his suit pocket. Sascha complied and began rounding up some cousins to join her for a drink.

Dale fiddled with his phone, and just as I was standing up, my clutch purse vibrated.

I quickly pried open the magnetic snap and pulled out my phone, already knowing who it would be. The timing was not coincidental. Sure enough, Dale's name appeared in a notification. I stared at it, worried and curious.

"Don't take too long," he said in a low tone before leaving the table and ushering Sascha towards the bar. It didn't take a genius to figure out he wasn't referring to opening the message.

My curiosity peaked and I pressed the notification. A link took me to a social media site for Uni Bar and the current livestream. I'd seen advertisements around campus all week about Dream of Darcy's unplugged show. I swallowed. Darcy wasn't the only one on stage tonight.

Everyone had vacated the table. I was alone and far enough away from the speakers that I could hear the sound if I turned up the volume.

So I did.

I tuned in just as one song finished and Darcy spoke into the microphone. "Not that he will admit it, but this next duet goes out to Justin's would-be sweetheart." The crowd, which sounded like it was full of women, cheered as Justin pulled a guitar into his lap. He was sitting on a stool beside Darcy, a microphone set up in front of him. Unless Justin went around admitting he had feelings for multiple women, she could only mean me.

I sucked in a quivering breath. I was the would-be sweetheart.

Justin plucked strings to start the song, followed by Darcy's melodic tones and lyrics I recognised instantly. It was the Jonas Brothers song I'd mentioned to him weeks ago when he asked me which was my favourite.

It wasn't until Justin began singing that I realised I'd been hold-ing my breath. His husky voice was shaky at first but it became smoother as his confidence grew. Darcy sang most of the lyrics, but my eyes were glued to Justin as if he was the only one on stage.

He'd learned and spent time rehearsing this song.

Did he decide to do this weeks ago or was this a recent reve-lation after our argument the other day? Why would he sing this song?

I glanced over at the bar, heart thumping in my chest. Dale was close to downing the rakija like a shot when Sascha stopped him, dramatically covering his mouth with her hand. Everyone around them laughed. One cousin even slapped him on the back as Sascha snuggled under his arm.

Grateful to be sitting alone, I looked up at the ceiling to blink away the wetness pooling in my eyes. Why couldn't I access the same kind of courage? The type it took to meet an entire family in one night. The type that helped you sing in front of a crowd, pouring your heart out without knowing if it would ever be recip-rocated. The type it took to blindly trust someone with your heart.

CHAPTER 24

I sat outside Justin's house staring at his front door from the safety of my car. This was the right thing to do. Deep down, I knew that. So why was taking the plunge so difficult? I'd driven here pumped with courage, but now that I faced the reality of seeing him, it was waning. Fast.

I'd spent the past week lost in my own mind, exploring the possibilities and what ifs of letting myself feel what my heart so clearly wanted. My head was in charge, it always had been, and it had a hard time relinquishing control.

I picked up my phone to call Sascha. She answered on the second ring.

"Are you here?" she asked in earnest.

"I'm here," I breathed.

"Well, are you coming in?"

That was still up for debate. "Is he home?"

There was a creak and Sascha's voice dropped to a whisper. "He is. He only just walked through the door."

"Maybe I should just call him, or text him."

The creak sounded again, followed by a sharp bang, and her voice returned to her usual volume. "No, no. You can't chicken out now. We talked about this."

"I know. I'm just..."

"Chickening out?"

"No, I'm not. I'm doing this. I have to do this." I was psyching myself up, but there were always doubts lingering in the back of my mind. "But, Sass, what if he's moved on?"

She sighed into the phone. "Babe, it hasn't even been two weeks. And from what I've seen of him in that time, there's no way he's even thought about moving on."

"What if it's not meant to be?"

"Don't start with the fate bullshit again. That's an excuse and you know it. If I have to come out there and drag you in here by the ear, you know I'll do it." The frustrated tone in her voice told me she would have no misgivings about that whatsoever.

"Okay," I groaned. "Keep your panties on."

"I'm not wearing any."

Ew! I hoped she was joking and not talking to me with her horny boyfriend in the room. It was best not to think about it. "Didn't need to know that. Okay, I'm getting out of the car."

"Good girl." She hung up.

Sascha's pep talk worked. This was it. With a new burst of courage, I got out of the car, locked it, and sauntered up to Justin's door. The last time I'd done this, it had set everything in motion. I'd given into desire and then all hell broke lose.

I took a deep breath before knocking on the door. It was so tempting to walk back down the path, get in my car and drive away. Especially when it seemed like no one was going to answer the door.

I knocked again, nerves flaring.

Eventually, there was a shuffling noise, and when the door opened, I came face to face with Justin. He looked confused. And he was wearing a suit!

"Hey," he said after several beats of silence.

"Hi," I breathed, distracted by his appearance. "I'm sorry, were you on your way out?"

"No, I just got in, actually." Taking note of my curiosity and wandering eyes, he offered an explanation. "I went into the office with my father today. Are you here for Sass? I didn't realise she was here."

It would be so easy to tell him I was here for my best friend. It would also be a lie. "No, I'm not. I'm actually here to see you."

"Right," he said, eyebrows raising. "Come in."

I stepped over the threshold, closing the door behind me. Justin walked down the hallway to the kitchen, passing the living room without a glance. Perhaps that was on purpose. Maybe he didn't want to be reminded of what happened in there the last time I visited.

"Can I get you a coffee?" A familiar offer. I always said yes, but not today.

"Do you mind if I make it?"

He looked surprised, but let me step up to his fancy all-in-one machine. "Do you know how to use it?"

"Do you really need an answer to that?" I frowned, carefully placing my bag on the counter.

"Guess not," he mused, leaning back against the granite.

"Every time we have coffee you get mine with macadamia, and I realised that you've never tried it before. You're missing out." I reached into my bag and pulled out the small bottle of macadamia syrup.

"Am I? Seems like it would be an acquired taste."

"You'll see."

I busied myself making coffee, acutely aware of his gaze following my every move. I ground the beans and used the inbuilt tamper to flatten them. Then I set the machine to pour two shots of espresso into mugs I took from the rack of clean dishes. Carefully, I swirled a small amount of syrup into the espresso. After heating and frothing the milk, I gently poured it into the mugs, finishing it off with a heart pattern. Well, I attempted that part. I could grind, pour and froth with the best of them, but latte art was a skill I did not possess.

After cleaning down the machine, I slid the mug along the counter to Justin. He looked down at it with a raised brow.

Ignoring the butterflies in my stomach, and avoiding ogling him in that suit, I walked around the counter and took up a stool. "Are you going to try it."

Justin turned to face me on the other side of the counter and picked up the mug, eyeing it with caution.

"It's not laced with poison. Promise."

Carefully, he brought the mug to his mouth and took a sip.

"What do you think?"

He licked his lips and I took another sip of my own coffee, attempting to hide the traitorous and uncontrollable reaction of my body. "It's sweet. And nutty."

"You hate it."

"I don't hate it," he replied, taking another careful sip. "Like I said, it's an acquired taste. It's just very sweet."

It made sense that he wasn't a fan, especially since he took his coffee with a double shot and no sweetener. "Well, if you don't want it, I'll be happy to take it off your hands."

He finally smiled as I reached for his mug. "Hey now, don't be greedy," he said, lifting it out of my reach. "I'll be finishing it."

His took another large sip to prove his dedication and for a brief moment, things felt like they use to.

An awkward silence fell between us once the natural banter dissipated. I was here for a reason and we both knew it.

Before I could get a word out, Justin interrupted.

"Wait. Before you start, I need to apologise to you." He leant both elbows on the counter, frowning down at his clasped hands. Then he took a deep breath and lifted his blue eyes to meet mine. "I said some things last week that I really had no right saying. I let my own feelings dominate what you needed and I'm really sorry for pressuring you. I shouldn't be trying to influence your choices with my own greediness."

"Did you speak to Caroline?" I questioned, warmth flushing my cheeks for an entirely different reason.

"I was there when you called her," he admitted softly. "But she left the room straight away. I didn't hear a word, and I didn't ask."

The anger bubbling in my chest at the potential deception settled. Caroline hadn't betrayed my trust, and neither had Justin. "Okay," I said, looking down at the mug nestled between my hands. Holding tightly stopped them from shaking.

"So, you came here to talk to me?" There was hope in his eyes. I knew it would be there, but I worried it wasn't going to be enough.

"I came here because I owe you an apology." Looking into his eyes now sent my heart into a flutter.

"What for?" he asked, confusion furrowing his brows.

"The way I treated you, last week on the field and after..." I glanced over my shoulder, eyes landing firmly on the corner of the couch visible through the doorway. The place we'd shared the most intense kiss of my life! "I have a lot of things I need to work through, and you got caught in the crossfire. I'm not very good at dealing with my emotions and sometimes I don't know how to talk to people."

"You don't need to apologise for having emotions," he said, straightening up to take hold of his mug.

"It's not for having these feelings, it's for the way I treat other people, the way I treated you when I didn't know how to deal. I'm not good at opening up. I'm not good at letting other people in." This was the harsh but truthful reality I was coming to terms with. I'd done a lot of reflection recently, and it was like I was seeing myself with new eyes.

"Why is that?"

"Because until recently, I didn't see the point. People pass through your life, nothing is ever permanent. I couldn't see the point in starting something when it's going to end eventually anyway."

"What about your Dad, and Sascha? How come it's not an issue with them?"

I shrugged. "They've been a constant in my life as long as I can remember. They've never done anything to make me think they were leaving."

"Have I done something to make you feel that way?"

I shook my head. "No, but that's what scares me."

"I don't understand." His worry turned to confusion. I wasn't explaining myself clearly.

"I am insanely attracted to you," I admitted, staying strong and holding his gaze. It was time to lay it all out on the line. "And it's not just physical, which is what petrifies me the most. I've never felt this way about anyone and I don't know how to deal with these feelings. I don't know what I'm suppose to say, or how to act. I don't know what it all means. And I don't know if you feel the same way, either."

Justin reached across the counter to take hold of my hand. "I think you know I do, Ellie."

Sighing, I looked down, but I didn't pull away from his warm touch. He was right. I knew. "Okay, so how do I know you won't be turned off by my crazy? It will be too much and you'll leave."

"You can't predict that."

"Exactly." He would get tired of me and he would bail. I wasn't sure I could deal with him leaving. If the last week was any indication of how I'd react, it wouldn't be pretty.

Justin kept hold of my hand as he rounded the counter. He sat down on the stool beside me, pulling it closer. He turned me to face him, his thighs brushing the outside of my knees. The layers of pants and tights between our skin did nothing to quell the spark of electricity.

"I can't promise that things are always going to be perfect. Any relationship that looks perfect all the time is probably toxic as fuck."

I couldn't really argue with that.

"But Ellie-bean, do you really want to live your life like this? Scared to even try?"

I shook my head, still unable to look at him. "No, I don't. That's why I'm here."

Justin's warm fingers found my chin and tilted my face up. The motion caused a swelling tear to break free. "I'm scared," I whispered. "I've never really been in..."

I couldn't bring myself to say it. A relationship. Not since my first boyfriend broke up with me, and I'm not sure I could even count that as a real relationship.

"I have a lot I need to work through," I continued, trying to explain my intentions clearly. "I'm going back to therapy, but she can't fit me in until the end of next month."

He nodded slowly, coming to terms with my words. "Therapy is good, and if I have to wait until then, or for however long it takes, then I will. Until whenever you're ready."

"I don't want you to wait."

My response caught him off guard and he instantly took it the wrong way.

I slid off my stool and stepped between his legs, bringing us face to face. Mustering every ounce of confidence I had, I placed my hands firmly on his chest. His own rested on his knees and I wished he would just wrap his warmth around me. "In all the mess being thrown around right now, you are the one thing I see clearly. I'm petrified, but I'm ready. And if you're willing to deal with the crazy whenever it appears, I want to try all of these scary things with you."

His blue eyes glistened, but they also scanned me with caution. I couldn't blame him for his uncertainty. I'd been hot and cold for so long when all he'd ever done was be honest with me.

Justin's arms finally snaked around my waist and pulled me against him. My hands slid slowly up his chest to rest at the nape of his neck. "You're not crazy," he whispered. "I want to know you. I want us to know each other. That means being there for each other, and supporting each other, especially when one of us is going through something. But Ellie, relationships aren't easy. We need to be open. Can you do that? Can you let me in when you need help? When you're struggling?"

The sincerity in his eyes told me all I needed to know. "I'm going to try my best, I promise. You might have to call me on my shit if I mess up though. I'm new at this."

"I think I can do that." The corners of his lips turned up as he tried suppressing his smile. "Now before I kiss you, promise you won't freak out on me again?"

I pressed in closer, lips just a breath away and voice low. "I can't promise that, but if I do, it will be a completely different type of freaking out."

Without another word, his lips covered mine in the most gentle of kisses. It was slow and heated, and the taste of him mixed with coffee set every nerve in my body on fire. The physical attraction was running rampant between us, just as it did last time. But this was something else, something more than I'd ever experienced.

This kiss was a promise.

"You're freaking out," Justin murmured against my mouth when he came up for air.

"Very much so," I admitted, before pressing my lips firmly back to his feeling like I was floating on air. How wrong I'd been about taking chances. How wrong I'd been about a lot of things.

He chuckled. "I like this type of freak out."

"Me too."

A loud knock sounded nearby. I jumped back out of instinct, but Justin held on tight, keeping me close to him.

"Can we come in yet?" Sascha whined, poking her head through the door. When she spotted that we'd disengaged, she confidently stepped into the room, followed by Dale.

Justin looked up to the ceiling, clearly annoyed. "Just once, I would love it if we weren't interrupted," he mumbled, only loud enough for me to hear.

"Maybe if we chose places with a little more privacy it wouldn't be an issue," I offered, amused by his reaction. I spun in his arms to face Sascha and Dale.

"Noted," Justin whispered in my ear, resting his chin on my shoulder. It felt strange to be wrapped in his arms with other people in the room. Strange, but comfortable. I liked it here.

Sascha eyed me with the smuggest of expressions as Dale rummaged through the fridge. She didn't say anything, but she didn't need to.

"I'm starving," Dale complained, not even acknowledging the position Justin and I were in. Maybe it was a guy thing. He either didn't care or he didn't want to make a fuss. "Barbecue?"

Sascha agreed and started pulling things from cupboards as Dale searched for utensils to open the meat packages. I watched, amused by the domestic nature of their relationship. They moved around each other with ease, as if they knew exactly where the other would be.

"Speaking of barbecues," Sascha began as she washed lettuce in the sink. "Baba want's to celebrate my birthday before she flies back to Adelaide."

I reached for my mug. Justin's tight grip on my waist made it difficult, but he refused to let go. "Your birthday isn't for another month."

"I know, but it's my 21st, so my parents are throwing an impromptu barbecue next Saturday." Sascha started slicing cucumber and throwing it into a salad bowl. "Everyone is invited so be there or be a loser who misses out on my awesomeness."

I smiled at her antics, grateful that she'd found a line for the conversation to take and that she didn't focus on the fact that Justin was playing with my hair.

"Do you want to stay for dinner?" he offered quietly, tucking a loose strand behind my ear.

I glanced over my shoulder and he moved slightly to give me some room. "Sure," I murmured back. Then I did something bold. I kissed him again, not caring that our friends were here or that they may judge us for such a public display of affection.

"Hey, cut it out you two," Sascha criticised with feigned outrage. Dale slapped her butt with a spatula and she elbowed him in the ribs.

I couldn't contain my smile. This floating on air thing? Yeah, I could get use to it.

CHaPTer 25

Sascha's last minute birthday barbecue didn't look last minute at all. Her parents had set up their yard with outdoor furniture, a fire pit, and a long table of delicious food. Baba waltzed around chatting to her children and grandchildren with a bright smile and made sure they had all eaten. She'd been to our table twice already and kept piling Dale's plate with more food. It was amusing to see the strained look on his face. He was full, but he couldn't deny her, not that she would let him if he tried.

Sascha was beaming. Not because she was dolled up (excessively so for a backyard barbecue), but because she was happy. Her family and her boyfriend were getting along. She'd always been worried about her boyfriends meeting her family and she never imagined it could go this well.

After dinner, and Dale's fourth helping of apple burek, some of Sascha's family said their goodbyes, opening up opportunities for games. Some revolved around drinking, but we'd chosen cards. Bullshit to be specific.

I shivered in the chilly air. Spring was here, but the nights were still cold. Attuned my need, Justin placed his free hand on my thigh and rubbed up and down, attempting to warm me with friction. I snuggled into his side as much as the armchairs would allow. He was so warm.

"Suck it, Drummer Boy!" Emily squealed, throwing her final cards down. I was already out of the game, having been the first to put down all my cards. Justin moaned beside me and threw his own deck onto the table. He'd come last.

"This game is bullshit," he whined dramatically.

"Yes dear, that's what it's called," Sascha quipped, making everyone laugh.

Emily stood up, pushing her chair back and almost falling into the potted plant behind her. "Who wants another drink?" she asked excitedly.

"Hun, I think you need more cake to soak up what you've already had first," Sascha called, chasing after her.

A cousin sauntered over and took Sascha's vacated seat next to Dale. They immediately launched into a conversation about an up-and-coming artist they were both interested in. It was nice to see he'd bonded with her family so easily.

Justin leaned down to place a kiss on my temple. "You're cold," he stated, moving the hand on my thigh to my shoulders.

"Just a little," I shivered, leaning into him.

"Come on, let's go and sit by the fire." Standing up, he took my hand and led me over to the fire pit. There were a few people spread out in the yard, but none of them seemed interested in the fire. I recognised two girls from high school and gave them a timid smile. One gave a small wave back but the other just looked at me and requested her friend's attention.

If Justin noticed the awkward interaction, he didn't say anything. He let go of my hand to pick up another log. As he tended to the fire, I stood straight, wrapping my arms around myself. He made quick work of stoking the fire before stepping back beside me.

"Is that better," he asked, checking me over with concern.

"It's okay," I shrugged. Unless I was standing a metre away from the fire, it wouldn't do much so soon.

"Come here," he said in a low tone, pulling me to his chest. I tunnelled my hands beneath his jacket, finding a warm spot to link them around his waist. He wrapped his arms around me and look down into my eyes. "Better now?"

"Much," I smiled, snuggling in closer.

"You're still shivering."

"Just give it a minute."

Justin leant down, his warm breath tickling the skin behind me ear. "You know," he continued in a suggestive tone that sent a different kind of shiver down my spine, "I can think of a much better way to warm you up."

"Oh really?" I challenged, tone matching his.

"Yeah," he nodded, adjusting his hold on me to give himself more space to press his lips to mine. He kissed me slowly and I melted against him.

One week. That's how long it had been. In that time, we'd locked lips plenty. Sometimes it was a quick hello when we met up for coffee on campus, or a lingering goodbye kiss when he walked me to class. Other times, in the relative privacy of our favourite place by the soccer field, there was little to hold us back. We'd gone for dinner and a movie last night, and I had no idea what was happening to the characters. I was more interested in what was happening to me and how I felt like a giddy teenager in the back row of the cinema.

This kiss could lead to something similar if circumstances were different. Reluctantly, I pulled back to clear my head. "If Baba wasn't here and Sass's parents weren't inside, maybe I'd let you try," I murmured against his lips.

"Would you now?" he chuckled, squeezing my hips.

I so wanted to let him try. There was no doubt that he'd succeed, but it was too soon. Kissing like our survival depended on it was one thing, but sex was something else. There were more implications and we both needed to be ready. Even though my body was screaming for his touch, there was so much that could go wrong.

"Maybe." I pressed my lips to his in a soft peck before burrowing back into his chest.

"Question," he began in a soft voice after a few moments of snuggling. "What's with Twiddle-dee and Twiddle-dumb over there?"

I didn't need to look up to know who he was talking about. The girls sitting across the fire, my old classmates.

I shrugged. "They're Sascha's friends, really. I went to school with them too, but we weren't close." In fact, the only time I really spoke to them was during lunch time, and that was because we were all friends with Sascha. Other than our mutual friend, there really was no reason to keep in contact after we'd graduated. "I'm pretty sure they think I'm a snob," I mumbled, eyes trained on the orange flames. They were likely surprised by my catch of a boyfriend, not that I could blame them for that. He was insanely attractive and sinfully charismatic.

Justin, ever sensitive to my needs, tightened his arms around me before lightening the mood. "Well if they're going to keep staring, we might as well give them the show they're clearly after."

I looked up to catch his mischievous grin. "That's a little mean."

"I don't care," he laughed, leaning closer.

He didn't need to ask twice. Any chance to kiss Justin was a chance I was taking.

Shame it didn't last long.

"Get a room!" Dale's voice called. It was followed by a giggle from Emily.

Reluctantly, I pulled back from Justin's warm lips and buried my face in his shirt. My chest fluttered thinking about the room we had also just been talking about.

Justin reached out to punch his mate in the shoulder as he walked by. Dale just laughed and took up a seat next to us. "Where's Darcy tonight?" Justin asked.

Dale looked to his feet. "No idea."

Emily tucked her hands into her pockets and sat on the edge of a garden bed. She looked pointedly at the fire, a glum expression on her face. Letting go of Justin, I went to sit beside her. "Hey."

"Hey," she smiled. The alcohol was either wearing off or doing its job.

"Everything okay?"

She shrugged.

I had a hunch. "Is it something to do with Darcy?" They were usually inseparable.

After a few moments and one heavy sigh, she nodded. "She and Isaac broke up."

"Oh."

Emily turned to me. "You're not surprised?"

Honestly? No, I wasn't surprised. "Sometimes things seemed a little tense between them. I heard them arguing over the phone once." Between that and the way Emily reacted around her best friend's boyfriend, there had to be something real going on. "Did that happened often? The arguing?"

She tilted her head back to look up at the sky. "More and more recently. This has been a long time coming." The tone of her voice was more relieved than concerned, which was odd considering she was always so worried about Darcy.

"So how come you're here? I thought Darcy would want your company after something like this."

"Actually, she doesn't want to see me right now." She was still focussing on the sky, her eyes blinking profusely. "Or anyone."

"Makes sense." I wasn't sure of the appropriate thing to say. I'd had experience with Sascha's break ups, but this was different. Emily wasn't dumped, but she clearly needed comfort for some reason. There was so much more to this situation than she was sharing. There had to be. "She'll call you when she's ready."

"Hope so," she sighed, unconvinced.

Before I could ask any more questions, Sascha's excited tones interrupted the chatter around the fire pit.

"So I did a thing," she called, trotting over in her shiny heels.

"Are those marshmallows?" Emily queried, seeming grateful for the distraction.

Sascha beamed. "Yes, yes they are."

"S'mores are not a thing," I reminded her. "Wagon Wheels would be much easier, and they have jam."

Sascha raised her brows at me. "They are when you're camping. And I think that's the laziest thing I've ever heard you say."

"We're not camping. And we're not in North America."

"But there's a fire. And I'm pretty sure my cousin may pass out here later tonight, so same, same really."

"How do you even make one?" Emily asked, standing up to help Sascha.

"I goggled it. It's actually really simple."

Sascha launched into her explanation and I wondered how long it would take them to realise they didn't have skewers or sticks.

"So what are we doing about rehearsals?" Dale asked, redirecting my attention. "Our last gig is coming up."

Anthony groaned. "I've been so busy with exam prep I haven't even thought about it."

"We can do a few extra rehearsals at our place this week," Justin chimed in.

Dale considered it for a moment. "As long as Darcy is cool with it."

"Why wouldn't she be?" Justin queried, a look of confusion in his expression. Her break-up must have been so recent that not all housemates had heard yet.

Dale shrugged as if to say the news was inevitable. "She broke up with Isaac."

Unsurprised, Justin sighed. "Ah. That might throw a spanner in the works."

Dale shrugged again. "She'll be fine."

Would she? The final gig was only two weeks away. I couldn't imagine anyone getting over a breakup so quickly, not enough to focus on exams, rehearsals and her final show. If Justin decided he didn't want to be with me after only a week, I would be devastated. Darcy and Isaac were together for a few years, so I couldn't fathom what she must be going through.

Sensing my sudden bout of over-thinking, Justin sat beside me on the edge of the planter. He leaned in, his proximity an instant balm. "You're definitely coming, right?" he asked in a low tone.

"Of course I am," I smiled up at him. "I wouldn't miss it."

I rather enjoyed watching Justin on stage. He was a vision and now that he was my boyfriend, I would feel no shame in ogling. In fact, I hoped he ogled right back.

"Good." He pressed a sweet kiss to my temple, leaving a tingle behind. Then he stood up. "Do you want another drink?"

"Sure."

"I'll be right back," he nodded, eyes looking me over. "Then maybe we can talk about this trying to warm you up thing."

I flushed at the mere mention of Justin trying to warm me up. My body was desperate for his touch, screaming for it actually, and I had no doubt that I'd give in to temptation sooner than planned.

Chapter 26

"Do you want another shot?" Emily yelled over the thump of music and Darcy's melodic voice.

I shook my head, keeping my body moving with the beat. "No, I'm good."

"You sure?" Sascha chimed in, leaning in to my ear. "You look a little nervous."

I rolled my eyes at her assumption, even though it was completely accurate. "I'm good," I repeated, a blush rising to my cheeks. Maybe I shouldn't have told her.

Sascha giggled and ignored Emily's curious look as they squeezed through the crowd and off the dance floor.

Alone in a sea of sweaty bodies, the weight of his gaze felt heavier. An intentional wiggle of the hips and glance over the shoulder was all it took for that blush to turn into a full body tingle.

Justin didn't miss a beat. The way he looked in his black, low cut shirt, with his tattoo peeking out, only added to my nerves. And when he licked his lips after looking me up and down, I thought maybe I could do with another shot after all.

Sascha knew me so well. When she and Emily returned to the dance floor, drinks in hand, she handed me a third glass. I took it and downed the vodka concoction in two gulps. Emily cheered me on and Sascha raised her brows knowingly.

"Shut up," I mumbled, unheard over the music. Sascha caught it though, and laughed again.

That's how the night went. Dancing and drinking, although I did refrain from more alcohol. It was Dream of Darcy's last show and the atmosphere was wilder than I'd ever seen it. Uni Bar was at capacity and there was no sign of it slowing down, not even when Darcy thanked the crowd for their support over the years and all band members stood up front for a never-ending applause.

The after party seemed to go on forever. I watched keenly as Justin mingled with his friends and his fans. His smile was contagious as he spent time with classmates he would probably never see again after graduation. I hung back with Emily and Sascha, letting the band do their thing.

Eventually, people moved on from congratulating Dream of Darcy and flocked to the bar and dance floor. When the questions and praises stopped flowing, Justin made his way over to me.

He slipped passed the red rope separating our booth from the rest of the crowd and slid into the seat beside me, trapping me in the corner.

"How are you feeling?" I asked, placing a hand on his arm.

Justin sighed, putting his nearly empty beer on the table. "I don't know, really. Can you feel exhilarated and sad at the same time?"

My fingers fiddled with a loose thread on the hem of my dress. I wasn't one for understanding emotions, but you could definitely feel more than one thing at once. "Absolutely."

He nodded with a smile. "Then that's how I feel. Exhilarated and sad." I had little doubt that the melancholy would take over soon. He puckered his lips, looking down at his beer and then up at the stage.

"You'll miss it." There was no question about it. Justin enjoyed playing the drums and performing with his friends.

His attention back on me, he spoke in a low voice. "I will miss it. But I guess it's time for a new chapter."

I let him have his moment before I turned my body to face him. We were alone in the booth and I was mostly blocked from view. Knowing that wandering eyes wouldn't see, I felt the bravery bubble.

Reaching out for his hand, I linked our fingers and asked quietly, "Are you tired?"

Justin turned, giving me his full attention and matching my tone. "Exhausted. Why do you ask?"

The bravery was mounting, and so was my heart rate. Slowly but deliberately, I led our interlocked hands to the hem of my skirt. Letting go, Justin's fingers splayed over my stocking-clad thigh and gave a gentle squeeze.

"So exhausted that it's time to go home?" I whispered, guiding his hand further under my skirt until it reached the clip of my suspenders. I'd put them on with confidence earlier, but that confidence had rescinded to anxiety. Would they have the desired affect? Did he want this? Did he want me?

Justin's eyes widened with realisation. Before he could react further or say anything, I lent forward to press my lips to his, making my intentions clear.

His fingers gripped my upper thigh a little tighter as he kissed me back. Exhausted would not be how I described his energy in this moment.

When we pulled away, only a breath apart, his eyes glistened. "Are you suggesting what I think you're suggesting?"

I pressed my lips together, holding in a giggle. "Do you need me to show you again?"

"I'm just making sure."

I kissed him again, this time giving him a sweet peck on the lips. "I am suggesting what you think I'm suggesting."

His eyes darted from mine, to his hand under my skirt and back again. Clearing his throat, he let me go. "I just have to make the rounds and say goodbye."

"Okay."

He leaned back in to give me another kiss. "But then you and me, we are out of here."

"Sounds good to me."

"I won't be long," he said in a reluctant tone, sliding back out of the booth.

When he was out of the VIP section and no longer looking me over with that dangerous glint in his eyes, I scanned the room around me. No one was paying attention.

While in the moment, I hadn't thought about what others might have seen. I'd been bold, more so than I had ever been in public, but it seemed I didn't have anything to worry about to begin with. Not a single person had been looking our way.

It took another half hour before we waltzed out of Uni Bar, Justin's arm wrapped around my shoulders. We hadn't even made it inside his car before he kissed me again. He pushed me up against the passenger-side door, enclosing me in his warmth. Reaching up to pull him closer, I kissed him back with an eagerness that had been bubbling for weeks.

Completely lost in our own world, it took a wolf-whistle from a stranger to break us apart. Blushing, I reached behind me to the door handle. "We should probably take this somewhere more private."

"Definitely," Justin agreed, letting his hands drop.

The car sizzled with tension and the drive back to his place seemed to take twice as long as it should. His hand rested on my thigh for most of the ride, and every so often he'd snap my suspenders.

When we finally made it back to his place, his hands were on my hips before the front door closed. Our lips found each other without a word and danced with an intense fervour, one we'd never tapped into for fear of going too far. Now all inhibitions were off the table and there was no room for holding back.

Between kisses, Justin backed me through the foyer towards the staircase. When my ankles bumped into the wood and our lips broke apart, he caught me around the waist. His breath was heavy when he spoke.

"Not to spoil the moment," he said in a low tone, "but I really need to shower before we..." He trailed off, his light eyes travelling the length of my body, or as much of it as they could see with him holding me so close. It was more than enough to show exactly what we would be doing. "I get pretty gross when I play."

He didn't seem gross to me. In fact, he smelled amazing. "Okay," I smiled, taking him by the hand and leading the way up the stairs to his bedroom.

Justin flicked the light on and swung me around. "I'll be two minutes, promise," he murmured, pressing a sweet kiss to my lips. He let go reluctantly and strode across his room to another door. He turned back to me, concern spreading across his face. "Two minutes," he confirmed before disappearing into the en suite.

I closed his bedroom door before going to sit on the edge of his bed. The shower was already running, but his brief absence was already enough time for the nerves to creep back in.

Should I undress and position my self on the bed? Should I sneak into the bathroom and surprise him in the shower? Should I just sit here? My heart was pounding.

To distract myself, I stood up and approached the bookshelf. Besides the first morning I woke up alone in his bedroom after a drunken night out, I'd been in here a few times. I'd seen it all before, but focusing on the mixture of textbooks, novels and trinkets helped steady my mind.

I'd barely made it through reading the titles on the top shelf when the en suite door opened. True to his word, Justin had only needed two minutes. In my periphery I could see he wore nothing but a navy towel, hanging loosely on his hips.

My body tingled, each nerve burning with anticipation before his hands even found me. Approaching from behind, Justin gently wrapped his arms around my waist, his touch so light it set my skin alight even with the fabric of my dress keeping us from truly connecting.

"Snooping?" he teased, hands splaying across my navel.

With his chest pressing into my back and his lips on my shoulder, my heart lost control again. I reached up and pointed to a wooden box in the middle of the bookshelf. "What's in this?" I asked, my voice barely a whisper.

Justin feathered kisses along my neck, mouth resting just beneath my ear. "I'll show you later." His breath was warm and tickled my neck, actions speaking louder than words. He had other things on his mind. "Do you still want to?" he asked, hope and worry both lacing his tone.

Turning in his arms, I planned on telling him exactly what I wanted, but when I came face to face with his bare chest, my voice vanished. My hands found their own way to his abdomen and he shivered under their initial touch. Shirtless Justin was nothing new, but each time he quivered like that, it sent a thrill through me.

My fingers traced curves up to his chest. Applying pressure, I aimed to lead him backwards. Taking the hint, Justin backed up until we reached his computer chair and sat down, trying to drag me with him.

I let him go and took a step back. Slowly, and fully aware of his wandering gaze, I reached for the hem of my dress. He watched intently, wiping his hands on his towel as I pulled it carefully over my head.

I'd spent ages choosing the matching lingerie set and it seemed to achieve it's purpose. Justin sucked in a breath before reaching for me. He pulled me eagerly into his lap without a word.

Knowing exactly where to find the most comfortable spot atop the thin fabric of his towel, I straddled him and wasted no time in bringing our lips together. Our earlier fervour returning, Justin deepened the kiss and squeezed my hips, pulling me closer.

"This feels familiar," he murmured between heated kisses along my jaw.

I smiled. "Maybe we won't get interrupted this time." It was a frequent occurrence and seemed inevitable, no matter where we were.

"Hold on," he said, tightening his grip on my waist before pushing backwards. I nearly lost balance as he rolled the chair over the floorboards to the bedroom door. He turned the lock before redirecting his attention to me. "Shouldn't be a problem now."

He might not have noticed, but I certainly did when the movement caused the corner of his towel to break loose and slide beneath me. His thigh was bare and only a small corner of terry cloth and the thin lace of my panties separated us.

Justin reached up to tuck a loose strand of hair behind my ear. "You didn't answer before," he said in a low tone. "Do you want to? I just need to make sure."

To prove to him that I was in this, I pushed my hips firmly into his and placed my lips against his ear to tell him exactly what I wanted to happen here tonight.

Brows raised and eyes glistening, Justin licked his lips as I pulled back to gauge his reaction.

Seemingly speechless and potentially surprised that such words had come from me, he breathed deeply. "Yes Ma'am," he smirked, hands moving to cup the back of by thighs.

He stood up with me wrapped around him and moved towards the bed, the towel finally falling to the floor.

CHAPTER 27

There was no denying waiting a few weeks before sleeping with Justin had been the right choice. Not because I would have regretted it if we'd made it here sooner, but because this moment was absolute perfection.

Justin's chest was warm, and a little tacky with sweat against my cheek, but also the most comfortable place in the world. I drew in a content breath as his fingers traced circles on my bare shoulder.

"What are you thinking about?" he asked quietly, pressing his warm lips to my hair.

I'd been examining the intricacies of his tattoo, not really thinking about anything other than what we'd just shared. "Nothing and everything," I admitted. "What are you thinking about?"

His chest shook a little and I could tell without seeing that his lips had curved into a smirk. "Just replaying a few moments."

I turned to rest my chin on his chest. "Hmm, and which moments were those?" I asked, trying hard to conceal my smile. Without a word, he leant forward to capture my lips and tell me exactly what he'd been thinking about. "Yes, those were good moments," I agreed when he pulled back. He settled against the pillows with me against his chest.

After a few more minutes of cuddling, I found my eyes wandering around his room again. They soon rested on the small wooden box, the one I'd asked about earlier. While that may not have been the right time to bring it up, I was genuinely curious.

"So," I began with slight caution, "What's in the box?"

Justin followed my gaze, his chin brushing against my hair. He sighed but didn't hesitate to reveal its mysteries. "They're letters from my mum."

I froze. "Oh. Sorry, I didn't mean to pry," I apologised, propping myself on my elbow to look down at him, hoping I didn't just spoil the moment by bringing up painful memories.

"No, it's okay," he smiled, noticing my panic. "They're a good thing."

"When did she write them?"

Justin glanced back at the box. "I'm pretty sure she wrote them when she was in the hospital. There's one for each of my birthdays. Dad gives me one each year."

"That must be lovely, but also hard."

He shrugged. "A little. This year more than others."

"Why's that?"

His eyes glazes over for a moment. "The last letter came on my 21st birthday."

A letter each year until a few months ago. How do you respond to something like that? "Oh."

Justin sensed my uncertainty. "It's okay. I came to terms with mum's passing a long time ago."

"Do you still read them?"

"All the time. They're full of my mother's sage life advice, and her hopes for me. It's nice to pull them out every now and then."

What a beautiful gift Lillian Hart had left her son. I couldn't even imagine what writing those letters would have been like for her, or how they made Justin feel each time he received one.

When silence fell again, I moved to get out of bed. "Be back in a moment." After cleaning up a little in the en suite, I re-entered the bedroom to find Justin sitting with his back against the headboard. He'd put on boxer shorts.

Glancing around the floor, I gathered my undergarments and put them back on. When I sat at the edge of the bed untangling the suspenders, which had somehow gotten twisted in the stockings, Justin bounced over to me, his warm lips pressing a small kiss to my waist.

"Why are you getting dressed?"

I shrugged. "I should probably get going," I admitted softly. "It's really late."

He rested his head in a palm, watching me curiously. "Do you want to stay?" There was a glimmer of hope in his eyes alongside the worry that always seemed to be there. It was a genuine offer. "You can wear some of my things and I'm pretty sure Darcy keeps a pack of toothbrushes in the main bathroom," he offered, knowing those things would be at the forefront of my decision.

The question was not foreign to me, but I'd always had the same answer until now. "Sure," I agreed without hesitation, leaning down to kiss him.

He shot up almost immediately. "Shirts are in the second draw. I'll go find that toothbrush." Justin was out the door a few seconds later in nothing but his boxers.

I shook my head and fell back against the sheets. For someone who claimed to be so exhausted earlier tonight, he still had an unbridled amount of energy.

The dim sunlight peaked through the gaps of Justin's curtains. Barely daybreak and I was wide awake.

Justin lay face down beside me, cheek heavy against his pillow, shoulder blades rising and falling with steady breaths. He was a heavy sleeper. I'd already been out of bed to tidy up in the bathroom. While I attempted to be quiet, it was a small space, and the walls were thin. Even climbing back under the covers didn't jostle him. Now, I sat up against the headboard planning my week on my phone, waiting for him to wake. It was another half hour before he did.

With a groan, he rubbed his face against the pillow. "This isn't going to work," he mumbled, voice muffled by cotton and down.

I looked to him quickly. "What?"

The corners of his lips curved at my reaction. He reached up to take the phone out of my hands. He locked it and threw it carefully onto the comforter near our feet before reaching for me. "You're a morning person," he continued in a husky voice, pulling me down and wrapping his arm around my middle.

"And you're not," I guessed, a sense of relief coursing through me as I nestled into him.

Justin kissed my shoulder with warm lips. "Sometimes," he admitted, snuggling into my back.

We lay together, embraced in each other's warmth. Content in his arms; it felt like the most natural thing on Earth to be so close with him.

"You're wide awake," he sighed when I started to squirm, a little restless.

I rolled in his arms, bringing us face to face. His eyes were closed. "Sorry. When I'm up, I'm up." I also wasn't accustomed to waking up next to someone in a bed that wasn't my own.

His hooded eyes barely opened. "It's okay, I can be up too."

Reaching through the circle of his arms, I brushed the dark hair from his eyes. "How about you rest a little more while I go downstairs to make us some coffee."

The corners of his mouth curved. "That would be nice," he murmured.

I kissed the tip of his nose before bounding out of bed. "I'll be right back."

"You better be." So much for being sleepy. His gazed followed me around the room as I rustled through his draw looking for pyjama pants and stayed on me until I walked out the door.

The house was quiet, and I couldn't deny it felt a little strange to be walking through it barefoot and wearing my boyfriend's clothes. This was a first. I smiled to myself walking down the front hall, already thinking about being upstairs with him again and liking how it warmed my chest.

Those thoughts were thrown out of my mind the moment I walked into the kitchen.

"O-oh," I stuttered, taking a step back. "Sorry."

Emily and Darcy pulled away from each other, both attempting to tame their dishevelment by patting their hair and straightening their pyjamas.

I took another step back, ready to leave them be. "I'm so sorry, I didn't mean to interrupt."

Darcy's face glowed a bright red and she avoided my gaze. Emily also blushed and tried hiding her smile behind her hand. "It's okay," she said, tone bright.

Darcy cleared her throat. "I'll be upstairs." She grabbed a teacup from the bench and gave me a sheepish smile as she passed through the door. "Morning."

I turned back to Emily, who could no longer contain her bright smile. "Clearly I've missed something huge!" I whispered, unsure if Darcy was out of earshot.

The last thing I expected to see this morning was the two of them locking lips by the kettle. Things started clicking in my mind. The tension between Emily and Isaac. The arguments between Isaac and Darcy. And all the little things I'd assumed were the acts of a close friend but were clearly something else.

"How long?" I trailed, attempting to put it all into a timeline.

"Technically it's only just happened," Emily admitted. "But it's been building for a while."

I paused before asking my next question but did so anyway. I needed to know. "Is this why she and Isaac broke up?"

Emily shrugged, playing with her cuticles. "Partly, but they had a lot of other issues before this became one."

Now that the shock had worn off a little, I could see the concern in her eyes. "Well, I'm very happy for you both," I smiled, hoping to ease her worries.

It worked. "Thank you." Emily straightened up, shaking her hands. "We've been close for so long, and so comfortable around each other, but now I'm nervous all the time."

I could empathise with that. "You'll both get used to it," I said, unsure how I could possibly give advice on the matter when I was still a bumbling ball of nerves myself.

Her smile faded again. "I know, I just hope I don't screw it up."

"You won't." The confidence in my tone seemed to help.

After a moment of silence, Emily grabbed her teacup and started towards the door. "I should go and check on her."

While I had so many more questions to ask and memories that needed clarifying, I let her go without another word. Did this just start last night? How long had they kept their feelings a secret, from each other and from their friends?

Needing to find out more, I made quick work of the coffees. A double shot for Justin and sweet macadamia syrup for me. Then I walked swiftly up the stairs and opened the bedroom door with my elbow. As soon as I closed it behind me, the words were out of my mouth. "You won't believe what just happened in the kitchen."

Justin sat up to lean against the headboard. He took the coffee I held out to him. "You made me two cups?" he queried jokingly.

"You wish," I laughed, walking around to my side of the bed, placing the mug on the table. "No, I just walked in on Emily and Darcy."

"And?" he pressed, taking a sip of his cappuccino.

"And they were kissing!"

Justin let out a laugh and looked to the ceiling. "Finally!"

"What? You knew?"

He continued with an apologetic tone. "It was just an assumption. The sexual tension has been driving me nuts for weeks."

"I can't believe you didn't tell me," I mumbled, exaggerating my disappointment.

Justin placed his mug on the bedside table and reached for me. "I'm sorry. Like I said, I wasn't sure and I'm too scared to ask Darcy what's going on. She can be terrifying when people get in her business. They need to figure it for themselves, and they'll tell us things when they're ready."

That was fair. While my curiosity was flaring, I knew I needed to respect their privacy. Emily and I had a rough start when we first met, but now things were different. If she was happy, then that was all that counted, and if she considered me a friend the way I did her, then she would tell me more when she was ready.

I turned towards the bedside table, ready to start my morning coffee, but Justin had other plans. He grabbed at my waist, spun me around and pinned me in one swift movement. With his weight on me, I barely had an inch to move, not that I wanted to.

"So," he began, voice low and lips barely a breath away from mine. "Any big plans for today?"

I sucked in a deep breath, relishing the scent of him mixed with coffee. Two of my favourite things in one. "Well, actually," I feigned disinterest. "I was planning on having a lazy day. Might spend it all in bed."

"Oh really?" he smirked, readjusting his position on top of me. "Need a companion for that?"

"Well, it is your bed, so if you happen to be lazing about as well, I'd have no objections." I couldn't keep hold of the serious tone and let out a giggle.

"I also have no objections," Justin mumbled before capturing my lips in a warm kiss.

CHAPTER 28

Dad wanted to meet Justin. Formally, that is. He'd met my boyfriend a couple times before, when Justin came to pick me up, but it wasn't enough to simply greet each other and make small talk. Dad preferred a sit-down meal, a proper conversation, a real chance to interrogate the man his daughter had been seeing for over a month. It was a father's prerogative, or so he said.

Maybe things would have been different if Justin wasn't the son of his former friend and the stepchild of his ex-wife. He may have waited for my relationship to develop more before requesting Justin came over for a barbecue.

Another person might think I would be the nervous wreck in this situation, desperately worried about my father liking my boyfriend. Me being me, that made sense. Tonight, however, it was not the case.

"Do you think he'll like it?" Justin asked, slowing his Jeep to a crawl in search of a kerbside car spot.

I reached across the console to take his hand. "He will enjoy whatever you brought."

"But is it good enough?" he continued, eyes darting from one side of the road to the other.

To distract him, and to avoid answering the same question I'd already answered three times, I steered the conversation to parking. "There will be more spots open in the next street," I suggested. We'd already driven by my house knowing there was no room in the driveway. It barely fit my own car and would in no way accommodate another, especially one the size of a Jeep.

Justin continued driving and sure enough, there were a few free spots. He whipped into the first one he saw. The houses on this road were larger and had more kerbside parking. My street was full of thin terraces, and it was a tight squeeze.

"Stop worrying," I sighed, closing the door. Justin rounded the car to meet me on the footpath. "Dad likes you, trust me."

It was the truth. If I had any doubts, I'd be the one freaking out. I knew for a fact that Dad was happy with Justin because I was happy. He'd told me so many times in the past few weeks.

"He does drink whiskey, right?"

I laughed. "Yes. Cheap, expensive, and everything in between." The bottle Justin currently held in his hand was on the expensive side.

He took hold of my hand, pulling us to a standstill. "I'm sorry," he started, a frown forming on his brow. "I'm just really nervous."

Taking a step closer, I said, "You've met him three times already."

"This is different. What if he doesn't like me?"

I shook my head. "How on Earth could he not like you?"

Justin's brows rose, stating the obvious.

"He's a very open person," I began, hoping my words would convince him until he experienced it for himself. "The past doesn't matter to him, he told me so. And even if it did, he would never hold it against you. What happened had nothing to do with us."

It had taken me a while to accept my father's words, so I couldn't blame Justin for feeling the way he did. When it came time for me to meet his family—in a formal way, considering I'd already met his sister and Caroline was, well, Caroline—I would be a mess as well. I dreaded the day.

"Okay," he finally agreed with a sigh.

I stood on my tiptoes to give him a quick kiss. "You ready now?

"Yep, let's go."

Hand in hand, we continued walking. When we rounded the corner onto my street, a compulsion took over me. I jumped up onto the short brick fence, just as I use to when I was a kid, and balanced as I walked along it.

Justin kept hold of my hand, laughing at my antics.

"Now what?" he asked when I reached the first driveway and end of the fence.

I turned to him and pouted.

"Piggyback?" he suggested, amusement in his tone.

I smiled sweetly. "If you insist." Then he offered his back to me and I jumped on without hesitation, wrapping my arms around his neck and legs around his waist. He hooked a hand under one of my knees, the other keeping hold of the whiskey.

One driveway from my own, he couldn't contain his squirming. "Keep going," he murmured, leaning into my lips as they trailed kisses along his neck, "And I'll either drop you or we're going back to the car."

"I vote for the second option," I laughed, continuing my work on his neck.

Justin slowed his pace and stood up straight. I nearly fell off.

"Is your dad going through a mid-life crisis?" he asked uncertainly. "Nice bike."

My eyes quickly found the road bike tucked into the driveway near the front of my car. My heart dropped and I slid down Justin's back, letting go of him. "Sawyer's here."

Justin took a moment to respond. "Oh."

"I'm sure he's not staying," I said quickly, hoping that was the truth. "He's probably just sorting out something for work with Dad." I glanced up at him to gauge his reaction. Sure enough, his expression was strained.

"It's fine," Justin nodded, attempting to straighten his face. "It's not a big deal."

Slipping my hand into his, I hoped to ease both our worries. "Come on, it will be fine."

We continued up the front path and were barely halfway when the door opened. Sawyer was backing out the door, shaking dad's hand as he went. When he turned around and spotted us, his smile dropped.

"Hi," I said, voice soft.

After a moment of taking us in, he responded, lips tight. "Hey."

Justin didn't let go of my hand.

Sensing the tension, Dad stepped over the threshold. "You made it. Good evening."

Without hesitation, Justin replied. "Good evening, Mr Newcombe."

"Richard, please," Dad insisted. "What's that you've got there?"

Justin looked down at his hand as if he was seeing the whiskey bottle for the first time. "It's a single malt," he said, offering it to my father.

"Wonderful," Dad continued, taking the bottle Justin held out to him. "I finished a good one the other night. Why don't you come in and pour me a glass?"

Justin looked to me with worried eyes and I squeezed his hand. "I just need a minute out here," I said, hoping he would understand.

He did, squeezing my hand back before letting go. I was grateful he didn't kiss me. This was awkward enough. He walked up the stairs, nodding to Sawyer as he went. Sawyer nodded back, lips still pressed together. It was a much more civil interaction than the last time they'd met.

When Justin was through the door, Dad closed it and I stood alone with Sawyer in my front yard.

After a long moment, he broke the silence. "Are you happy?" he asked, not with an accusatory tone as I was expecting, but with one of genuine curiosity. It was one thing to know that I was with Justin, it was another thing to see it.

"Yes," I admitted. There was no point in lying or playing it down.

Sawyer nodded, fiddling with the strap on his helmet. I hadn't noticed he was wearing his leathers, something that once caught my eye instantly for how attractive he looked in them. While he was still one of the best-looking men I knew, I saw him differently now. We both knew it. "That's good. You deserve to be happy."

I swallowed, taking a step forward. "I owe you a gigantic apology," I began, shaking my head. "More than one, actually."

He held up a hand, as if to wave off my apology. "You don't owe me anything, Elle."

"Yes I do," I insisted. "In my confusion and uncertainty, I led you on."

"We both agreed it was a casual thing, no labels."

"Even so, we both know there was more to it after a while." There were times when we'd leaned on each other, needing a comfort and support no one else could provide at the time. That held meaning, I saw that now.

"Maybe if I'd said something sooner, there would have been. But that's my own fault, not yours. You made your intentions clear from the beginning." Even now, he tried to keep the blame off me when I should be shouldering most of it.

"And I could have done or said something about what was going on with Justin sooner, and then maybe it wouldn't be like this between us."

Sawyer sighed, keeping eye contact. "I don't think it would have mattered. Justin or no Justin, this would have happened eventually."

I nodded. After much reflection and taking the time to explore my own thoughts and feelings, I knew we would have ended up in a similar position, regardless of who came into my life. "You're right, and that's what I'm sorry for. You deserve so much better than that."

"Don't worry about me, Elle, I'll be fine."

He would be. I was merely a blip in his existence.

"You won't see me much. I'm not going to be working at the hotel anymore, except when you're desperate to cover a shift."

"That's a shame," he said, before quickly adding, "Not that you're pursing what you really want to, that we won't see much of each other, I mean. Besides all the other stuff, I thought we had a pretty good friendship going. It would be a shame to let that go."

"We did. We do."

His tone was thick with sincerity. "Then I hope you know I'll always be here for you. If you need someone to talk to, about anything, I'm here."

"Anything?" I teased, hoping to lighten the mood.

He looked towards the door, suppressing the upward curve of his lips. "Well, maybe Sass can be the ear for certain things."

"That's fair," I smiled. I wasn't ignorant; there was no chance I'd talk to him about my relationship.

"Come here." His tone was soft as he held out an arm. I stepped into his warmth, linking my hands around his middle. "I'll see you soon."

"See you soon," I murmured into his chest before letting go.

Sawyer walked over to his bike, only glancing back at me when he was seated with helmet on and backing it out of the driveway. I waved goodbye and watched as he took off down the street.

I let myself have a few more moments before going inside. I'd barely noticed Sawyer's absence the past few weeks, having been so caught up in Justin. Now it was painfully obvious. His offer of friendship was sincere though, even if I didn't deserve it.

When I walked into the kitchen, Justin was standing at the island bench, pondering three empty scotch tumblers. Through the patio doors, I could see Dad fiddling with the barely used barbecue. Dinner tonight would either be good, or we'd be ordering take away.

"You okay?" Justin asked cautiously when I came to stand beside him. His concern wasn't about Sawyer and me. He was worried about my head and where it was at.

"Yeah, everything's good," I smiled. Sorting things out with Sawyer felt like a weight had fallen from my shoulders, only to be replaced with another. "You know that Sawyer and I will always be friends, right? It's not like I'll be hanging out with him or anything, but he will be around. You know, with the hotel and all."

At the end of the day, Sawyer worked with my father. Friends or not, he would always be a part of my life in one capacity or another. It would make things a lot easier for everyone if we could get along. Was it selfish of me to ask Justin to accept that?

Justin sighed, putting the whiskey bottle down to give me his full attention. "I do know that. I completely understand and I'm okay with it."

Surprise and relief filled me. "Thank you." With nothing weighing me down, I reached up to wrap my arms around his neck. "How did I ever get so lucky?"

"Well..." he began, hands resting on my waist.

"That was a rhetorical question," I interrupted.

"Sure it was." Justin laughed, placing a kiss to my neck before letting me go. "So, does your dad prefer his whiskey straight or on the rocks?"

"Definitely straight." I wandered to the freezer and pulled out an ice cube tray. "But I..."

"Prefer yours weakened by a handful of ice," he finished for me with a smirk, holding up the third glass. "I know."

EPILOGUE

"My name better be the only thing written in your diary today," Justin mumbled as he rolled over. He rubbed his eyes and nuzzled a little into his pillow before sliding over and snuggling in to my side.

I pressed my lips together in a smile, scrolling through my digital calendar to today's date before showing him the phone screen. "What else could I possibly be doing today?" I shook my head. He knew his name was the only thing written in my schedule.

Justin's warm hands found my waist. "I'm a who, not a what," he murmured against my ear after pulling me into his embrace. My giggles filled the room as we sank back into the sheets.

An hour later, we finally rolled out of bed. Our definitions of a lazy Saturday morning were still not on par, but the compromises over the last few weeks were slowly helping them come together. Half-past eight was a sleep-in for me but still an early wake-up call for Justin. So, while I got ready for the day, he trekked downstairs to make us coffee, mumbling dramatically about a double shot and that both mugs were for him.

I'd been staying at Justin's place more and more over the past few weeks. We'd only just decided that I should have a toothbrush here. While it felt a little strange, I liked the way it looked in the cup on the vanity, right next to his.

Keen to get the day started, I brushed my teeth and took a quick, steamy, shower.

When I emerged from the bathroom fully dressed and ready to fight for my morning coffee, it was to the sound of Justin yelling.

"Do not go in my room!"

"Why?" came a whine before the thumping of shoes on the stairs ceased.

I froze, staring widely at the bedroom door. It was slightly ajar, the voices in the foyer travelling easily through it.

"You said I could borrow your Lord of the Rings books," Claire continued, clearly annoyed.

"You can, just not right now." Justin's tone matched his sister's.

"What does it matter? You're not reading them right now are you?"

Justin continued, the strain clear in his voice. "That's not the point."

Another, deeper voice entered the conversation. "Claire, please don't argue. Go and wait in the kitchen."

There was a momentary pause before Claire finally gave in. "Fine," she moaned, obeying her father and slowly thumping back down the stairs.

I released a heavy breath, still staring at the door. Justin's father and sister were here. Did that mean Caroline was nearby as well?

"Dad, I'm sorry, I forgot about today," Justin apologised.

"Clearly. I'm sure you wouldn't be entertaining a... guest, if you'd remembered your thirteen year old sister was coming over." Michael Hart didn't sound pleased.

Unsure if I should be listening in, I sat down in Justin's computer chair, fumbling for a distraction. The easiest thing to do would be to close the door, but I couldn't. What if they noticed? Instead, I continued watching it, waiting for what came next.

"I still need you to take Claire to her ballet classes today. Carol's in Melbourne and I've got that meeting with the investors from New Zealand at ten."

"Yeah, I've got it, I'll take her," Justin agreed without hesitation.

"Thank you." There was a long pause before Mr Hart continued, the judgement clear. "I'll go and sit with your sister while you say goodbye to... your friend."

"It's not like that," Justin replied immediately, a harsh edge to his tone.

Disbelief, and perhaps a little caution, laced his father's next question. "What is it like then?"

My heartbeat quickened.

"She's not just a guest, or a friend." The way he spoke, with so much confidence and sincerity, even his father couldn't deny it. There was no repressing the smile that spread across my lips.

Mr Hart took his time before responding. "Okay. If you've got a girlfriend, you should bring her around for brunch."

"I'm not sure that's a good idea." The confidence disappeared.

"Why wouldn't it be?" Mr Hart questioned. "I think we should meet the person our son is dating."

"Maybe one day, but she's not ready. Not yet."

She's not ready.

"It's Elizabeth, isn't it?" It was a wonder it took so long for him to put it together. There was only one person in Justin's life who wouldn't be ready to meet his parents. "Have you even thought about Caroline? Considered her feelings?"

I had. In fact, I thought about it often.

She's not ready.

"It's got nothing to do with her."

"Of course it does."

"My relationship is my relationship," Justin insisted, the edge returning.

"You don't think this is a unique situation?" his father argued, matching his tone.

Justin didn't give in. "Yeah, I know it is, but it's still new. I don't want to mess things up by forcing past trauma to resurface before she's ready."

She's not ready. Was I that transparent?

"Have you met Richard?" Mr Hart asked after another tense pause.

Justin hesitated. "Yes." Dinner with dad was becoming a weekly event. Justin was always so willing and open to spending time with my father, whether it was at home or out at a restaurant. He never complained. In fact, he often seemed excited in the lead up. Knowing how much my dad meant to me, he made the effort.

I wasn't doing the same for him.

She's not ready.

Did that make me selfish?

"I see," Mr Hart continued. "So it is serious enough to meet the parents. Just not yours."

"Dad, stop!" Justin demanded. "If and when Ellie is ready, however long it takes, we'll come around for brunch. Until then, you'll just have to accept things as they are. Okay?"

"Fine. Okay," his father conceded. "Thank you for taking Claire today. I'll see you when you drop her home this evening. We'll talk more then."

"Sure. No problem."

The conversation ended there, the front door closing a little harder, and louder, than necessary.

It wasn't long before there were footsteps on the stairs again. When Justin pushed the door open with his elbow, I felt a sense of relief rush through me. He carefully monitored the rims of two coffee mugs as he carried them across the room, still shirtless and wearing nothing but boxers.

"Hey," he breathed, handing me one of the mugs.

"Hey."

"Are you folding my socks?" he questioned with a smirk and a raised brow.

Glancing down, I noticed the matching pair I'd just dropped into my lap. The basket of clean clothes beside me also held a few folded pairs. I hadn't realised what I was doing. "Yeah, I just... I don't know."

But Justin did. "You heard all that?"

I nodded, eyes focused on my mug.

"I'm sorry. My dad, he can be really..." Justin trailed. I wasn't sure what to make of Michael Hart. I suppose he had his reasons, and he seemed like a protective father and husband looking out for the ones he loved.

I shrugged. "It's okay."

"No, it's not." Justin reached for my coffee and placed both mugs on the desk behind me. Then he took hold of the computer chair and rolled me towards him. He sat on the edge of the bed, bringing my chair as close to him as possible before resting his elbows on his knees and taking my hands.

After a momentary pause, he shared his thoughts, the words coming out in a rush. "Listen. I know some things have been difficult for you, for both of us. It took us a while to get here, and I'm so happy." Justin paused again, gauging my reaction with concerned eyes. "The thing is, my family, well, they're my family. You and Caroline have a complicated history, and if we continue this, it will eventually mean meeting the family. Christmas. Easter. Other unavoidable events. I don't want to put you through more trauma. So, I understand if being with me isn't... I mean, if you don't want to—"

"Stop." He wasn't about to say I could leave if I wanted to. I wouldn't let him.

"Ellie—" he began, but I interrupted again.

"No. Listen." Unfolding my legs, I moved onto the edge of the bed with him, straddling his lap. I rested my arms against his bare shoulders to bring us closer. He needed to understand. "You have been the best thing to happen to me in a really long time. Yes, some things have been hard to deal with, but none of that was you. The truth is, I would have had to deal with my Caroline issues eventually."

He sighed, hands grasping my waist softly. "I know, but it's still not something I want to put you through."

"But it's something I need to go through. I know that. I accept it. Caroline is a very tender spot, and I'm constantly petrified I'm hurting my dad, but I can't hide from this anymore." Whether I'd met Justin that first night at Uni Bar, or I never ran into him at all, my feelings towards Caroline would have surfaced at some point. He may have been the reason I needed to face them sooner, but he wasn't the cause. "My first session with my psychologist is next week and I think she'd be proud of how far I've come without her," I added, hoping to lighten the mood.

Justin reached up to brush a loose strand of hair behind my ear. "I agree," he whispered.

"It's because of you, and the way you make me feel so safe and cared for." My heart fluttered. I couldn't suppress it, not any more. "It's because I..."

The words stuck in my throat.

Ever the empathetic, Justin gave me a way out. "It's okay, you don't have to say it. I know."

I also knew. "And that's exactly why I feel I can say it. You're in my heart, Justin, and you give me the courage to face the things I've avoided for years, the difficult and devastating things. I want this. I want you."

I was ready.

"I love you." I was confident he'd reciprocate, but my heart raced faster in anticipation than it ever had.

The corners of his lips turned up before they brushed mine and he whispered, "I love you, too."

I took a deep, relieving breath. The words solidified the feelings that swelled between us.

I kissed him back, softly at first, but then feverishly. Needing, and wanting, to be as close to him as I could be, I pushed him back against the mattress. Justin didn't protest. He knew exactly what I needed and gave it to me, as he always did, hands wandering hotly from my waist to my thighs.

We carried on like that for a while, my heart still pounding and showing no signs of slowing down. Well, until a loud banging on the door, followed by Claire yelling loud enough for the neighbours to hear, finally tore us apart.

"You both have twenty seconds to put your clothes on before I come in there. I'm going to be late, and Miss Violet does not tolerate tardiness."

I glanced down at Justin, who somehow managed to keep a straight face. Unaccustomed to the antics of little sisters, I stifled my giggles in his neck.

"What do you say we drop Claire at her dance class and then grab some brunch by the beach?" he asked softly before pressing a sweet kiss to the side of my head.

Pulling myself together, I reluctantly rolled off him, sat on the edge of the bed and took hold of his warm hand. "Sounds like a date."

A few months ago, the joy that swelled inside me seemed impossible. I knew not everything would be this easy and that there was still so much to work thorough—love didn't magically fix everything, after all—but I'd face those challenges over time.

I had a lot to look forward to—starting with brunch—and for the first time, I wasn't afraid of where my life was heading.

www.ingramcontent.com/pod-product-compliance
Lightning Source LLC
Chambersburg PA
CBHW071754190726
48292CB00003B/972